THE BERMONDSEY POISONER

Penny Green Mystery Book 6

EMILY ORGAN

First published in 2018 by Emily Organ

emilyorgan.co.uk

Edited by Joy Tibbs

Emily Organ has asserted her right under the Copyright, Designs and Patents Act 1988 to be identified as the author of this work.

ISBN 978-1-9993433-2-3

THE BERMONDSEY POISONER

Emily Organ

Books in the Penny Green Series:

ALSO BY EMILY ORGAN

Penny Green Series:
Limelight
The Rookery
The Maid's Secret
The Inventor
Curse of the Poppy
The Bermondsey Poisoner

Runaway Girl Series:
Runaway Girl
Forgotten Child
Sins of the Father

CHAPTER 1

"This is all you need for your travels is it, Francis?" asked my sister Eliza as we stood in the Great Hall of Euston Station. She pointed at the leather trunk by his feet.

"Yes, it contains everything I need, thank you." He grinned. "I have never stopped to admire this hall before. Isn't it beautiful?"

I followed his gaze to the grand stone staircase, immense columns and coffered ceiling, which was flooded with light from a high row of windows. Beside us stood the statue of a man in a frock coat with a scroll in his hand.

"But you're to be away for several months," continued Eliza. "Surely you'll need more than a single trunk!"

"It will be perfectly sufficient for my needs," he replied. "Most important of all is taking the correct clothing." He gestured at his light brown suit. "This looks rather pale and out of place in a London train station, but it will serve me well in the tropics."

"I'm sure it will, Francis," I said.

He held my gaze for a moment, his green eyes twinkling

with anticipation behind his spectacles. I realised how much he was looking forward to searching for my father and felt slightly envious of him.

"Time to say goodbye to Mr Stephenson," he said, glancing up at the statue next to us.

"Who's he?" asked Eliza.

"George Stephenson, the father of railways."

"Oh, him."

"His early engines were designed for the coal mines," continued Francis, "but he turned his hand to passenger trains for the Stockton and Darlington Railway, and after that the Liverpool and Manchester line. Before long, railroad builders were travelling all the way over from America to learn from the great man."

"I'm sure Mr Stephenson wishes you well on your travels," interrupted Eliza. "However, I'm worried that you're about to miss your train to Liverpool. Which platform does it depart from?"

Francis looked up at the clock. "Oh yes, I must go. Platform twelve."

He picked up his trunk and we hurried through an archway toward the platforms. Plumes of smoke rose up into the lattice girder roof.

"Platform twelve is this way!" my sister shouted over the hiss of steam and the shrill of guards' whistles. She strode on ahead of us, attracting a few bemused glances in her practical woollen suit with its skirt divided like breeches.

Francis and I followed her as she darted around porters pushing trolleys filled with luggage and people embracing each other with hearty hellos and goodbyes.

"Where are you meeting your translator, Francis?" bellowed Eliza.

"Liverpool. My sister will also meet me there. She and her husband are going to see me onto the boat."

"How lovely that your sister will be there. Oh, this must be your train!"

Francis handed his trunk to a porter and we began to stride purposefully alongside the brown and cream carriages.

"Are you headed for first class at the front?" Eliza called out.

"No, I'm travelling in second," replied Francis.

"Oh, Francis, you should have afforded yourself a little comfort!"

"Second will suffice."

"Just as one trunk suffices, I suppose!"

"Don't forget that Francis has to travel by mule for a few hundred miles to Bogotá," I said. "He can't take too much luggage."

"Here we are!" said Francis as we reached a carriage marked second class. The letters LNWR – denoting London and North Western Railway – were etched onto the side in gold.

I felt a lump in my throat as he opened the carriage door.

Eliza suddenly embraced him, and he took a step back, his eyebrows raised in surprise.

"Good luck, Francis!" she said. "You must write to us as often as you can. We'll be thinking of you every day, won't we, Penelope?"

I nodded fervently. "We will."

Francis brushed his sandy fringe away from his spectacles and turned to face me. "Goodbye, Penny."

I could barely hear him above the noise of the station.

"I'll accompany you into the carriage," I replied.

I didn't feel ready to say goodbye. I was struggling to believe that it would be many months before we saw him again.

"Careful, Penelope, you don't want the train running away with you," warned Eliza.

Francis moved aside as I lifted my skirts and stepped into the quiet compartment, sitting down on one of the blue carpet seats. He closed the door behind him so that we could hear each other more clearly. Then he removed his bowler hat and placed it on the luggage rack above my head.

"I hope you have a comfortable journey," I said, "and I hope all your travelling companions are agreeable. You will write to us as Eliza asked, won't you? Please do send word to us once you have arrived in Colombia. Or perhaps you could send a letter from one of the stops along the way."

"Of course I will." He gave a quiet laugh.

"What's funny?"

"If only you had been this interested in hearing from me before I made the decision to leave."

I paused, surprised by the candidness of his comment.

"I have always been interested in you, Francis."

"Not quite interested enough, though." He smiled. "Never mind, there is nothing more to be said on the matter."

The train guard's whistle sounded, and Eliza hammered on the window.

"Please be careful, Francis," I said, rising to my feet. "Colombia is a dangerous place, and crossing the Atlantic Ocean is also hazardous."

"I shall be fine."

"And good luck. I hope you manage to find Father."

"I shall do my best, Penny."

I embraced him, but my movement was so impulsive that I pinned both his arms down by his sides. There had once been an opportunity for me to marry Francis, but the chance had now passed. *Had it been a mistake to turn away a man who loved me?*

The train hooted its whistle.

We separated, and I adjusted my spectacles as I felt a tear roll down my cheek.

"You need to disembark," said Francis. "You don't want to end up coming with me!"

I didn't rush toward the door; indeed, I quite liked the thought of accompanying him. An adventure in South America sounded rather appealing. *Besides, what was left for me in London?* The man I loved, Inspector James Blakely, was to marry his fiancée, Charlotte, in a little under four weeks. I wasn't sure how I would cope with it when the day came.

"Please write," I said again.

"I've told you I will, now get off the train!" He laughed.

The carriage gave a jolt. I glanced out of the window and saw that the train was beginning to move. Eliza was marching along beside the window with an alarmed expression on her face and wildly gesticulating arms.

I flung the door open and readied myself to step out onto the platform, which was beginning to flash past with increasing rapidity.

"Careful, Penny!" said Francis.

"Goodbye!" I said tearfully and hopped out, stumbling as my feet connected with the platform.

I recovered myself and managed to slam the door shut just in time. Eliza and I held on to our hats as we jogged alongside the train. Francis lowered the window.

"Goodbye!" we shouted. "Good luck!"

The train picked up speed so that we were no longer able to keep up. We stopped, breathless, and watched Francis' waving hand until it disappeared from view.

The last of the carriages pulled out of the station. The train gave a whistle, reached a bend in the railway line and was gone.

"Doesn't he remind you of Father, Penelope?" asked Eliza, her voice cracking. "I used to feel like this whenever he went away."

The aching lump in my throat returned. "What if we never see him again, Ellie?"

"Oh, we will, we will." She draped an arm across my shoulders. "He's going to find Father, I feel sure of it. Just imagine what it will be like to welcome both of them home!"

"Do you really think that could happen, Ellie?" I turned to look at her.

"I like to believe so, don't you? I have every confidence in Francis, and I know that he'll write regularly so we shall know exactly how he's getting on. He's a good man, Penelope, but perhaps it's just as well that you didn't agree to marry him. He would never have gone to search for Father then, would he? On reflection, this is the best outcome for all of us. We have someone we can trust searching for our father, and Francis gets to go on a great adventure!"

"Perhaps I should have gone with him," I said. "I rather wish that I had now."

"Nonsense, Penelope. You couldn't possibly go travelling across South America. It would be completely unbefitting for a woman."

"You campaign for women to be given the vote, yet you believe women are incapable of becoming explorers?" I asked.

"The two issues are quite distinct. Now, shall we find somewhere to have an early lunch? If I recall correctly there are some quite pleasant dining rooms at this station."

CHAPTER 2

A *South American Adventure*

A second search for the plant-hunter, Mr. Frederick Brinsley Green, is to be carried out by Mr. Francis Temple Edwards. Mr. Edwards has no previous experience of international exploration and was, until recently, employed as a clerk at the British Library. Through his acquaintance with Mr. Green's daughter, Miss Penelope Green, Mr. Edwards has forged an interest in discovering the whereabouts of Mr. Green, who has not been seen since the March of 1875. Mr. Edwards will sail from Liverpool tomorrow, Wednesday 20th August, to the United States of Colombia on the SS Pampero.

A previous search was conducted by the explorer Mr. Isaac Fox-Stirling eight years ago in the March of 1876. Although Mr. Fox-Stirling was unsuccessful in establishing the whereabouts of Mr. Green, he discovered a hut which had recently been inhabited by Mr. Green close to the Falls of Tequendama, twenty-five miles southwest of

Bogotá. Mr. Edwards plans to return to this location and make further enquiries with the assistance of a Spanish translator.

Mr. Edwards has compensated for his lack of expeditionary experience by conducting exhaustive research into the South American continent and her peoples.

Before he was declared missing, Mr. Green made a number of trips to South America and transported many exotic plants back to the shores of Britannia. At the time of his disappearance, the plant-hunter had been collecting orchid specimens on behalf of Kew Gardens.

Mr. G. W. Brice of Kew Gardens spoke to our reporter: "For nine years mystery has surrounded the supposed disappearance of one of our brave plant-hunters, and with no confirmation that Mr. Green lost his life in Amazonia it is everyone's hope that Mr. Edwards finds him in good health. It would be marvellous indeed if Mr. Green were to return home and be reunited with his wife and daughters."

"I think the article places an unfair emphasis on Francis' lack of experience," I said, folding up my copy of *The Times*.

"Well, it's rather an ambitious expedition, isn't it, Miss Green?" replied my glib colleague, Edgar Fish.

We were sitting in the newsroom at the *Morning Express* newspaper, which was a cluttered place with piles of paper on every surface and a grimy window looking out onto Fleet Street.

"You can't blame the reporter for pointing it out," continued Edgar. He was a young man with heavy features and small, glinting eyes. "The chap's probably never been further west than Kensington."

"I'm certain he must have," I replied curtly.

"Has he been on a ship before?"

"I don't know."

"Because if a chap's never been on a ship before he's bound to find a two-week Atlantic crossing a bit rough."

"Especially if there's a storm," added my curly-haired and corpulent colleague, Frederick Potter.

"That's right, Potter, and the storms are not infrequent, are they?"

"Sometimes they can last for days," I said, "though Mr Edwards is fully aware of that. We were forced to listen to Mr Fox-Stirling's never-ending tales of Atlantic crossings enough times."

"Getting there is one thing," continued Edgar, "but managing the natives is quite another!"

"They lead a somewhat primitive life in that part of the world," added Frederick.

"Do they practise cannibalism in Amazonia?" asked Edgar. "Mr Edwards had better watch his back, else he'll end up in a native's cooking pot!"

"Don't be so ridiculous!" I snapped.

"What's ridiculous?" asked our editor, Mr Sherman, as he strode into the newsroom, leaving the door to slam behind him.

"Edgar suggested there is a possibility that Mr Edwards will be eaten by cannibals while he searches for my father," I said.

"May I suggest, Fish, that if you've nothing intelligent to say, don't bother saying anything at all," scolded the editor. He had a thick black moustache, and his hair was oiled and parted to one side.

"That means he'll be silent forevermore!" laughed Frederick.

His comment was met with a scowl from Mr Sherman, who took a puff on his pipe before turning to address me. "Miss Green, have you heard about a chap called John Curran?"

"No, sir."

"He seems to have been maliciously poisoned. The inquest into his death will take place tomorrow at The Five Bells in Bermondsey Square."

"Do the police have any suspects?" I asked.

"I understand the wife is under suspicion, but she has vanished."

"Damning herself by her absence, eh?" said Edgar. "There is no surer way to convince people of your guilt than by running off and hiding somewhere."

"It may be a little more complicated than that, Fish," said Mr Sherman. "The woman may have her reasons for disappearing, or perhaps I'm not in possession of the full facts of the case. I'm relying purely on a conversation I overheard down at the Turkish baths yesterday evening."

"Where would we be if we didn't all have our ears to the ground in one way or another, eh, sir?" said Edgar. "You hear your news at the Turkish baths and I hear mine at Ye Olde Cheshire Cheese. Where do you hear your news, Miss Green?"

"From my landlady," I replied. "She hears it all from a neighbour of ours, Mrs Wilkinson. I don't know how Mrs Wilkinson manages it, but I swear she's always the first in London to know anything."

"Well, I'd say that between the bathers, drinkers and neighbours of this good city we're on the ball!" said Edgar. "And let's not forget your connection at the Yard, Miss Green. It's always useful to have a friend down in the CID. We may only have a few reporters, but between us we seem to have most of London covered."

"Well done, Fish," said the editor. "Perhaps once you've finished congratulating yourself you might like to get on and write something."

"I was congratulating everyone, sir."

"That's most kind of you. Now then, don't forget that the *Morning Express* is only as good as its last issue, so let's get on with it. We have circulation numbers to worry about! Miss Green, get yourself down to The Five Bells tomorrow and find out what you can about the poisoned man and his wife."

CHAPTER 3

I walked down to the river the following morning, passing the stone walls and turrets of the Tower of London. It was a warm, late-summer day but the sky was grey. I removed my jacket and unfastened the top button of my high-collared blouse in an attempt to cool myself down. Beyond the river, the chimneys of south London darkened the air with clouds of smoke.

I had heard that a new bridge had been proposed that would cross the Thames from the Tower of London to Bermondsey, but for the time being the quickest route was via the Tower Subway.

I paid my halfpenny toll and climbed down a long spiral staircase to the tunnel, which ran beneath the river.

The Tower Subway was not designed to delight the senses; it was a tube lined with cast iron and lit by a row of dim lights. Water dripped down the walls and the wooden walkway was unsteady in places. The slightest noise echoed along the tube so that a conversation being held fifty yards away sounded as though it were level with one's shoulder. I strode as quickly as I could and thought about Francis, who would be departing from Liverpool at that very moment. I had already encountered his replacement in the reading room at the British Library. His name was Mr Retchford, and he was a dough-faced man with small, pig-like eyes and a shrill voice. I couldn't imagine him being anywhere near as helpful as Francis had been.

The warm scent of exotic spices from the warehouses lingered in the air as I emerged from the dingy subway staircase on the south side of the river. I walked beneath the railway lines from London Bridge station and found that a new smell assaulted me as I reached Crucifix Lane. Beneath the railway arches were heaped piles of animal dung collected for soaking and softening leather in the tanneries. My stomach turned as a hard-faced woman, seemingly impervious to the stink, emptied a small crate of dog excrement onto the foul-smelling mound. Flies buzzed in my ears and my throat gagged. I covered my nose with my handkerchief and strode along as quickly as possible.

Bermondsey was a lively, busy place, where rows of cramped little houses sat cheek by jowl with factories pumping out fumes of chocolate, glue and sulphur. Every spare corner was given over to industry of one sort or another. Machines rumbled and hammers pounded. As I neared Bermondsey Square the acrid odour from the large tanneries caught in the back of my throat.

The inquest into John Curran's death was held in an upstairs room at The Five Bells public house.

The coroner, Mr Robert Osborne, was a wispy-haired man with a thick moustache, and he sat at a table with a small group of gentlemen. The jury of twelve men sat on chairs along one side of the room, while the press reporters and members of the public were crammed into what remained of the floor space. I did my best to write everything down in my notebook, squashed as I was between two other reporters.

The coroner stated that John Curran had been a labourer at a local tannery and was thirty-one years old when he died at his home, 96 Grange Walk, on the seventeenth of August. Proceedings were halted for a short while at this point as the jury paid a visit to the mortuary in the nearby church to view the body.

Once the jury had returned, Mr Osborne called on the first witness, Dr Jacob Hill, who stated that Mr Curran had been unwell for about a week before his death. Mr Curran's wife, Catherine, had on two occasions summoned the doctor to the home they had shared while he was unwell.

"Can you describe the symptoms Mr Curran presented with, Dr Hill?" asked the coroner.

"He complained of pain in his bowels and diarrhoea."

"And what treatment did you recommend?"

"I ordered for him to take soda water and milk."

Dr Hill reported that there had been no improvement in Mr Curran's condition by the time of his second visit and stated that he had found Catherine to be an extremely concerned and attentive nurse. He had last seen her when she visited him at his surgery to request a certificate of death.

A man representing Prudential Life Insurance Limited deposed that Mr Curran had been insured with the company for the sum of fifty pounds, and a representative from the General Assurance Society confirmed that Catherine Curran had effected a policy on her husband's life for the sum of thirty pounds. Both policies had been taken out with Mr Curran's full consent.

Mr Osborne then called for William Curran, the brother of John. A young, clean-shaven man with a heavy brow and scruffy fair hair walked up to the table. He held a cap in his hand and wore a smart but ill-fitting suit, which I guessed he had borrowed for the occasion.

William Curran stated that he lived in Paulin Street and worked at the same tannery where his brother had been employed.

"Were you concerned about your brother before he died?" asked the coroner.

"Yes, sir, I was, 'cause 'e'd taken to 'is sickbed."

"And what was his sickness?"

"What the doctor 'ere said. Diarrhoea. An' vomitin' an' pains such as 'e'd never 'ad afore."

"And prior to this spell of sickness, would you say that your brother had been in good health?"

"Yes, sir. Never 'ad a day of sickness 'is entire life."

"He was ordinarily a fit and healthy man?"

"Yes, sir."

"And did you have any idea as to the cause of his sickness?"

"Not ter start wiv. I thought 'e'd get better, but it was when she stopped me seein' 'im, that's when I begun ter get suspicious."

"Can you explain who you mean by *she?*"

"Yeah, 'is wife, Caffrine."

"Mrs Catherine Curran prevented you from visiting your sick brother?"

"Yeah. I've seen 'im once, and when I've went back to see if 'e was gettin' better she ain't never let me back in."

"Mrs Curran would not readmit you to their home?"

"Nope."

"Did she give you a reason for refusing to do so?"

"She tells me as 'e's tired and don't want no visitors. Well, that don't sound like our John! I ain't never known 'im refuse ter see me."

"Did you attempt to visit your brother again after that?"

"Yeah, twice more I tried ter see 'im."

"And you were unsuccessful?"

"She weren't lettin' me in the door."

"In your statement to the police you say that you visited your brother on the twelfth of August, and that was the last time you saw him. Is that correct?"

"Yes, sir."

"And why did you inform the police about your brother's death?"

"'Cause she wouldn't let me see 'im, like I said! I told 'em she's done summink to 'im. I dunno what, but she's done summink. It weren't right."

"What made you think Mrs Curran had *done something*, as you put it, to your brother?"

"'It just weren't normal. I smelt a rat."

Detective Inspector Charles Martin of M Division was the next witness. He was a young, fair-haired man with a round, pleasant face and fair whiskers.

"I was informed that Mr William Curran had concerns that his sister-in-law might have had a hand in his brother's death," he told Mr Osborne.

"And what caused you to give credence to his accusation?" asked the coroner.

"I wasn't sure whether to believe it or not initially, sir. It's not uncommon for the police to receive false accusations pertaining to all sorts of crimes, including murder. However, it is my duty to establish whether there is any basis for the accusation."

"And did you find any such basis?"

"My suspicions were aroused, sir, when I went to the address, number 96 Grange Walk, and found no sign of Mrs Curran there. The enquiries I made with her neighbours suggested that she had taken off."

"Have you since established the woman's whereabouts?"

"No, sir. M Division is currently carrying out an extensive search for the woman."

"Can you speculate on the reason for Mrs Curran's disappearance?"

"One possible explanation is that she is guilty of her husband's murder, as Mr William Curran has suggested. The sudden death of a usually healthy man, the disappearance of his wife, and the existence of not just one but *two* life insurance policies, led us to decide that a post-mortem examination of Mr Curran's body was necessary. And the findings of the autopsy suggest that—"

"Thank you, Inspector Martin. I shall stop you there as we will hear about the autopsy from the police surgeon next."

Dr Montague Grant had a long ginger beard and wore half-moon spectacles. He confirmed that he had carried out the post-mortem examination and explained that the stomach and bowels had shown signs of inflammation and ulceration, which suggested Mr Curran had consumed an irritant.

"And you suspected this irritant to be a poison?" asked the coroner.

"Yes indeed, sir, so I removed sections of the viscera and sealed them into three jars, which were then passed to Mr Irving at the Royal Institution."

The analytical chemist from the Royal Institution, Mr Joseph Irving, spoke next.

"I examined the contents of each jar according to Reinsch's test and obtained evidence of arsenic being present," he said. "I also conducted an examination according to Marsh's test, which provided the same result. An extraction of the poison from the viscera was then conducted by the Fresenius-von Babo method, which yielded a quantity of arsenic equivalent to one-and-a-third grains from the stomach and intestines. A further quantity of arsenic, equal to one grain, was obtained from the liver, kidneys and spleen. I should add that the intestines had a golden-yellow appearance, which suggests that arsenic was present throughout, and that this was not a case of a single incident of poisoning."

"You believe that more than one dose was administered to the deceased?"

"I do, yes."

"And that the amount of arsenic present was enough to kill a man?"

"Yes."

Once all the witnesses had spoken, Mr Osborne addressed the jury: "My judgement on the matter is that we must adjourn for two weeks in order to allow the police time to search the home of the deceased for further evidence of arsenic poisoning, and to locate the whereabouts of Mrs Catherine Curran. I propose that this inquest be resumed on Wednesday the third of September."

CHAPTER 4

"So in summary, Inspector, you believe that Mrs Curran poisoned her husband and then ran off with the life insurance money," I said to Inspector Martin as we stood outside the pub in Bermondsey Square after the inquest.

"It seems that way, although there could be another explanation."

"Such as?"

"I don't know yet, but I'm reluctant to jump to immediate conclusions. *Morning Express* did you say?"

I nodded.

"My father takes the *Morning Express*. I try to read it when I find the time; you never know what snippets of intelligence may be picked up from the reading of a newspaper."

"Some claim that newspapers contain no intelligence at all," I commented.

Inspector Martin laughed. "We all know those types, don't we? The grumbling sort of chap who perpetually complains that his glass is half full."

"I hope you find Mrs Curran very soon," I said. "She has a lot of questions to answer."

"She certainly does. Have you seen that photograph of her?"

"No, which one would that be?"

Inspector Martin opened the folder he had been holding under his arm and pulled out a piece of card, which was about five by eight inches in size.

"I've shown it to a few of the press chaps," he continued. "It's a photograph of her with Mr Curran. A local photographer contacted me shortly after Mrs Curran went missing. He'd heard that she had run off, and it seems she was so quick to get away that she never visited his studio to pick this up."

He handed me the photograph, which showed a couple sitting side by side on a small settee. The woman looked about thirty and was fair-haired and dark-eyed with a pretty, heart-shaped face. She wore mourning dress with black gloves and a black bonnet. The man sitting beside her wore a buttoned-up jacket, a starched collar, a dark tie and a peaked cap. The expression on his face was oddly fixed, and whereas the woman was looking directly at the camera there was something about the man's eyes which didn't seem quite right.

Inspector Martin must have noticed my quizzical expression. "The photographer has painted the eyes onto the photograph," he explained. "Mr Curran was deceased by the time this was taken."

I stared down at the couple incredulously. "I can understand why someone might wish to have a photographic memory of their loved one," I said. "But arranging for the photo to be taken when you have just murdered him? That seems highly unlikely."

"If it's true, it would certainly be a macabre thing to do, Miss Green," he replied. "This photograph was taken on the day Mr Curran died. After collecting the certificate of death from the doctor, Mrs Curran requested that the photographer visit her home and take this photograph in one of the rooms they occupied in the upper storey of the house. By the following day she was gone. We were admitted to the house by the lady who lives downstairs, and when we gained access to the upstairs room we found poor Mr Curran sitting in the same position he had been arranged in for the photograph."

"Good grief!" I shivered.

"That's when we realised something was amiss and had him removed to the mortuary. We have since discovered that Mrs Curran was successful in swiftly obtaining from the insurance companies the amount of money she effected on the life of her husband."

"It's difficult to believe that someone could be so cold and calculating," I said with a sigh. "Catherine Curran looks like an ordinary woman in this photograph. She even looks as though she might be friendly. I simply cannot see how she might be capable of something like this."

"We can't be certain that she is, but it's all rather suspicious, isn't it? We haven't found many people who know her well yet, but from what we hear she's a friendly lady who was apparently very concerned about her husband's illness and nursed him up to his final moments."

"Presumably to feed him as much arsenic as possible."

"Possibly. And if that's what happened the poor fellow probably never realised she was the cause of his ailment."

"How dreadful," I said, taking one last look at the photograph before handing it back to the inspector. "Could he really have had no suspicion that he was being poisoned?"

"By all accounts arsenic has no flavour, so it's impossible to taste the poison in a mouthful of food or drink."

"Have you any idea where she obtained the poison?"

"Not yet. Its sale is carefully controlled, as you probably

know. But we are still collecting items from the home and the analytical chemist will test them for the presence of arsenic. We're also making enquiries at the local stores to find out whether any of them sold vermin powder to her."

"And you have no clues at all as to her whereabouts? Have you visited her family and friends?"

"We have only been able to locate a few acquaintances so far. William Curran recalls her telling him that she had some family in Kent."

"Do you know much about her?"

"Not much at all, but hopefully we shall learn a lot more presently."

"The money from the life insurance has presumably facilitated her escape."

"No doubt it has. It means she can afford both board and travel. My fear is that she's taken a train somewhere and left London altogether."

I sighed. "I suppose she could be anywhere."

"We mustn't lose hope, Miss Green. We'll do whatever we can to find her. You could help us by publishing an appeal for her whereabouts in the *Morning Express*. The general public can be very helpful at times such as these. Someone must know where she is."

CHAPTER 5

I returned to The Five Bells after my conversation with Inspector Martin. As I had hoped, William Curran was already drinking inside. He had removed his tie, which was lying on the bar next to his mug of beer.

"Yer don't see many women writin' for the papers," he said after I had introduced myself. Dark eyes observed me from beneath his heavy brow.

"Not yet," I replied. "I hope there will be more in due course. Please accept my condolences for the sad passing of your brother, Mr Curran."

"That's kind o' yer, Miss Green. Still can't believe he ain't 'ere no more. People will tell yer that we didn't always see eye to eye but 'e's still me brother."

William Curran seemed reasonably polite, but his movements were heavy and there was something unpleasant about his gaze that I couldn't quite put my finger on. He struck me as the type of man who possessed a violent nature.

"I pray that your sister-in-law is found soon. If it's proven that Catherine poisoned him she will need to face justice."

"It's obvious it's 'er, ain't it?"

"It does seem that way."

"They reckons it's arsenic, don't they? Who else would've given 'im arsenic? And with the life insurance an' ev'rythin'. All she wanted was the money! She should swing fer it."

He wrapped a large hand around his mug of beer and lifted it to his lips.

"What's she like?" I asked.

"I used ter fink as she was a good 'un! Thought she loved 'im, I did."

"How long were they married for?"

"Near on a year."

"Do you know where they met?"

"Down The Butcher's Arms on Long Lane."

"And did they know each other for long before they were married?"

"Can't recall now. Few months, proberly."

"So they first met early last year?"

William took another sip of his beer while he considered this. "S'pose it would be, yeah."

"Your brother was about twenty-nine or thirty by then. Had he been married before that?"

"No, it were the first time fer John."

"And Catherine was presumably of a similar age?"

"I dunno really. I s'pose she is. She ain't much younger than 'im."

"Did you know anything of her life before they met? Perhaps she had been married before."

"I fink 'e said as she was, but I can't be certain of it."

"Did she talk much about herself?"

"Not much, no."

"Any family members? Parents? Siblings?"

"Never met any of 'em."

"You didn't meet anyone from her family at the wedding?"

"Not as I can recall. Weren't many of us there."

"Catherine Curran strikes me as rather a mysterious lady."

"I can't say as I knows 'er too well. She's kind and everyfink, always asks 'ow you are an' that. She's quiet-spoken and John got no answerin' back from 'er. I remember finking as she was a good 'un, but I don't fink it no more!"

"You mention that you didn't always see eye to eye with your brother. Had you fallen out at the time of his death?"

"Not as such. I jus' wanted ter see 'im and make fings right. When I 'eard 'e was took bad I wanted to tell 'im I was sorry."

"What for?"

"There ain't no need ter go into all that now." His dark, stony stare prompted me to change the subject.

"Are you married, Mr Curran?"

"Yeah, my missus is called Ellen."

"Does Ellen know Catherine well?"

"No, Caffrine works a lot. She's a fellmonger down the leather market."

"Do you know which tannery she worked at?"

"I can't say as I'm sure. One o' the ones 'round 'ere, though."

"You say that your sister-in-law was kind, and a good wife. You must have thought it out of character for her to refuse you entry to your brother's home."

"Yeah, it weren't like 'er. She tells me as 'e's taken sick. I sees 'im the once and 'e's in a bad way. An' I asks her, ''Ave yer 'ad the doctor out?' An' she says, 'Yeah, I've 'ad the doctor out and I'll 'ave 'im out again 'cause John's real bad.' She tells me it's 'is job 'as made 'im sick. She says it's the filth what's used in the tannin' that's done it. Well, I've worked at the tanneries since I were a lad and it ain't never made me sick.

And John's worked there since 'e were a lad and the first time 'e gets sick is when 'e's married to 'er!"

"It's fortunate that you informed the police of your suspicions. Some people would have simply believed what Catherine had told you."

"Yeah, well I didn't, see. Summink weren't right. We're goin' out lookin' for 'er this evenin', all of us. We're gonna find out where she's bin 'idin'."

"Hopefully she won't have gone far," I said optimistically, but I thought of the money she had at her disposal to aid her getaway. "Inspector Martin has asked me to publish an appeal in the newspaper, so we shall soon have as many people as possible on the lookout for her."

I left The Five Bells, crossed the road, and made my way along Grange Walk, where the Currans had lived. The street was lined on both sides with small terraced houses and a pall of smoke from the factory chimneys hung overhead.

Children played in the road and an emaciated dog padded about, sniffing at patches of damp on the walls.

A large-framed woman of about twenty-five leant up against a wall, watching me. She wore a dirty apron over a dark dress, but there was no sign of a bonnet or shawl. Her unkempt hair was the colour of straw and hung loosely about her shoulders. As I passed her she gave me a lopsided smile. She appeared to me like an overgrown child.

"Can I help you?" I asked.

She shook her head in reply and continued to smile.

A constable stood outside the modest-sized house numbered ninety-six. I stopped and gazed at the upstairs window, thinking of the morbid photograph of the Currans. I recalled Catherine Curran's pretty features and tried to comprehend her thoughts at the time the photograph had been taken. Presumably she believed she had got away with murder. That explained why she had felt confident enough to arrange a post-mortem photograph of her and her dead husband.

And if it hadn't been for William Curran she probably would have got away with it.

CHAPTER 6

I passed by the newspaper reading room at the British Library to check the shipping news. After searching through the small print I felt a pang of sadness when I saw a mention of Francis' ship:

LIVERPOOL
   SAILED – 20th August – Tintore *to Barcelona;* Ericson *to San Francisco;* Prince Leopold *to Quebec;* Pampero *to Savanilla.*

There it was confirmed, in black and white, in front of me. Two days previously Francis' ship, the *Pampero*, had left port bound for Savanilla on the northern coast of Colombia.

I lifted my spectacles and wiped a tear from my eye, silently scolding myself for my sentimentality.

Once I had pulled myself together, I worked on my article about the farewell letter New Zealand's Māori king, Tāwhiao, had written after visiting London over the summer. I kept expecting Francis to appear at my shoulder as I worked. Every now and then I was certain I had caught a glimpse of him walking between the desks, speaking to the head librarian at his rotunda in the centre of the room, or making his way along one of the galleries which circled beneath the great dome. His disappointing replacement, Mr Retchford, bustled about, scolding anyone who dared utter a sound.

"Penny?" whispered a voice at my shoulder. I shook my head, absent-mindedly assuming I had imagined Francis' voice. As I turned, my heart performed a flip in my chest.

It was James.

I returned his broad smile and was struck by how handsome he looked in his dark blue suit.

"What are you doing here?" I whispered. "You surprised me!"

"No talking!" came a high-pitched rebuke from Mr Retchford.

I gathered up my papers from the desk and shoved them into my carpet bag.

"We were just leaving," I said to the dough-faced clerk.

James and I walked out onto the steps of the British Museum. I had last seen him with Charlotte, and the awkwardness of that meeting still lingered in my mind.

"How are you, Penny?"

"I'm all right, thank you."

His blue eyes fixed mine as if he didn't quite believe me.

"I'm guessing you've heard about the poisoning in Bermondsey," I ventured, keen to keep the conversation moving.

"Yes, and there is still no sign of the wife."

"I'm not sure how they intend to find her. I imagine she'll have travelled as far away from London as possible by now.

She has plenty of money from the life insurance policies to ease her passage."

"She took out more than one policy?" asked James. "That should have aroused suspicion even before she attempted to give her husband the poison."

"I don't suppose many people would have known that she had taken out two policies, would they? The insurance salesman who sold her the second one probably had no idea that there was already one in place."

"I suspect you're right, Penny. Let's hope she hasn't travelled too far from here. If she gets away with this she might attempt the same crime in another city many miles away. She could easily change her name and no one would be any the wiser."

"You don't really think she would risk doing this sort of thing again, do you?"

"I should hope not. Perhaps she desperately needed the money to pay off debts or something along those lines. And perhaps the woman will eventually listen to her conscience and hand herself in. I'd like to go down to Bermondsey and find out how they're getting on there. I know Inspector Charles Martin well. We were constables together at T Division, and he's a fine police officer."

"I didn't realise that. He seems a pleasant chap and doesn't mind me asking questions. The same can't be said for certain other officers."

"Indeed. He's a good man."

"What did you come to see me about?" I asked, pausing on the steps.

"Oh yes, I came to ask about the journal you consulted when you were carrying out your research into the Forsters' murder case. What was it called?"

"*The Homeward Mail.*"

"That's right, I remember now. I should like to look through a few editions."

"That means you'll have to go back inside the British Library and contend with Mr Retchford."

"Is he the chap who told us off for talking?"

"Yes, the man whose voice somehow doesn't match his appearance. Don't you find it off-putting when someone speaks differently from the way you might expect?"

James laughed. "Hopefully Mr Retchford will be more helpful when I ask him about accessing copies of *The Homeward Mail*."

"I wouldn't be so hopeful. I realise now what an asset Francis was."

"He certainly did a lot of research on your behalf, Penny."

"And to think that he's in the middle of the Atlantic Ocean at this moment! His ship is due to call at the coaling station of Terceira in the Azores soon, so I shall look out for that in the shipping news. I've already seen confirmation that he has left Liverpool."

"You've been keeping a close eye on him, I see."

"He's searching for my father! I still can't fully believe that he has taken on the task. And to think that he has never done this sort of thing before! I think it incredibly brave of him."

"It certainly is admirable."

"When I was sitting in the reading room just now I kept thinking I had caught a glimpse of him going about his work, just as he always used to."

"You're missing him, then?"

"I suppose I must be. I'll get used to it, and I'm looking forward to receiving his next letter. Hopefully he'll be able to send one from the Azores Islands."

"That would be a comfort." James glanced at his pocket watch as if he were losing interest in the conversation.

"Would you like me to introduce you to Mr Retchford so you can take a look at some editions of *The Homeward Mail*?"

"That would be useful, but there is no great urgency. I just need to look something up for the trial."

"I see. Are you all right, James?"

"Yes, I'm fine. Why do you ask?" His manner had suddenly become formal and distant.

"I thought you had come down here to look at *The Homeward Mail*."

"Yes, and I will do. I just hadn't expected to hear you singing the praises of Francis Edwards in this way."

"I wasn't singing his praises; I merely mentioned that he is on a ship out in the Atlantic at this moment. This is a very important venture! It means an enormous amount to me."

"Yes, and I suppose he knew that all along. His gallant adventure is a thinly disguised attempt to win the heart of his fair lady."

"You have no idea what you're talking about!" I snapped. "Francis undertook this journey because he knew there was no chance that I would ever marry him. He told me he had no wish to spend the rest of his days stuck in a library hoping that I might one day change my mind. Those were his very words! And I feel terribly guilty about it all."

"I shouldn't feel guilty if I were you, Penny. He's off on an adventure knowing that the Green daughters now consider him the greatest hero who ever lived."

"Now you're acting like a child."

"He's *brave* and I'm a *child*, am I? Well, thank you, Penny. The truth is finally confirmed, isn't it?"

"I have work to be getting on with."

I turned to walk back toward the library, but James caught my arm.

"Don't go, Penny. I'm sorry. I have no desire to argue with you."

"Likewise," I replied, my throat feeling tight. I turned back to face him.

"And yes, you're right. I am being a child about this," he continued. "And I didn't come here to read the cursed *Homeward Mail*. That was nothing more than an excuse. I came here to see you."

"Oh?"

"Three weeks from tomorrow I shall be married."

"I don't wish to be reminded of that."

"I have known Charlotte's family for a very long time."

"And what difference does that make?"

"It means that our marriage was first considered long ago; so long ago, in fact, that I have been accustomed to the idea for many years."

"Well that should be of great help to you when you come to make your vows."

"But then you appeared, Penny."

I gave a dry laugh. "I *appeared*? As if I were a work of magic?"

"Perhaps it was magic."

"If I remember rightly you accosted me at the foot of these very steps."

"I did. I remember it well."

We both smiled.

"James, I cannot deny that I enjoy hearing these words from your lips," I said, "but they are only words. They change nothing."

His manner grew more distant again. "My marriage needn't affect our working relationship."

"Even though Charlotte no longer allows us to meet at the Museum Tavern?"

"There are ways around that."

"Everything will be different when you marry, James. You

know that as well as I do. And I think that's why you're here today. You have suddenly realised it."

"It won't be any different; I shan't allow it to be."

"Your wedding is still going ahead in three weeks' time, is it not?"

There was a pause as he looked at me, a guilty expression passing across his face.

"On the thirteenth of September?" I asked.

He nodded. "Yes."

I shrugged. "Then there is little else for us to discuss, is there? Please excuse me, but I must get back to my work."

CHAPTER 7

D earest Penny and Eliza,

Tuesday 19th August 1884

I write to you from the Royal Corinthian Hotel in Liverpool! Tomorrow morning I shall embark the SS Pampero at the Prince's Landing Stage. I had a good look at her through the telescope this afternoon, and I must say that I'm terribly excited about my impending adventure.

I would like to thank you both for giving me this opportunity of a lifetime. I vow to do my utmost to find out what has happened to your father and will write whenever I find the opportunity. I'm told there aren't many post boxes in the jungle, but I shall do all I can to get word to you whenever possible!

Ever your friend,
Francis Edwards

I folded up Francis' letter, which had been left on the hallway table for me, and glanced around for any sign of my landlady, Mrs Garnett. She appeared to be out, so I made my way up to my garret room, where my cat Tiger was meowing at the window to be let in.

I ate some bread and butter, then made myself a cup of cocoa before loosening my stays and sitting at my writing desk to continue my work on the book about my father. Francis' journey to Colombia had provided me with the encouragement I needed to spend more of my time transcribing Father's letters and diaries. I hoped that the outcome of his search would inform the conclusion of my book.

I tried not to think about James as I worked, but when Tiger clambered onto my lap the brief distraction gave me a moment to reflect on our conversation from earlier that afternoon. James knew he was making a mistake in marrying Charlotte, I felt sure of it. But was his conviction strong enough to make him call off his wedding? I knew that he couldn't bear the thought of upsetting Charlotte or her family, not to mention his own family and friends, or the many guests who had been invited. The boulder had begun to roll down the hill some time ago, and as it gathered speed James had felt increasingly powerless to stop it.

Sometimes I felt sympathy for him in his predicament and at other times I felt angry. *How could he have allowed the situation to descend to this point?* He had made it clear that he harboured an affection for me; he had even kissed me on one occasion. Charlotte would have been horrified had she known about it. *Perhaps I should tell her*, I mused.

The thought was tempting, but I knew that by doing so I would be held responsible for ruining the betrothal. All the blame would fall upon me, and I risked losing the man I loved at the same time. I maintained a faint hope that James would come to his senses and realise he wasn't as devoted to his future wife as he should be.

I tried to distract myself by making another cup of cocoa. As the water was heating up on the little stove in my room my thoughts turned to the poisoning of John Curran. Something James had said about Catherine Curran lingered in my mind: '*She might attempt the same crime in another city many miles away. She could easily change her name and no one would be any the wiser.*'

My conversation with her brother-in-law had revealed that he knew little about her past or her character. Had Catherine purposefully revealed as little about herself as possible? Had she done this sort of thing before?

I heard a door slam downstairs, heralding the return of Mrs Garnett. As I finished making my cocoa I heard footsteps on the stairs, and then came a knock at my door.

"Mrs Garnett!" I said as I opened it. "Have you enjoyed an evening out somewhere?"

"You could say that."

She was breathless with exertion and still wore her bonnet and shawl. Her dark skin glistened with perspiration and her brown eyes left my face, focusing instead on the papers that covered my writing desk.

"How can you ever get anything done with all that clutter everywhere, Miss Green?"

"There's an order to it."

She sucked her lip disapprovingly. "I can't see any order going on over there."

"It all makes perfect sense to me."

"Good. I suppose that's all that matters."

"What did you come to see me about, Mrs Garnett?"

"Oh, that's right. I found Tiger lurking in my parlour again this morning."

"Oh dear, I am sorry."

"She made me sneeze. I've told you before about the sneezing. Once she sets me off I sneeze all night and don't get a wink of sleep."

"I apologise. I really don't know how she gets in there. Your sneezing appears to have stopped for now, thankfully."

Mrs Garnett winkled her nose, as if testing it. "Only because I've been outside for a while."

"Where have you been?"

"Mrs Wilkinson and I have been helping with the search around Bermondsey for that despicable woman who poisoned her husband!"

"Was there any sign of her?"

"No, none. But we're all determined to keep looking. If everybody keeps looking we're bound to find her, aren't we?"

"She may not be in Bermondsey any longer."

"Oh, I don't know about that. If it's an area she knows well, and I'm sure she does, she'll know all the best places to hide around there. There's no use in her travelling somewhere else to hide in a place she doesn't know, is there?"

I considered this, and it seemed a logical surmise. "Until now I had assumed she would have travelled as far away as possible, but what you are saying makes sense, Mrs Garnett."

"It was Mrs Wilkinson who suggested it. She has a good nose for these things."

"Did you come across anyone who knew more about her?" I asked. "Family or friends, for example?"

"There was talk of a sister or cousin in Rotherhithe, but I'm not sure which it was. Some of the others told me they had been to the house, but no one had discovered anything there. Mrs Wilkinson and I looked around the wharves near the brewery. There are lots of hiding places in those warehouses."

"She can't hide there forever, though, can she?" I said.

"Spending one's life in a warehouse wouldn't be much of an existence."

"You're right, Miss Green, which is why we looked around there. The chances are she's had enough of the place by now and is looking to emerge and make good her escape. She may well choose to do it at night, but they've got men with lanterns down there now. Mrs Wilkinson and I came home because neither of us likes the dark much."

"I never knew you went in for detective work, Mrs Garnett."

"Oh, I don't. I was just helping with the search."

"I'm sure the police in Bermondsey are grateful to you and everyone else who has been keeping a look out for her."

"I hope so. Now please keep your cat out of my parlour, Miss Green."

"I'll do my best, Mrs Garnett."

CHAPTER 8

"We had a good turnout for the search yesterday evening," said Inspector Martin as we stood in the parade room of Bermondsey Street police station. "Still no sign of Catherine Curran, though."

"My landlady thinks she's hiding in one of the warehouses down by the river."

"She may well be. We've had a number of constables staking out the riverside. Meanwhile, we have received an interesting report from a lady who resides on the Old Kent Road. She thinks she may have let a room to Catherine Curran on the night of her husband's death. We have a sergeant over there speaking to her now."

"That's encouraging news."

"And there's something else you might like to see, Miss Green." The inspector stepped over to a nearby table and picked up a buff envelope. "At the house on Grande Walk, we found another photograph."

He pulled out the piece of card and handed it to me. It bore the image of a couple seated on a chaise longue in a photographer's studio. The young woman was fair-haired and wore mourning dress. The man leaned rigidly against her and, once again, there was something about his eyes which seemed unnatural.

I shuddered.

"Is he?"

"Deceased?" said Inspector Martin. "Yes, he is."

I stared at the photograph and recognised Catherine Curran from the previous photograph I had seen of her.

"She's done this before," I said, feeling nauseous. "It's exactly the same situation, isn't it?"

Inspector Martin gave a firm nod. "We can't draw any firm conclusions just yet, but it certainly appears that way."

There was a border around the photograph, and the embossed gold writing at the bottom of it stated:

'E. Lillywhite. Photographer. Upper Grange Road, Bermondsey.'

"Have you visited this photographer?" I asked Inspector Martin.

"Yes, Mr Lillywhite has been quite helpful. It took a little while to jog his memory about the couple, but once he'd consulted his books he was able to tell us that this photograph is of a Mr and Mrs Thomas Burrell, and that it was taken on the eighteenth of May 1882. Two years and three months ago."

"Burrell? She was Catherine Burrell?"

"Yes. They were married at St Mary Magdalen church in Bermondsey on the twenty-second of July 1881. We found them in the parish register. Her maiden name was Peel."

"Catherine Peel, Catherine Burrell and then Catherine Curran. She has changed her name at least twice."

"She certainly has. We also found the record of her

marriage to John Curran in the parish register, and she was listed there as a widow with the surname Burrell, so there is little doubt that it is one and the same woman."

"Are we to presume that Thomas Burrell's death was not considered to be suspicious?"

"There was no inquest as far as we're aware. We've asked the coroner to check his records."

"So the cause of death was considered to have been natural."

"It seems that way; however, his body is to be exhumed from St Mary Magdalen's churchyard at dawn on Monday next."

"Oh goodness, really?" I handed the photograph back to the inspector.

"There's a lot to write about here, isn't there, Miss Green?" He gave me a friendly smile.

"There certainly is. I hardly know where to start. This woman needs to be found! You're going to tell me now that an insurance policy was taken out against Thomas Burrell's life, aren't you?"

"Indeed it was. So far we've found evidence of at least one policy, but there may be more."

"Why does she have these photographs taken after her husband's deaths? I cannot understand it."

"Some sort of macabre memento, I suppose. Under ordinary circumstances you could understand why a widow might wish to have a lasting memory of her husband, especially if no photographs had been taken of him during his lifetime. But to do such a thing after she has caused his death is completely unfathomable."

"Perhaps she felt it was the expected behaviour of a widow. Perhaps by accompanying her husbands in the photographs anyone who became suspicious would have considered her less likely to have been the poisoner."

"It's possible. The photographs certainly create the impression that she was a loyal, caring wife until the end."

"And even afterwards."

The inspector gave a dry laugh. "Indeed."

"Have you spoken to Thomas Burrell's family?" I asked.

"My constables are trying to locate them as we speak."

"Let's hope some of them live in this area. It's interesting that she remained in Bermondsey after the death of her first husband, isn't it? She didn't feel the need to run away after the event."

"Presumably because his death was attributed to natural causes. No one suspected her of any wrongdoing."

I shook my head in bewilderment. "She must have felt so pleased that she'd got away with it. I wonder how many other crimes she has pulled off."

"I hope there are no further incidents, but the discovery of this photograph means the investigation has been expanded. We've had to enlist the help of Scotland Yard."

My heart skipped. "Inspector James Blakely?"

"You know him?"

"Yes, and I believe you do too."

"I do indeed," he replied. "We've known each other for some time. Blakely will be a great asset to us."

"Which number Old Kent Road is Catherine Curran rumoured to have lodged at? I should like to interview the woman who lives there."

"Three hundred and fourteen, on the top floor. It's between the fire station and The Thomas à Becket pub. Ask for Mrs Hardy."

I travelled by horse tram along the busy Old Kent Road until the red-and-white-brick fire station came into view. The house where Mrs Hardy dwelt had once been a smart family home, but it had been clumsily divided into apartments and looked rather shabby.

"She only stayed 'ere fer two nights," said Mrs Hardy, who came down from her rooms to speak to me on the doorstep. She was a short, elderly lady with an old grey bonnet tied firmly under her chin. "I gets a lot o' folk stoppin' wi' me, but there was summink different about 'er."

"In what way?"

"Summink weren't right. Whenever there was a door slam or a loud voice she'd jump like a scared kitten."

"Did she tell you anything about herself?"

"Said she were runnin' from 'er 'usband as 'e were a drunk. She gave me a sovereign, an' then she gave me five shillin's for 'er food, an' then she said she 'ad more coins on 'er, an' that's why she couldn't afford ter be found by 'er 'usband, 'cause 'e were after the money, see."

"And did you believe her story?"

"Can't say as I did, she 'ad a bit of a look abaht 'er. 'Er eyes wasn't matching what she said, like. I felt bad for 'er abaht the drunk 'usband, but when I asked 'er abaht 'im, like where 'e lived and what pub 'e drank in, she 'ad to stop an' fink abaht it. That's why I reckoned she were lyin'. I told 'er so an' all, and next thing I know she's gone."

"She left immediately?"

"Middle o' the night. I woke up and 'er room was empty. So I tells Minnie abaht it."

"Minnie?"

"Me daughter, lives over in Astley Street. I tells 'er abaht it and she says she's 'eard of some woman what's gone on the run after a poisonin'. 'Er 'usband read abaht it in the paper. She gave me it. I can't read it, but I still got it."

Mrs Hardy shuffled off up to her rooms for a short while before returning with a copy of *The Southwark News*. It was folded open on the page where the news story appeared. I quickly read through it.

"Minnie says there's a 'scription of 'er, an' she read it out ter me."

"I see it now," I said, reading it out loud so Mrs Hardy could hear it again. "'Wanted in Bermondsey on suspicion of having caused the death of John Curran by administering arsenic is Catherine Curran, the deceased's wife. She is about thirty years of age and five feet four inches in height, with a slim build. Mrs Curran has a fresh complexion, dark eyes, fair hair, wears rings on her fingers and was last seen on the seventeenth of August dressed in a black dress, black shawl and bonnet.'"

"That's 'er, I'll swear to it," said Mrs Hardy. "She told me 'er name was Jane, but she musta been lyin' abaht that an' all."

"And you went to the police about it?"

"It was Minnie what done that; I don't walk too far these days. She told 'em an' then they come round an' I told 'em everyfink I know."

"I wonder where she is now," I said.

Mrs Hardy shrugged. "She weren't givin' nuffink away, an' now I knows why! Wish I coulda kept 'er 'ere fer longer and got 'er harrested. I shouldn't of haccused 'er o' lyin', 'cause I frightened 'er away, didn't I?"

"You couldn't have known she was a fugitive, Mrs Hardy," I said. "You mustn't blame yourself. You've helped the police as much as you can."

CHAPTER 9

A hansom cab brought me to St Mary Magdalen church in Bermondsey shortly before sunrise on a mild Monday morning. I paid my fare and tentatively stepped through the gate to the churchyard. To my left, the cream walls of the seventeenth-century church were spectral in the gloom, and around me there were dark, crooked tombstones to mark each silent sleeper.

I followed the path toward the dim lamplight at the centre of the churchyard. An early morning blackbird sang from a nearby yew tree, the gaiety of its song painfully at odds with the sombre mood of the occasion. As I approached the lamplight I saw a group of shadowy figures standing around the grave of Thomas Burrell. The sound of shovels digging into the earth made me shiver.

One of the figures detached itself from the group and walked toward me.

"Penny?"

It was James, and I could just make out his features in the grey light.

"I believe this is the second exhumation we've attended together," he said with a wry smile.

"I hear you're to help Inspector Martin with this case." I felt mindful of our uncomfortable conversation on the steps of the British Museum and feared that more tension would inevitably grow between us as his wedding approached.

"Yes, and we're beginning to wonder how many lives Catherine Curran has claimed. We're asking London's coroners to examine their records for any suspicious poisonings over the past ten years."

"That's even assuming that inquests were held into their deaths," I replied. "In some instances poison may not have been suspected, as was the case with Thomas Burrell."

"Sadly, you're right, and that's why we're digging the unfortunate chap up this morning."

"How long do you think it will take to determine the cause of death?"

"The autopsy will be carried out immediately at the morgue here, but samples of his body tissue will need to be examined by the experts."

"Presumably the chemist at the Royal Institution who identified the arsenic in John Curran's body."

"Yes, probably the same chap again. My guess is that it'll take a few days, and then there'll be the inquest, of course."

"And during that time Catherine Curran will be able to take further steps to avoid capture."

"It's a frustrating business," said James, "but we're doing all we can. Today we'll have men going through all the local parish registers looking for a reference to a Catherine Peel or any other names she may have used in the past. There may be more husbands, and there may even be children. We shall hopefully find out, and perhaps we may be able to trace some of her family members."

"I visited the landlady, Mrs Hardy, whom she stayed with on the Old Kent Road," I said.

"What did she tell you?"

"She thought Catherine was lying and confronted her about it. She wishes she hadn't done so now, as her actions frightened Catherine away."

"She shouldn't have any regrets. Everyone has a right to know the truth about a person who is staying under their own roof. She might have notified the police, I suppose, but at that stage she had no idea who Catherine really was. The fact that Catherine took flight when confronted indicates that it was a viable sighting, so we can be reassured about that at least."

"And the fact that Catherine is paying for lodgings suggests to me that she doesn't have any family or friends who might be willing to put her up," I added.

"Yes. We're asking the owners of lodging houses and hotels to be on the lookout for her. It's a bit of luck that she has already checked in to one of these places. If she had someone hiding her away it would be far easier for her to escape detection."

"The Old Kent Road location worries me, though," I said. "It's the main route from London to Kent, and ultimately the port of Dover. She could have travelled that way and then stowed herself away on a ship."

"She may have. But she could also have stowed away on a ship in the Port of London. If she flees the country there is very little we can do about it. We have to hope that she will stay close by, and the indications are that she hasn't ventured too far yet."

We were distracted by a flurry of activity at the grave site.

"It looks as though they're about to lift him out," said James.

We moved closer to the grave, which had a freshly dug

pile of soil beside it. A man stood inside the grave, examining the coffin.

"Some o' the wood's gone rotten," he announced. "Dunno 'ow much of 'im we got left in there."

I felt my stomach turn.

"Let's just lift him out, and get this over and done with," said Inspector Martin. "Has Dr Grant arrived yet?"

"He's waitin' up in the mort'ry."

"Get some ropes strapped around the coffin and lift him out. Every man and his wife will soon be turning up to watch these proceedings if we're not quick about it."

I shuddered as the coffin was hauled up. There seemed something inherently wrong about disturbing the dead. A section of the coffin's rotten wood splintered off and dropped back down into the grave.

I looked away, my stomach turning again.

"I should get back to the newsroom and write up this morning's sombre events," I whispered to James.

"I'll let you know what the police surgeon finds out," replied James. "However, I think we can already make an intelligent guess as to what caused this chap's death."

CHAPTER 10

"You're spending quite a bit of time south of the river, Miss Green," commented Edgar as I unpacked my papers onto my desk in the newsroom.

"There's a lot going on in Bermondsey at the moment," I replied. "It'll be interesting to find out how many people this Catherine Curran has poisoned."

"I hope I never come across her," said Edgar.

"She's hardly likely to poison you, Fish," laughed Frederick.

"I suppose not. But it makes you think, doesn't it? Perhaps I need to employ the services of a food taster in case Mrs Fish has it in for me. Isn't that what the great rulers of old did? I believe they had a chap taste their food before they ate it, and if he didn't die they would happily tuck in."

"Perhaps you could ask your housekeeper to undertake the task," suggested Frederick.

"I don't think she'd be amenable. Perhaps I could dose myself with small amounts of poison on a regular basis so that

I would become used to it. I'm sure I recall reading about a Persian king who did that."

"He poisoned himself before anyone else could?" asked Frederick.

"Yes, but only with very small amounts so that he became accustomed to it. That way if anyone had tried to poison him they would have failed."

"Did it work?" I asked.

"Do you know what, Miss Green? I have no idea whether his strategy was successful or not."

"Mithridatism," announced Mr Sherman, the door of the newsroom slamming shut behind him as usual.

"A what, sir?" asked Edgar.

"Administering poison to oneself. That's what you're talking about, isn't it?"

"It is, sir," said Edgar. "Although I wasn't aware of that word you used to describe it."

"It comes from King Mithridates the sixth, who was terrified of being poisoned."

"That's the chap I was talking about!" said Edgar. "I'm pleased to find that I still remember one thing from my school days."

"But did it work?" I asked again.

"We know that he was successful in building up a tolerance to poison because his actions worked against him in the end," replied Mr Sherman. "After being defeated by the Romans he attempted to take his own life. Guess how he tried to do it?"

Edgar laughed and slapped his desk. "Poison?"

"Exactly right, Fish."

"And it didn't work?" I said.

"Exactly, Miss Green. It had no effect at all, so he had his bodyguard run him through with a sword instead."

"Ugh," said Frederick.

"That's how it was in those days," said Sherman.

"Thank goodness we live in modern times," said Edgar. "I'm glad there's none of that falling on your sword business any more."

"You might feel like doing so yourself, Fish, if I don't have your article on the Abyssinian envoys shortly," said our editor. "Don't forget that it also needs to be typewritten."

Edgar gave me pleading look.

"Not me this time, Edgar," I said. "I have too much to do myself."

"I think I'm beginning to understand why a woman might wish to poison her husband," said Eliza as we dined at The Holborn Restaurant that evening. The clatter of silver on china and a mumble of voices filled the air.

"Ellie, that's a horrible thing to say!"

"Some men are exceptionally tiresome," she added as she sliced at a piece of boiled turkey.

"Being tiresome is no reason to be murdered. Perhaps if the husband is a violent drunk one might sympathise with an attempt to poison him, but there's no evidence to suggest that either John Curran or Thomas Burrell were unpleasant men. In fact, we know that Catherine Curran's motive was to claim the life insurance money."

"I suppose I'm thinking about something else entirely," said Eliza with a sigh. "There are moments when I have thought about poisoning George."

"You don't actually mean that!"

"Actually, Penelope, I do. The man has been so cantankerous and difficult since he went to live with his friend Mr Beale-Wottinger. I'm beginning to wonder what I ever saw in him."

"Well, you know my thoughts on the matter," I replied.

Eliza's husband, George Billington-Grieg, had moved out of the family home since becoming indirectly implicated in a murder case I had worked on.

"I know that he hasn't yet been found guilty of any wrong-doing," said Eliza, "but he's not a complete fool. I think he must have turned a blind eye when he shouldn't have, if nothing else."

"We shall find out in due course," I said. "If he's found to be blameless will you take him back again?"

There was a long silence.

"I'm not sure. I suppose there is my financial position to consider."

"You could find yourself a job, Ellie. You've always wanted to do that."

"I suppose I could. I must say that writing has always appealed to me."

"There's little money in writing, unfortunately," I said. "You'll need something which pays rather better."

"George's salary will continue to pay some of our expenses. We'll have to sell the house, I suppose, which is a terrible shame as I adore living in Bayswater."

"George's salary cannot be completely relied upon," I said. "If he goes to prison for his role in the murder he'll have no income at all."

"It won't come to that!"

"And if you decide to divorce, the amount of money he gives you will be decided by a court."

"Oh dear, no. This is why I think this could all be a big mistake. I don't want to have the courts involved. I couldn't bear the idea."

"George is a lawyer, Ellie. If the animosity between you grows stronger, who knows what strings he'll pull?"

"He wouldn't do that, we're his family!"

"I'd like to believe that, but you don't know what his intentions are. I expect he's as upset about the matter as you are, and his behaviour might be unpredictable. I think you should seek legal assistance, Ellie, especially when your estranged husband is a lawyer."

"We're not estranged!"

"Then what are you?"

"Briefly separated."

"Do you expect a reconciliation?"

"I don't know. I'm not sure what to do."

"Do you *want* a reconciliation?"

"Only if he's found to be innocent of all wrongdoing. And if he changes his ways."

"George isn't going to change, Ellie."

"How do you know that?"

"We've known him for many years. He's stubborn and set in his ways."

"So are you, Penelope."

"But we're talking about George."

"Oh dear, it's such a terrible mess. I despise having to pretend that everything is well between us to all our acquaintances."

"Then stop pretending."

"His parents would be horrified! I'm worried they'll find out if I drop my guard. I couldn't bear the thought of all that disapproval."

"If people are going to disapprove that's their problem, not yours."

"It is my problem, though. The stigma of being a divorced woman is quite dreadful!"

"It's not as terrible as it used to be."

"There's a danger that I shall be ostracised."

"Your good friends won't ostracise you, Ellie."

"Well that's just it. I sometimes wonder whether I have

any good friends."

"I'm always here for you. I don't care whether you're divorced or not."

"Thank you, Penelope. Sometimes I don't think I'm brave enough to go through with all this. It feels as though it would be so much easier just to allow him to come back home and continue as we were before. It would be easier for the children. They keep asking me where he is, and I have to tell them he's busy at the office. I'm going to have to explain the situation to them at some stage, and I really don't want to."

"That will likely be the most difficult part, Ellie. Perhaps you and George could explain it to them together."

"Can you imagine George ever doing such a thing? He would refuse to have anything to do with it."

"He needs to share the responsibility."

Eliza gave a laugh. "This may sound rather foolish, but of late I had started comparing George unfavourably with other men." She took a sip of wine.

"Such as who?"

"Well, embarrassing as it sounds, I had begun comparing him with Francis Edwards."

I laughed. "You couldn't find two men who were more different in nature!"

"Exactly! That's what I realised. As time went by I came to admire Francis very much, and when he announced that he was going to search for our father... well, my heart could have burst with pride and admiration. The man has so much courage; not to mention that clever mind of his. Such an interesting fellow. He was wasted at the library, of course, and although I'm desperately sad that he's gone away I'm also extremely pleased for him. I cannot think of anyone I would rather have out there looking for Father."

"He's never done anything like this before, Ellie."

"No, but I trust him. You trust him too, don't you?"

"Yes, I do."

I showed Eliza the letter he had sent from Liverpool, and noticed that her eyes grew damp as she read it.

"Isn't he marvellous, Penny? Such a good man. He wrote this before he left, I see. I wonder where he is now."

"Hopefully he's reached the Azores Islands by this time."

"Azores. The name alone sounds beautiful, doesn't it? I should think it's rather wonderful there. A tropical paradise."

"The islands are in the middle of the ocean," I said. "They're probably quite exposed to the elements."

"Don't ruin the image, Penelope. I don't want to wish wind and rain upon the Azores islanders. Anyway, I was thinking about Inspector Blakely the other day. Have you seen him recently? It can't be long now until his wedding."

"It's on Saturday the thirteenth of September."

"Which is how long away?"

"Nineteen days."

"I notice you're keeping a close count. How are you feeling about it?"

"My feelings are irrelevant. It will go ahead regardless of how I feel."

"It's probably for the best."

Eliza drained her glass of wine and I felt my teeth clench in response to her flippant comment. I wanted to tell her that his marriage wasn't *for the best* at all, but I resisted the urge to snap at my sister. I knew she was upset about her marital troubles, and sharp words from me would do nothing to ease her pain.

"Oh well," she continued. "Perhaps when Francis returns from South America you might feel like marrying him. The man will surely have proved his worth by then."

"Perhaps you could marry him, Ellie."

My sister's mouth hung open in surprise.

"You obviously hold him in high regard," I continued,

"and if you were to divorce George it might be something to consider."

She gasped. "Penelope! I would never... I couldn't possibly consider Francis in that manner. What a ridiculous suggestion!"

I noticed that her face had turned crimson.

CHAPTER 11

I found James at Bermondsey police station with Inspector Martin the following morning. They were accompanied by a young, long-limbed police officer with close-set eyes who was introduced to me as Detective Sergeant Richards.

"Penny!" James smiled as he greeted me, and I felt a warm twinge in my chest. His blue silk tie matched the colour of his eyes. "I take it you're here for an update," he continued. "Events are moving swiftly, so there will be plenty for you to write about."

"Good." I returned his smile. "Are you any closer to finding Catherine?"

"Not so far, but we've found another husband."

"Dead or alive?"

"Deceased, sadly."

"Oh goodness. Another one?"

"Before I tell you the details, Penny, you'll probably appreciate the added insight that Dr Grant, who carried out the autopsy on Thomas Burrell, has given. He believes the poor man was poisoned with arsenic. Samples of viscera have been passed to the analytical chemist at the Royal Institution; however, the police surgeon was somehow able to deduce—"

"The presence of inflamed and ulcerated intestines?" I asked.

"Why yes, Penny, I do believe he mentioned something like that. How did you know?"

"From John Curran's inquest."

"I'll tell you something else he mentioned," continued James. "He said that Thomas Burrell's body was remarkably well-preserved for one that had been buried in damp ground. The reason being that arsenic acts as a sort of preservative. Were you aware of that?"

"No, I wasn't."

"We must await the results from the chemist, of course, but it appears, as we feared, that Burrell was also poisoned by his wife."

"And the third husband you found?"

"We found him in the parish registers," said Inspector Martin. "A man named Francis Peel."

"Of course!" I said. "Catherine's surname was Peel before she married Burrell. I assumed that Peel was her maiden name, but it must have been the surname of her previous husband."

"Indeed," said Inspector Martin. "They married in November 1878 and Peel died on the ninth of February 1880."

"Where is he buried?"

"Believe it or not, in the churchyard of St Mary Magdalen," replied Martin with a smile. "If we'd found out a day or two sooner we could have dug both former husbands up at the same time."

I shivered. "Are you also planning to exhume Francis Peel's body?"

"We are indeed, at dawn tomorrow. And I expect we shall discover the same sorry scenario."

"Have you any idea where Catherine obtained the poison?" I asked.

"No, and it's something which is truly puzzling us," said Sergeant Richards, stepping forward to join the conversation. "The house at Grange Walk has been extensively searched and we can find no container that the poison might have been stored in or administered from. Enquiries are still being made among local shop owners to ascertain whether anyone recalls selling rat poison, or something of that sort, to Mrs Curran. The woman is quite the enigma. We're looking into William Curran as well, as several neighbours have reported witnessing arguments between the two brothers in the weeks leading up to John's death."

"He mentioned to me that they didn't always see eye to eye," I said.

"They didn't get on at all from what we're hearing," said Inspector Martin. "There could be motive on William Curran's part."

"But that cannot explain Thomas Burrell's death, can it?" I said. "Have you tracked down Thomas Burrell's family?"

"Yes, there's news on that front," said Inspector Martin. "The chap was from Somerset, where his relatives continue to live. This morning we received a telegram from his sister, who had read about her brother's exhumation in the newspaper."

"Oh dear, she must be quite upset about that."

"No doubt she is," said Inspector Martin. "She is to travel to London at her earliest convenience."

"She should be able to tell us a bit more about Catherine Curran," I suggested.

"Or Catherine Burrell, as she was known back then. We do hope so."

"It's difficult to keep track of all the names, isn't it?" I said.

"It certainly is," said James. "We haven't found a photograph of Catherine and Francis Peel, but I think it might be worth asking around at the local photography studios to find out whether any of them photographed the couple. We already have constables out and about looking for members of the Peel family."

"Do you mind if I help with that?" I asked. "I would be interested in speaking to anyone who happens to have met her."

"Of course," said James with a smile. "First we'll need to write out a list of photography studios from the Post Office Directory, and then we can split them between us. Let's begin with the two we know she has already visited."

❧

I went to the studio of Mr Lillywhite, the photographer on Upper Grange Road. He was a slight, neatly dressed man with an overly manicured moustache. I wiped the Bermondsey grime from my spectacles with a gloved finger and surveyed the room. A screen bearing a depiction of an Italianate balcony stood at one end, and beside it was an array of chairs of different heights and sizes. A couple of rugs were rolled up on the floor.

"Mrs Burrell had her photograph taken with her husband shortly after his death," said the photographer. "That's what I confirmed with the police officer the other day. I don't recall her ever coming here before then. There was a husband previous to him, you say?"

"Yes, Mr Francis Peel. I'm told that he died on the ninth of February 1880. Would you mind checking your records for their names?"

"Of course. I won't be a moment."

Mr Lillywhite retreated into a room at the back of his studio to take a look.

I surveyed the rest of the room as I waited. A theatrical red velvet curtain hung from the ceiling, and a bench and plinth stood side by side. They gave the impression of stone, but I suspected they were constructed from papier mâché. Vases of artificial flowers and plants were scattered about the room, and at the centre stood the camera on a three-legged stand, draped with a black cloth.

"I'm afraid I haven't been able to find anyone with the surname Peel who visited me in the month of February 1880," said Mr Lillywhite on his return. "I'm sorry I can't be of any help on this occasion. The woman you mention is suspected of murdering her husband, is she not?"

"Yes. What was your impression of her when she visited you with Mr Burrell?"

He stroked his manicured moustache as he gave this some thought. "I can't say that I recall her very well. She was upset, of course, and found the photographic session rather distressing. People in her position usually do."

I glanced at the chaise longue pushed up against a wall. It looked like the same one Catherine Curran and her dead husband Thomas Burrell had been seated upon for the photograph.

"How was the body of the deceased brought here?" I asked.

"The undertaker takes care of that. It can be a difficult time for the family, especially where children are concerned."

"I can imagine. So you don't remember anything specific about Mrs Burrell's visit? There was nothing which struck you as particularly unusual about her?"

"Not at all. From what I remember, she was a normal grieving widow. This was a few years ago, of course, so I only have a vague recollection of them. But I think if anything that had struck me as different about her I would have remembered it. If she did poison her husband, why would she bring him here? I can't imagine a murderer behaving in such a way."

CHAPTER 12

The next photographer I called at on Alscot Road had no record of a Mr and Mrs Peel visiting him. Neither did a photographer I visited on Fendall Street. Feeling despondent, I began to walk back toward Bermondsey Street. The air was warm and the sunlight had bathed the smoky sky a deep orange.

The stench from the tanneries grew stronger as I reached Page's Walk and I was pleased to bump into James beside a stable block on the corner. The expression on his face suggested his experience had been similar to mine.

"I suppose we'll have to venture further afield," he said, consulting the list he had compiled earlier. "I wrote a few other names down here. The question is, which direction do we go in? There's Rotherhithe to the east, Peckham to the south and Walworth to the west."

I sighed. "It could be in any direction, couldn't it? And we don't even know for sure that she had a photograph taken of herself and Francis Peel."

"Let's choose a few in Rotherhithe," said James. "And if

that yields nothing we'll have to get a few more constables knocking on photographers' doors."

We hailed a hansom cab, which took us beneath the South Eastern Railway lines to Jamaica Road. The small seat didn't allow much room between me and James, and when the carriage jolted over the bumps in the road my shoulder knocked into his. I was close enough to smell the pleasant scent of his eau-de-cologne. There were only eighteen days to go until his wedding. *Did he really intend to go through with it?*

"Are you all right, Penny?"

"Quite fine, thank you. Why do you ask?"

"You sighed just then."

"Did I? I didn't realise I had. How are the wedding plans progressing?"

"You're thinking about the wedding and that made you sigh?"

I turned to look at him. "Does that surprise you?"

"No," he replied, holding my gaze. "It makes me sigh too. Every moment of my spare time is taken up with discussions about the day. So much so that it's a relief to be investigating these murders instead."

I laughed. "You prefer murder to marriage?"

James laughed in response. "Of course not! That sounds... Well, I'm not sure at all really. What a question!" He rubbed at his brow, and I thought of confronting him about his feelings for Charlotte and for me. It was a conversation that I felt I needed to have with him before the wedding, but I was struggling to summon up the courage.

A photographer in Jamaica Road said that he had not come across the Peels himself but suggested another shop in nearby Paradise Street. The photographer at Paradise Street told us he could find no record of the Peels but had received word that a young woman matching Mrs Curran's description had been staying at The Angel pub down by the river.

"It may be nothing," said James as we left the photographer's studio, "but as The Angel is only a short walk away there seems to be no harm in investigating it. Here's the Paradise Street police station. Let's call in and find out if there's been any mention of a sighting."

A constable inside the station told James that the parish constable, Lopes, would know more, and that he was currently in position at The Angel. We walked down narrow Cathay Street between the tall wall of a granary and a line of grimy, terraced houses.

The Angel sat on the riverfront at the end of a row of wharves. To one side of it were steep steps that led down to the Thames.

"Smells like the tide's out," I said, wrinkling my nose at the stink wafting up from the mudflats.

A small, scruffy boy lingered at the top of the steps and a man with his hands in his pockets observed us as we paused to cross the road opposite the pub. Heavily loaded carts passed by, the horses sweating in the heat.

Inside The Angel we found Parish Constable Lopes sitting at a table beside a paned window which overlooked the river. He was laughing and joking with a group of men as we approached.

The parish constable hurriedly stood to his feet when James introduced himself, he swiftly dusted off his helmet and placed it back on his head. He was a brown-haired man with bushy whiskers and some considerable girth.

"A lady news reporter, eh?" said Lopes. "Times are a-changing, aren't they, Inspector?"

"They certainly are," replied James. "Can you tell me if you've heard anything about the woman who is believed to be staying here?"

"Believed to have *stayed* here. She's gone now, sir."

James cursed beneath his breath. "Do you have any idea where she was headed?" he asked.

"No."

"Did you see or speak to her at all?"

"No, I only heard about her. Landlord Figgins knows more."

"And where's he?"

Lopes looked over at the bar and raised his hand in the direction of a man with sharp features who was keeping a keen eye on us. On seeing Lopes' gesture he walked over to join us.

James introduced himself to the landlord. "Perhaps you can tell us about this young woman, Mr Figgins."

"I dunno if she's the one yer lookin' for. She stayed 'ere these past two nights."

"Did she tell you her name?"

"Jane."

"The same name Mrs Hardy told me!" I said. "That's the woman she stayed with on the Old Kent Road."

"Did she give a surname?" James asked the landlord.

"Taylor, I think she said," replied Figgins.

"So Jane Taylor stayed here on the nights of the twenty-fourth and twenty-fifth of August?" asked James.

Figgins nodded.

"Did she tell you anything about herself?"

"Said she's escapin' a bad 'usband."

"Did she give you any indication of where she had come from or where she was going to?"

Figgins shook his head. "Nope."

"Did you believe her story about the husband?"

Figgins shrugged. "I 'ad no reason not ter. Pretty little thing, she was. She don't deserve to be treated bad."

"Did she pay you for her board?"

"Yeah, three shillin's."

"And there was nothing about her conduct which made you suspicious?"

"None. Shame she ain't stayed longer, then you could've asked 'er yerself. I don't think she's the poisoner, but some folk think she looked like 'er, and one of 'em told Lopes 'ere so."

"What time did she leave this morning?"

"'Bout six."

"And you don't know where she was headed?"

"No idea. She tells me she can't stay nowhere too long in case the 'usband finds 'er, an' I believes 'er! Girl like that wouldn't do no 'arm to no one."

"That's the skill of these people," replied James. "If they were to walk around looking like murderers they wouldn't get far, would they?" He turned to face the parish constable. "When were you planning to tell your superior about the girl, Lopes?"

The constable looked uneasy. "After me drink, sir. I was about to send word to Bermondsey Street."

"When did you first hear that the girl was staying here?"

"I heard talk of it yesterday, sir, but I thought it unlikely that it was the same woman. I suppose I was guided by Figgins, sir. He didn't seem to think it was her."

James scowled. "You didn't feel the need to investigate, even though it's your job to keep an eye out for such things? You know that a murderess is on the run from the police and you don't feel the need to investigate reports of a mysterious young woman staying in a pub just two hundred yards from your police station?"

"I didn't think a murderess would choose to lodge two hundred yards from a police station, sir."

"It seems she must have assumed you would think that

way. She's made a fool of you, Lopes. Here she was right under your nose and you did nothing about it!"

"We ain't got no proof it was 'er!" protested Figgins.

"From this moment on, all solitary young women who match her description must be considered!" fumed James. "The very worst that can happen is that we offend a young lady who is busy minding her own business. We could have spoken to this Jane Taylor and quickly ascertained whether she was our Catherine Curran or not. Now she's slipped through our fingers and who knows where she'll turn up? She could have hopped onto a boat out there for all we know," he added, pointing at the river through the window. "Perhaps that's why she chose this pub, because of its proximity to the Thames."

"Yer don't often see a girl like 'er on a boat. Folk would suspect summink," said Figgins.

"She's capable of bribery," said James. "We know she's collected a fair bit of money from the life insurance policies. Now put your beer down, Lopes, and rally as many men as you can to get out there looking for her. Maybe she has remained local. She seems to have been keen to stay in this area until now, so let's do everything we can to find her!"

I followed James as he marched out of the pub.

"Hopeless!" he said once we were out on the street. "Completely hopeless!"

"It has to be her," I said. "The story she told the landlord about running away from her husband is the exact same story she told the lady on the Old Kent Road."

"It can only be her," agreed James. "And to think that we could have caught her if we'd known!"

CHAPTER 13

I travelled back to the *Morning Express* offices that afternoon, first by horse tram, then via the Tower Subway and finally on an omnibus to Fleet Street. While sitting on the omnibus I drafted another appeal for information on the whereabouts of Catherine Curran. I hoped that I would be able to persuade Mr Sherman to publish it in a prominent position so that as many people would see it as possible.

I felt sure that Catherine couldn't have gone far. Although it was conceivable that she had secured herself passage on a boat, she had so far remained in Bermondsey. I hoped this meant that she preferred to stay within an area she knew well.

There was a suggestion that something out of the ordinary had occurred when I discovered Mr Conway's large frame blocking the corridor to the newsroom at the *Morning Express* offices. Despite being the newspaper's proprietor, it was unusual for him to pay us a visit.

His trousers, jacket and waistcoat were of a baggy brown tweed, and his wavy grey hair sprawled into a pair of long, bushy side-whiskers. He was accompanied by a young, narrow-faced, pale-haired man holding a bundle of papers.

"Miss Green, isn't it?" Mr Conway wheezed.

"Yes. Good afternoon, sir."

"I suppose you're wanting to get past." He looked around, as if trying to locate a wider section of corridor. He grunted, then made his way toward the doorway of Mr Sherman's office. I walked past him and his assistant, thanking them as I did so.

It was unusually quiet in the newsroom, and to my surprise I found Miss Welton, Mr Sherman's secretary, sitting with Edgar and Frederick. She was fidgeting with the high collar of her woollen dress, staring glumly through the pince-nez clipped to her nose.

"Something's happened," I said cautiously. "What's happened? Why's Mr Conway here?"

"Mr Sherman's been arrested," said Edgar quietly. His face looked pale.

For a brief moment I felt the need to laugh, as if he had told me a joke. But the seriousness of his expression assured me this was no laughing matter.

"Arrested?" I asked. "What could he possibly have done?"

"They won't tell us."

"But when?" I asked. "And who arrested him?"

"It was last night," replied Edgar. "I don't know where he was or what he was doing; that's all we've been told. It was T Division in Kensington, I believe."

"We should go down there and find out what's happening."

"That was my idea too, Miss Green, but Conway has forbidden it. He knows more than he's letting on."

"I cannot understand the secrecy."

I realised as soon as the words had left my mouth that there might be a valid reason as to why the details of his arrest had been kept secret. The memory of the confidential matter he had imparted to me during our walk in Lincoln's Inn Fields earlier in the summer came back to my mind and my stomach gave a sickening flip.

"Sit down, Miss Green," he said. "You look shocked."

"I am," I replied, slowly lowering myself onto a chair. "Poor Mr Sherman. He must feel so humiliated; so frightened."

"What makes you say that?" asked Edgar. "None of us has any idea what has happened."

I glanced across at Edgar, Frederick and Miss Welton, realising they had no idea about Mr Sherman's secret life.

"We've been considering the possibility that he got himself into a fight," suggested Frederick.

"It's difficult to imagine, but a possibility all the same," I said.

"He would never get into a fight," said Miss Welton. "Mr Sherman wouldn't harm a soul. He wouldn't do anything wrong at all. I simply don't understand it."

"I'd like to know where he was when he was arrested," said Frederick. "Was he at home or somewhere he shouldn't have been? A bank, for example."

"Perhaps he was robbing it!" laughed Edgar.

"This is no laughing matter!" said Miss Welton, dabbing her eyes with a handkerchief.

"I suppose we shall find out in due course," I said sadly. "In the meantime, how is the morning's edition going to be printed?"

"We shall all have to work together on it," said Edgar. "Mr Conway has already told us it can be a slimmer edition on this occasion."

"But how will the compositors know what they're doing?" I asked.

"The chief one, Smith, is pretty good. He's already laid out a lot of it," said Edgar. "In fact, I should get back down there and find out how it's coming along. We just need to decide where the main stories will go."

"Do you have any idea what Mr Sherman was planning to lead with tomorrow?" I asked.

"Well it seems France and China are now at war after the sea battle near Fuzhou," said Edgar. "I think that should be the lead story, but Frederick reckons the prime minister's visit to Scotland should go before it."

"So we're already in disagreement on that," I said.

"Let's ask Mr Conway which he'd prefer," said Edgar.

"I was going to ask Mr Sherman if we could publish an appeal regarding Catherine Curran's whereabouts," I said.

"We can do that," said Edgar. "Have you written it?"

"Yes, it's two hundred words. I've included the details of when and where she was last seen."

"Right then, let's get on with it," said Edgar, rolling up his shirt sleeves. "Let's make Sherman and Conway proud."

The newsroom door opened and Mr Conway entered with the young, narrow-faced man.

"This is Crispin Childers of the *West London Mercury*," he announced. "He's a competent chap and just happens to be my nephew. He'll be taking over the reins here for the time being."

We stared in silence at the new arrival. His hair was so pale it was almost white, and his insignificant chin made him appear much younger than his years.

"Your nephew, sir?" said Edgar. "I can't see any obvious family resemblance."

I suppressed a chuckle as I surveyed the difference

between our oversized, tweed-wearing proprietor and the thin, insipid-looking man standing next to him.

"I think we can manage, Mr Conway, sir," said Frederick. "We've all worked on the *Morning Express* for a number of years."

"Nonsense," puffed the proprietor. "Childers here can see to the editing while you get on with your news reporting. I need to go and instruct my lawyers to ensure that Mr Sherman gets the best defence a chap can get in the whole of London. Now introduce yourselves to one another and get on with it."

Edgar and I exchanged a doleful glance.

My despondent mood was worsened by the group of reporters I found loitering outside the office that evening. Unfortunately, the *Morning Express* had become a news story in itself. I looked down at my feet and marched along Fleet Street to find an omnibus, but I wasn't quick enough to escape my constant nemesis Tom Clifford from rival newspaper *The Holborn Gazette*. He grinned as his slack jaw turned over a piece of tobacco.

"Is this the end for the *Morning Express*, Miss Green?"

"Not at all."

I continued walking but he followed behind me.

"No chance of Sherman gettin' his job back after this, is there?"

I shrugged, as if to pretend that I knew for sure what he had been arrested for.

"A total embarrassment, ain't it?" continued Clifford.

"Why?"

"Oh, come on, Miss Green! Arrested at the Hammam Turkish Baths on Jermyn Street with all them other men. Solicitin' to commit an unnatural offence!" He laughed. "That won't do for a newspaper editor, will it? They've arrested a lawyer an' all!" He laughed again. "Disgustin', it is. They should all hang for it."

I spun around in anger. "Don't be ridiculous!" I hissed. "Mr Sherman hasn't harmed anyone!"

"It's indecency, Miss Green. And it's morally wrong!"

"You're a fine one to comment on other people's morals," I snarled, turning away and looking for a cab to whisk me away from there as quickly as possible.

"But I ain't goin' around committin' unnatural acts, Miss Green," he called after me. "An' he's supposed to be a professional man!"

CHAPTER 14

P olice Raid on the Hammam Turkish Baths, Jermyn Street

A raid was carried out at the Hammam Turkish Baths on Jermyn Street just before 11p.m. on Monday 25th August. Police had received viable information that behaviour of an improper nature was taking place on the premises. Upon investigation, it was found that the suspicion was justified, and police officers duly arrested more than a dozen men.

Private information had been sent to Chief Constable Herbert Granger of Vine Street police station in February of this year, and he immediately commenced inquiries relating to the baths. Constables in plain clothes attended on frequent occasions and witnessed what appeared to be immoral activity.

At eight o'clock on Monday evening two constables attended the baths incognito once again. However, on this occasion Chief Constable Granger waited outside, accompanied by a dozen constables. After witnessing further morally questionable behaviour, the two plain-

clothes constables left the baths and informed Chief Constable Granger, who entered the premises with his constables. He explained the intentions of the raid to the owner, Mr. Patrick Caulfield, and proceeded to arrest 13 men, who are accused of soliciting to commit an unnatural offence. Several of the men are said to be respectably connected.

The article went on to describe the subsequent appearance of the men at Marlborough Street Police Court and the bail terms given. Beneath this it listed their names, ages and occupations. I had hoped Mr Sherman's name wouldn't be among them, but my heart sank when I saw it:

Mr. William Sherman, single, 53, newspaper editor, Bedford Row, Holborn.

He had been released on bail and had most likely returned to his home. I thought back to our conversation in Lincoln's Inn Fields and recalled how fearful he had been of anyone discovering his private affairs. He had been so frightened of losing his profession, and I struggled to believe that Mr Conway would ever allow him back into the office to edit the *Morning Express*.

I sighed as I sat in the newspaper reading room at the British Library, reluctantly leafing through *The Holborn Gazette*. I was afraid to read what Tom Clifford had written about the case, but I couldn't help myself.

The hitherto respected editor of the Morning Express *newspaper, Mr William Sherman, was one of 13 men arrested for soliciting to commit an unnatural offence at the Hammam Turkish Baths of Jermyn Street on Monday 25th August.*

I folded the newspaper, not wishing to read any more. Before I left the room I decided to find out whether there was any news regarding Francis' steamship. I found it listed in the shipping intelligence.

TERCEIRA - *arrived* - Pampero *[August 25th] destination Savanilla*

This piece of news brought a smile to my face. I was happy to read the confirmation that he had arrived in the Azores. I wondered what life had been like for him on board the ship.

CHAPTER 15

I returned to Grange Walk in Bermondsey later that morning, hoping to find out more about Catherine Curran and her former husbands.

The windows at number ninety-six looked empty and there was no longer a police constable stationed at the house. The air was warm and smoky. I called at some of the little terraced houses along the street.

"I only knowed 'er married ter John. I dunno about no one else," said a thin-faced woman with streaky grey hair at number ninety-two. A small girl clung to her shabby skirts.

"Did you know her well?" I asked.

"Never seen much of 'er. She was workin' down the leather market."

"Does she have any family or friends who live locally?"

The woman frowned as she considered this. "There's Dotty over the road," she said. "I saw 'em talkin' sometimes."

"Which number does Dotty live at?"

"Eighty-seven. Dunno if you'll find 'er at this time, though. She's a shop girl."

I thanked the woman and crossed the road to Dotty's

house. The little girl let go of her mother's skirts and followed me.

"I think you should go back inside," I said.

The girl looked up at me with her wide blue eyes and said nothing.

"Don't you want to go back to your mother?" I asked again.

I looked back at number ninety-two and saw that although the door still stood open there was no sign of the girl's mother. I heard another door open and three children came running over to us. The blue-eyed girl clearly knew them, as her face broke out into a grin.

"What's 'app'nin'?" asked one of the children, a boy of about eight.

"Nothing's happening," I replied. "Shouldn't you be at school?"

"You the school inspector or summink?" a harsh voice called out from the doorway the children had just run out of. I looked over to see a hard-faced woman leaning against the doorpost, regarding me with her arms folded.

"No," I replied. "I'm a news reporter." The woman scowled and the children began running in circles around me. "I'm here to talk to Dotty," I explained, trying my best to walk over to number eighty-seven without bumping into any of them.

An old lady tottered out into the road and observed me carefully, leaning on an even older-looking walking stick.

"Good morning," I said to her cheerily, trying to continue on my way. I became aware of curtains being moved to one side and other people watching me from their doorways. *Why was I such a point of interest?*

I hoped Dotty would be home and invite me inside, away from the neighbours' prying eyes. But there was no answer at number eighty-seven, and as I stepped away from the door more children joined me, two of whom began playing peek-a-boo with my skirts.

"What's in yer bag?" asked a dirty-nosed boy.

"Nothing exciting, I'm sorry to say."

"Ain't you got no sweets?"

"I'm afraid not."

Someone stepped in front of me and I saw that it was the woman with the dirty apron and unkempt hair who looked like an over-sized child. She had small, wide-set eyes and a short, upturned nose.

"Hello again," I said, forcing a smile. "How are you?"

She gave me a lopsided smile but said nothing.

I stepped to the side of her and continued on my way as best as I could with three children still tugging at my skirts.

"I dunnit," the woman called out.

"I'm sorry?" I turned to look at her and saw that she still had the same odd smile on her face.

"I dunnit," she repeated.

"Done it? Done what?"

"The murder. I dunnit."

"The murder of John Curran?"

The woman nodded and grinned.

"You're confessing to the murder of John Curran?" I asked, incredulous that the childlike woman who stood before me might have had something to do with it.

"And them others."

Until this moment I had thought she was joking with me, but this statement made me reconsider.

"What do you know about the others?" I asked.

"Tom. And the other one too. Don't remember 'is name."

"What's your name?" I asked her.

"Sally."

"Sally, are you sure about this? You're quite certain that

you had something to do with the deaths of John Curran and Thomas Burrell?"

Sally nodded again.

"But how did you do it?"

"Put it in their beer, I did."

"Put what in their beer?"

"Poison."

"How?"

"Got the beers from Noakes and stuck it inside 'em."

I had heard of the brewery, which was close to Bermondsey Street.

"You gave them poisoned beer?"

Sally nodded and gave another smile. Her awkward conversation and childlike manner led me to believe that she was not of sound mind. I would have dismissed her confession as pure fantasy had she not demonstrated some unexplained knowledge of the case. Putting arsenic in a bottle of beer seemed to be a feasible method of poisoning someone.

I felt a shiver run up my spine as the children began dancing in a ring around me and Sally. Although I struggled to believe what she was telling me, I felt I couldn't completely dismiss her claim. This woman might not have been responsible for the murders, but it was possible she knew something that might prove useful.

"Sally, I think you need to speak to the police," I said. "Do you know where the police station is on Bermondsey Street?"

She nodded in reply.

"I can walk there with you if you like."

Sally nodded and smiled, and I felt it best to leave Inspector Martin to decide what to do about her. He seemed an understanding man, and I felt sure that he would be kind.

"Do you need to tell anyone where you're going?" I asked. "Your mother or father, perhaps? Or your friends?"

Sally shook her head.

"And do you have everything with you that you need to bring? Did you want to fetch your bonnet and shawl?"

"No need," she replied.

Sally spoke little during our slow walk to Bermondsey Street. She seemed to have no interest in me, and instead stopped regularly to peer in at windows or examine pieces of rubbish which lay on the ground.

It seemed impossible that this woman could have murdered three men. So why was she claiming that she had?

CHAPTER 16

J ames was chatting with Inspector Martin and Sergeant Richards when Sally and I arrived at Bermondsey Street police station.

"Penny!" he said with a grin. He was wearing the dark blue suit he always looked most handsome in. "You've arrived at an opportune time. We're just about to meet with Dr Grant to discuss what he has found out from the autopsy on Francis Peel."

"And I think I recognise this young lady," said Inspector Martin. "It's not Sally Chadwick, is it?"

Sally nodded in reply and gave an odd laugh.

"Sally has told me something which I think you all need to hear," I said. "You may be rather surprised."

"Is that so?" said Inspector Martin. He gave me a knowing glance, which suggested that he was well aware of her state of mind.

The four of us took a seat around a table in a spartan interview room, which smelt as though it had recently been scrubbed with soap. We listened as Sally told us in slow, stilted sentences how she had bought beer from the Noakes brewery on three occasions and put poison in it before giving it to John Curran, Thomas Burrell and another man whose name she couldn't remember. I wondered if she meant Francis Peel.

Her story sounded quite convincing, and James listened intently, looking perplexed. Inspector Martin had a faint smile on his face, as if he didn't believe a word she was saying.

"Well, thank you, Sally," he said once she had finished. "May I ask which type of poison you added to the beer?"

"Arsenic."

"Interesting. And how did you come by it?"

"Soakin' fly papers."

Inspector Martin raised an eyebrow. "Really? And how did you go about doing that?"

"Bought 'em from Gibsons."

"Gibsons on Tanner Street?"

Sally nodded, prompting Inspector Martin to pull his notebook out of his pocket. He seemed to be taking her story a little more seriously now.

"I suppose that will be easy to verify with Gibsons themselves," he said as he made a note. "How many packs did you buy?"

"A fair lot of 'em. Mebbe twelve."

"I see. And how did you go about soaking them?"

"Put 'em in a bowl o' water overnight, then poured it into a jug, then poured it into a bottle."

Inspector Martin scratched his temple with the end of his pencil. "There's no doubt that doing such a thing would enable you to extract the arsenic from the papers. How did you know to do it?"

"I've read about it."

"You can read, Sally?"

"Yeah, I can read. Maggie taught me."

"Maggie?"

"Maggie at the church."

"Ah yes, I know who you mean. What did you do next with the bottle of water and arsenic?"

"I poured it into the beer."

"I cannot understand how you managed that. How did they not notice?"

"I done it afore I give it to 'em."

"You poured the poison into the bottles of beer you had bought from the Noakes brewery, as you have already explained to us?"

She nodded.

"I shouldn't think there would be much room in a bottle of beer for arsenic-laced water to be added," said Inspector Martin.

"I pulled out the stoppers, poured a bit out then put the poison in 'n' put the stoppers back."

"And you gave these poisoned bottles of beer to John Curran and Thomas Burrell?"

"Yeah. I took 'em round as a gift."

"Why?"

Sally shrugged and a long pause followed.

"S'pose I wanted to see what would 'appen," she eventually said.

"Those men died horrible deaths, that's what happened!" snapped the inspector.

Sally shrank back in her chair and raised her hands defensively in front of her. If what she had told us was true it was truly a despicable act; however, I couldn't help but feel a little sympathy for this grown-up child.

"Perhaps Sally is mistaken," I ventured.

She turned toward me, her mouth twisted. "I ain't mistaken! I done it!"

Inspector Martin sighed as though he didn't know what to make of it.

"Sergeant Richards, could you fetch some tea, please? I have a feeling this is going to be a long day."

The sergeant nodded and left the room.

"Very well," continued Inspector Martin. "We'll carry out some investigations into this. If what you tell us is correct, Sally, I assume we'll find evidence of the soaked fly papers and empty bottles in your home?"

"Yes."

I was surprised by her conviction. *Surely there couldn't be any truth in what she was saying?*

James seemed equally puzzled. "Evidence, or the lack of it, will quickly clarify the matter," he said. "You should send some men to Miss Chadwick's home straight away, Martin."

"Better still, I'll go myself," replied the inspector. "And I'll take Sally with me so she can show us around her alleged arsenic manufactory. Before we do that, Miss Chadwick, I need to ask you to write down your confession. You've told us you're able to read, so does that mean you're able to write as well?"

Sally nodded.

Inspector Martin passed her a piece of paper and a pen, and she began to write in a slow, laborious hand.

Sergeant Richards returned a short while later.

"The sister of Thomas Burrell has just arrived," he said. "She says she sent a telegram to inform us that she would be paying us a visit."

"Yes, I recall it. It's all happening at once, isn't it?" said Inspector Martin. "Ask her to sit in the waiting room for a moment, please."

Sergeant Richards nodded and left the room.

"Would you like me to speak to Miss Burrell while you finish your conversation with Miss Chadwick?" asked James.

Inspector Martin wiped his brow. "Yes, that would be useful. Thank you, Blakely."

CHAPTER 17

James and I left Inspector Martin's office together and made our way toward the waiting room. In the corridor we met the police surgeon with the long ginger beard and half-moon spectacles, whom I recognised from John Curran's inquest.

"Ah, Dr Grant," said James. "What did the results of the autopsy on Francis Peel reveal?"

"Looks like it's the same old story, I'm afraid," he replied. "Undeniable signs of poisoning in a body which is unusually well-preserved considering that it was buried four years ago."

"And it is definitely arsenic that has caused the effects you've seen?" I asked. "It couldn't be any other poison?"

"Not that I know of," said Dr Grant. "I've removed some tissue from the intestine, liver, kidney and spleen for the analytical chemist to examine. He'll attempt to extract some arsenic from the viscera, just as he did with Mr Curran, and that will confirm it for sure. If for any reason he is unable to do so I'm sure he will test for other possible poisons. But I would place my bet on the outcome being arsenic."

"We're still waiting for the results of the tests on Thomas Burrell's remains, aren't we?" I said.

"Yes. We should hear any day now," said Dr Grant. "I think we can safely work on the assumption that these three men were deliberately poisoned."

"And we now have a lady who has confessed," said James. "Inspector Martin is with her at the moment."

"That's news indeed," said Dr Grant. "It wasn't the wife after all, then?"

"We cannot exonerate her yet," said James. "For all we know the two women have worked together on this. It seems one of them has run off and the conscience of the other has got the better of her. I'm beginning to think that's the most likely explanation, but I suppose we may be surprised again."

We continued on our way toward the waiting room and saw Sergeant Richards leaving the parade room with a lady carrying a travel bag.

"I'm sorry." There was a tone of distress in her voice. "I'm afraid I got lost. I don't often come to places like this."

"It's quite all right, Miss Burrell," said Sergeant Richards. "The waiting room is this way. Inspector Blakely will have a conversation with you now. He's from Scotland Yard."

Sergeant Richards introduced us to Florence Burrell, the sister of Catherine Curran's deceased second husband, Thomas. She wore a dark shawl over a plain blouse and skirt, thick-lensed spectacles and a headscarf with a faded floral design over her dark hair. Most striking of all was the puckered skin which stretched from just beneath her left eye down to her chin. It was an angry red.

"Scotland Yard?" She spoke with a slight West Country burr. "I've never met anyone from there before."

"Please come and join us in the waiting room, Miss

Burrell," said James. "You must be in need of some refreshment after your long journey."

"Thank you, but I'm all right. I got something from a stall on my way."

We sat down in the waiting room.

"We heard you've dug him up," she said.

"Your brother Thomas?" replied James. "Yes, sadly we had to exhume his body because there is a growing suspicion that his wife may have poisoned him."

"She can't have! We were told he died from natural causes. They said it was his heart."

"That was the initial conclusion, yes. But some further analysis has revealed that the cause of death was poison."

"You looked at him yourself?" Her eyes were wide and sad behind her spectacle lenses.

"Not personally, no. The police surgeon carries out that sort of work."

"You should've asked us," she said. "You should've asked permission."

"I apologise, Miss Burrell, this must all be rather upsetting for you," said James. "The police did attempt to contact the family, but upon discovering that there was no one local, and with time being rather pressing, the decision was made to exhume your brother. The only official permission required is that of the coroner, but of course efforts are always made to speak to the family where possible. I apologise that we were unable to do that. Please rest assured that your brother was quickly returned to his resting place."

"That's something, I suppose. So you're saying he was poisoned?"

"We suspect it, yes. However, it is likely to be proven by the analytical chemist once he has succeeded in extracting the poison from the body."

"How's he going to do that?"

"Samples had to be taken from your brother's body for examination purposes."

"What sort of samples?"

"Pieces of the viscera, such as the intestine, liver—"

Miss Burrell clasped a gloved hand over her mouth. "You've cut him up?"

"No, it's not like that."

I felt sympathy for James having to explain such a difficult procedure to a relative of the deceased.

"During an autopsy an incision is made from the top of the chest down to the base of the abdomen," said James. "In this case the incision allows the police surgeon to inspect the organs of the body in order to ascertain whether there was any foul play. We are satisfied that there was in your brother's case. Small portions of tissue have been removed and sent to a chemist, who is an expert in detecting poisons. I know this is alarming to you, but please remember that we have done all this in the pursuit of justice. When your brother died no one had any idea that someone might have caused his death. It was assumed that he had died of natural causes."

"His heart."

"That's right. But the doctor who signed the certificate of death was mistaken."

Miss Burrell rubbed her forehead. "And she did it? Catherine?"

"We don't know. She's gone missing, and we would very much like to speak to her."

Miss Burrell sighed and shook her head. "There has to be some mistake. It can't have been poison. I was living in London when he was taken sick. He'd have known if he'd been poisoned, wouldn't he?"

"Not necessarily," said James. "We believe arsenic was used and the poison is almost tasteless. Hidden in well-flavoured food or drink it often escapes detection. Death isn't immediate unless the victim has consumed an extremely large dose, and the symptoms of sickness and diarrhoea can be attributed to many other causes. We suspect that in your brother's case a number of sizeable doses were consumed over the duration of a week or two. Eventually, his body would have been so weakened that he could endure no more."

Miss Burrell emitted a sob and James looked alarmed.

"Oh dear, I apologise," he said, giving me an awkward sidelong glance. "I was concentrating so hard on explaining it to you, Miss Burrell, that I didn't realise how distressing my words must have sounded."

"It is what it is, Inspector," she said, retrieving a handkerchief from a pocket in her skirt and dabbing at her eyes with it. "You know what you're talking about. I'll have to somehow explain it all to Ma and Pa when I get home. They'll find it hard to hear." She sniffed and wiped her nose.

"I realise that," said James sadly. "But there has been an interesting development just this morning. We have spoken to a lady who claims she had something to do with it, so we are now wondering whether she and your former sister-in-law might have colluded."

"Who is she?" asked Miss Burrell sharply.

"A lady by the name of Sally Chadwick."

Miss Burrell gasped. "Sally?"

"You know her?"

"Yes, I remember she lived near them."

"I haven't had the opportunity to speak with her myself," said James. "But I understand that she has confessed to poisoning your brother as well as Catherine Curran's latest husband, John Curran, who passed away only last week."

Miss Burrell shook her head. "I can't hardly believe it."

"We suspect that another of Catherine's husbands, Francis Peel, was also poisoned. Whether Miss Chadwick will also claim responsibility for his death remains to be seen."

"Another husband of Catherine's? How many has she had?"

"We have found three so far, and we suspect they were all poisoned. As you can imagine, this makes Catherine Curran appear rather guilty."

"Especially now that she has taken flight," I added. "That is not the usual course of action for an innocent woman."

"But hasn't Sally confessed?"

"Yes."

"Then it must be her! She always was a strange one. People called her the idiot girl." Miss Burrell shook her head in disbelief. "To think that Tom's been dead for two years and I never would've thought something like this could happen. I think Sally must've done it." She lowered her voice. "Tom told me she'd approached him."

"About what?"

"I meant what I said." Her eyes grew wider behind her thick lenses. "She approached him for his *attentions*," she added in a whisper. "He said no, of course."

"Oh, I see," said James. "She propositioned him, you mean?"

"Call it that if you like."

I struggled to imagine Sally doing such a thing. However, given that I barely knew the girl I concluded that it was feasible.

"Are you quite sure about that?" asked James. "It wasn't simply a misunderstanding on your brother's part?"

"I'm just repeating what he told me. He wasn't the sort to *misunderstand* people."

"Did he tell you what Sally's response was when he refused her?" I asked.

"I think he said she was a bit annoyed. Ashamed, too, I reckon. She probably didn't think he'd refuse her."

"Was Catherine aware of this incident?"

She shrugged. "Can't say. I don't know if he ever told her or not. I don't think he would've."

"What makes you say that?"

"It would've upset her, and he wouldn't have wanted that. Tom loved Catherine, but there were lots of things he couldn't tell her."

"Such as what?"

"About his stealing."

"What sort of stealing?"

"Getting into houses and taking money and jewellery. Sometimes they'd go north of the river and do the big houses in the City."

"*They?* Who were his accomplices?"

"I'm not at liberty to say. I don't mind telling you about Tom now that he's gone and no one can go arresting him for it, but I don't want to go getting anyone else in trouble. Besides, I can't remember any of their names, and for all I know they've probably been caught by now anyway."

"Was your brother ever arrested?"

"I think he was in the cells a few times for being drunk, but that's all I know about it."

"Did you get to know Catherine well in the time she was married to your brother?" I asked.

"Yes, of sorts. She wouldn't have poisoned anyone, though. Catherine wasn't like that. She loved Thomas. You should have seen her after he died. Broke her heart, it did."

"Do you know anything about her family?" asked James.

"They live down Kent way. Orpington."

"Both her parents?"

"I think so. Only time I saw them was when they came to Tom and Catherine's wedding. There were some sisters and all."

"All living in Orpington?"

"I think so."

"Do you have an address for any of them?"

"I don't, sorry."

"There have been some sightings of Catherine," said James. "And it seems she has remained local for the time being. We believe she took lodgings on the Old Kent Road for a few nights and also stayed at The Angel public house on the riverfront. To your knowledge, Miss Burrell, does she have any family members or friends in those areas?"

"I don't know. She may have, but it's a good few years since I saw her and people move about, don't they? I can't say for sure about friends, but I know she wouldn't poison anyone. That's not like her at all."

"Did she have a close friendship with Sally Chadwick?" asked James.

Miss Burrell shook her head. "I don't think so."

"Do you have any idea how Miss Chadwick might have known each of Catherine's husbands well enough to give them all poisoned beer?"

She shook her head again. "I've got no idea. Sally approached Tom, so maybe she did the same thing with the others. But when and how she did it... I just don't know. Has she been arrested?"

"I'm not sure yet. Inspector Martin is currently speaking with her."

"Can I see her?"

"I'm afraid not."

"I want to see her!" Her eyes flashed with anger. "I want to ask her why she murdered our Tom!"

"That's what we are all trying to find out, Miss Burrell," James said calmly. "Please leave the matter with us so we can uncover the truth. If it transpires that Miss Chadwick is responsible for the murders of these three men I'm sure a fair number of people would wish to see her in person. There's no doubt they would wish her some harm, and it wouldn't be a safe situation for her to be in. Please rest assured that she will face judgment in the proper legal manner."

I struggled to imagine Sally appearing in court. I felt sure that she would have no real understanding of what was happening to her. I hoped her confession would be dismissed as mere fantasy.

"There's no evidence yet to support what Miss Chadwick has told us," I added. "Perhaps she wasn't responsible for poisoning your brother after all."

I didn't care for the sharp look Miss Burrell gave me in response. She clearly wished to believe that her brother's murderer had been apprehended.

CHAPTER 18

"Where have you been, Miss Green?" asked a white-faced Mr Childers when I arrived back at the newsroom.

"Bermondsey," I replied. "A woman has confessed to being the poisoner in the Curran case."

"You've been in Bermondsey all day, have you?" he asked, checking his watch.

"I completed some work in the reading room to begin with."

"You are in the habit of working there, are you?"

"Yes," I replied, baffled by the question. "I need to consult the books and periodicals stored there for my articles."

"And you leave it until three o'clock to visit the office, just an hour before deadline, I see."

"I've been out reporting, Mr Childers."

I cast an exasperated glance at Edgar and Frederick, whose glum expressions suggested they had been subjected to a similar inquisition by the stand-in editor.

"And what of your article on the Sudanese campaign?"

"I was planning to speak to you about that on my return," I replied. "As the confession from the alleged poisoner in Bermondsey is important news I thought it should take precedence over Sudan for tomorrow's edition."

"The editor decides which stories take precedence, Miss Green, not the reporters." Spots of red appeared high on Mr Childers' white cheekbones. "Do you mean to tell me that you haven't written your article on the campaign?"

"I've carried out the research, Mr Childers. It wouldn't take me long to write it up."

"Good, because you only have an hour."

"I also have the article about the Bermondsey poisoner to write, Mr Childers."

"If you have time to write it before the deadline and there's enough space we will do our best to publish it."

"But it's rather more important than the Sudanese campaign, which is a long, ongoing story if I may say so. The poisonings in Bermondsey are of great interest to our readers because they happened here in London."

"Our readers are interested in a wide range of topics, Miss Green. The gory details of a poisoning might not appeal to many."

I felt irritated by the manner in which Mr Childers referred to '*our readers*' as if he had been working at the *Morning Express* for years.

"Two, possibly three, poisonings," I corrected. "This is a big story, Mr Childers."

"A big story if you live in Bermondsey, perhaps. It is of less interest to our readers in Kensington."

"Scotland Yard is now involved, and another possible culprit is still on the run."

"So I understand, and we must leave it all in the capable hands of the police. I expect to see you at your desk first thing each morning, Miss Green, so we can discuss the stories you are to write about."

"I am here sometimes," I replied, "but often I go to the reading room or another location first, depending on the story I'm working on."

"You come to this office first!" Mr Childers wagged a long, thin finger at me and I felt my jaw clench in anger. "I don't expect you to make your first appearance at three o'clock in the afternoon, full of plans to write about something I have never even asked you to!"

"It's an ongoing investigation I have been reporting on!"

"And being argumentative about it, to boot. This is what happens when you allow women into the workplace. Did Mr Sherman allow you to speak to him in this manner?"

"There was no need to. Mr Sherman had full confidence in my capabilities as a news reporter."

"It seems as though he let his reporters rule the roost."

"Not at all!" Edgar piped up. "You should have seen the roastings he gave me. And I deserved them most of the time, I'll admit that."

"Mr Sherman trusted us to do our jobs properly," I added.

Edgar stood to his feet. "Mr Childers, there is no one here who works as hard as Miss Green, I can vouch for that. She's a spinster and has little family to speak of, and that means she is able to devote every hour of every day to her work."

"Thank you for the veiled compliment, Edgar," I said.

"Veiled? I thought I had spoken very highly of you, Miss Green."

"I can see that it was well meant. Thank you."

Mr Childers' face was red and damp with perspiration. I could see that the confrontation was making him quite distressed.

"Less of the talking, Miss Green. Just get on with it," he

said bitterly. "We are now five minutes closer to the deadline than we were when you arrived."

He left the room and I sat down at my desk, my fists balled in fury.

"Who does that upstart think he is?" I snarled.

"Mr Conway's nephew, that's who he is," replied Edgar. "And he certainly hasn't been given this job based on his skill and expertise. But don't worry, Miss Green. Frederick and I have it all under control."

"What do you mean?"

"He'll regret talking to any of us in that manner, won't he, Potter?"

Frederick nodded with a smirk.

"What are you planning to do?"

"Just a little jiggery-pokery, Miss Green," replied Edgar.

"What does that mean, exactly?"

Edgar lowered his voice to a whisper. "I've already put a tack on his chair, haven't I, Potter?"

Frederick giggled like a naughty schoolboy.

"But we don't know if he's sat down on it yet. There have been no yelps forthcoming from the editor's office."

I sighed.

"But he deserves it, Miss Green!"

"Of course he deserves it, but antagonising him isn't going to help us, is it? It's just going to make him worse."

"What do you propose we do?"

"I don't suppose there's a lot we can do, is there? Perhaps we should just allow him to believe he's in charge."

"I see what you mean, Miss Green. His behaviour suggests he is a nervous sort of man who may be worried that he's not going to do a decent job of running his uncle's paper. I bet he has a nickname for Conway, such as Blimpy or something of that ilk."

Frederick chuckled. "Why Blimpy?"

"Because you can just imagine him saying it, can't you? *Uncle Blimpy*, in a whiny sort of voice."

Frederick and I laughed.

"Oh dear," I said. "I can't bear the thought of Mr Sherman being permanently ousted. Surely we're not going to be stuck with Childers forever."

"I can't imagine Uncle Blimpy getting rid of him and putting Sherman back in," said Edgar. "And how could Sherman possibly come back here after what's happened? He may face trial, and if he's found guilty he might end up doing a few months of hard labour."

I shuddered. "Mr Sherman would never cope with that."

"He wouldn't have a choice," said Edgar. "I have a lot of respect for the chap, but if you break the law you have to be ready to face the punishment."

"The whole thing was rather a surprise," said Frederick. "He often told us about his visits to the Turkish baths, but I had no idea that any untoward activities took place there."

"I had heard stories of untoward activities in some of those places," said Edgar, "but I have visited them in the past and never encountered anything out of the ordinary. I never imagined that Mr Sherman would have got himself caught up in any of it. Perhaps it's a mistake. In fact, it must be a mistake. I know the chap's not married, but that doesn't mean he would get involved in any funny business. He just hasn't met the right lady yet."

"I don't think he wants to meet the *right lady*," I said.

"You know better than us on this matter, do you, Miss Green?"

"No, it's just a guess."

Despite Mr Sherman's arrest, I still wished to keep the secret he had imparted to me down in Lincoln's Inn Fields. "I'm worried about him," I continued. "From what I've read, all the men who were arrested have been granted bail, but I can't see him coping well with this situation."

"It's the shame more than anything," said Edgar. "And the ruin of one's reputation. I should think his friends will be quick to desert him."

CHAPTER 19

Defying Mr Childers' orders to report to the office at the beginning of each day, I went straight to the reading room the next morning. I climbed the steps to the upper gallery, where I hoped to find some books which would help me with my ongoing articles about the Sudan campaign. From here I could look down on the circular room and watch the readers working quietly at the long desks which radiated out from the head librarian's dais. The sight of Mr Retchford bustling about proudly made me feel the absence of Francis even more keenly.

As I watched, a familiar figure in a dark blue suit and bowler hat entered the room. I smiled as I quietly observed James looking for me. It wasn't long before he looked up and gave me a wave. I climbed down the staircase to meet him.

"Hello, Penny," he whispered. "I have something here you might be interested in." He gestured toward a leather folder tucked beneath his arm.

"Tell me more outside," I whispered, spotting a reproachful glance from Mr Retchford. I quickly packed up my papers.

"How's Mr Sherman?" asked James once we had left the quiet confines of the reading room. "With all that business going on in Bermondsey yesterday I didn't have a chance to discuss it with you."

"I should think he's in rather a bad way," I replied. "No thanks to your colleagues at Vine Street station."

James sighed. "They had to follow up on those reports, I suppose."

"But who bothers to make these reports to them in the first place?" I asked. "Haven't they got better things to do? The police would be better off spending their time catching dangerous criminals."

"A police officer's work is full of variety, Penny."

"That's one way of putting it," I said scornfully. "I'm struggling to believe that such a thing has happened. Mr Sherman doesn't deserve to be treated like a criminal. He's a good man, and he would never hurt anyone."

"I agree, Penny, and so would many others. However, the police don't make the laws of this land; we only enforce them."

"No, but they could consider doing what is really important. They have been watching those baths since February! And has any real crime been committed? The allegations all seem to be based on gossip and vague suspicion. Meanwhile, Mr Sherman has lost his livelihood and the *Morning Express* has lost its best editor."

We stepped outside, where a brisk, warm wind was whisking around the columns of the museum's portico.

"What's in your folder, anyway?" I snapped.

"There's no need to be curt with me, Penny. I'm not Chief Constable Granger."

"I'm sorry, James. I'm just upset about the whole thing, and Blimpy Childers isn't helping matters either."

"Who? Who on earth is...? What name did you say?"

"You don't want to know." I sighed, instantly regretting using Edgar's new nickname for the man.

We paused on the steps of the museum as James opened his folder and pulled out a photograph. Once again, it showed a couple at a photographer's studio. The woman looked familiar.

"Catherine Curran?" I guessed.

James nodded. "And the chap next to her is, or was, Francis Peel."

Catherine looked younger in this picture and appeared quite upset. The eyes of the young man next to her had the usual glassy look about them.

The photographer's name was embossed onto the bottom of the photograph and I saw that he was situated at an address in Walworth.

"We have the constables of M Division to thank for this," said James. "They eventually found the photographer you and I had been looking for. He'd kept a negative copy of the photograph and had it developed for us."

"Catherine looks like a woman who is genuinely mourning for her husband," I said. "Perhaps she had nothing to do with his death."

"Maybe she didn't," replied James. "Perhaps Catherine is entirely innocent. There's a good deal of evidence to substantiate Miss Chadwick's claim."

"Really?"

"After interviewing her yesterday, Inspector Martin visited the room where she lodges. It's at a house in Grange Walk, not far from where the Currans lived. Martin and his constables found packs of fly papers there, some opened and some not. They also found bottles filled with a substance which Miss Chadwick claims is the arsenic-laced water she obtained from soaking the fly papers. They have been passed to the analytical chemist for testing. It has also been verified with

Mr Gibson, who owns a general store on Tanner Street, that Miss Chadwick purchased these fly papers from him. There is no doubt that the woman is of a rather unusual character, but she does appear to be telling the truth about her involvement."

"But it couldn't have been her!" I protested. "What would her motive be?"

"The only motive I have come across so far is the one suggested by Miss Burrell."

"You think Sally was angry that Thomas Burrell had rejected her advances? I struggle to believe that."

"Me too," said James. "However, though the motive may be intangible, the intent is clear. We cannot pretend that Miss Chadwick's mind is sound. I suspect she may have a touch of insanity about her. If a murderer is insane there is a fairly good chance there is no motive to speak of. At the very best there may be a twisted motive which makes sense to an insane mind but not to a rational one."

"But even if Sally committed the murders for some reason related to her insanity, how do you explain Catherine Curran's sudden disappearance? And the insurance policies she took out on her husbands' lives?"

"Good point, and we know that she was quick to claim on those policies," said James.

"Exactly. So Catherine must have had some involvement in the murders."

"It's possible that the two women worked together."

"They could have done," I replied. "And now Catherine has taken flight, leaving poor, simple Sally Chadwick to take the blame."

"But no one would ever have suspected her if she hadn't confessed," said James. "Why would she confess?"

"I have no idea," I said with a shrug. "A guilty conscience, perhaps?"

"We need to persuade Sally to implicate Catherine in all this. Hopefully she can explain exactly what happened and why they did what they did."

James sat down on the museum steps and withdrew his notebook from his pocket. I took a seat next to him as he leafed through his notes. The warm breeze threatened to lift my cotton skirts, so I hugged them close to my legs.

"Why is Miss Burrell's face so terribly scarred?" I asked. "Did she tell you?"

"Apparently, she mentioned to Sergeant Richards that she had suffered serious burns during an accident at a lead works here in Bermondsey."

"Poor woman," I said. "Is that why she returned to her family in Somerset?"

"I don't know. It could be, I suppose. I should think she left the lead works after it happened." He stopped turning the pages in his notebook. "Here we are. This is what we know so far. The lady we call Catherine Curran was named Catherine Vincent when she married Francis Peel in 1878. They were married for two years before he died in 1880, and the autopsy after his exhumation suggests that his death may have been caused by arsenic poisoning. Catherine married Thomas Burrell in 1881, a year after Francis' death. The autopsy on Mr Burrell suggests that he also died of arsenic poisoning, although we are awaiting the results of the toxicology tests to confirm it. He died in 1882."

"And then Catherine married John Curran."

"Yes, in November of last year. Their marriage lasted ten months before he died a death which we know to have been caused by arsenic poisoning."

"Three husbands in six years."

"Quite an achievement, isn't it?"

"Sally mentioned that she poisoned 'the other one', but she couldn't remember the man's name."

"Presumably she means Francis Peel."

"She must do. You mentioned the surname Vincent. Does that mean Vincent is Catherine's maiden name?"

"In the record of her marriage to Francis Peel she is described as a spinster, so I think we can be confident that Francis was her first husband."

"So we're not going to find any more deceased husbands from her past?"

"I sincerely hope not. And with a matrimonial record like that I'm surprised the life insurance companies allowed her to take out any policies with them at all!"

"If Sally Chadwick poisoned all three men she must have known Catherine for at least four years."

"Yes, she must have. But she won't talk about Catherine at all."

"And where is Sally Chadwick now?"

"Inspector Martin arrested her after they visited her home. She is currently being held in the cells at Bermondsey police station."

"Oh dear."

"She claims to have murdered three men, Penny!"

"Without truly realising what she was doing, I should think. She is clearly not of sound mind. Will a physician pay her a visit?"

"I should think Inspector Martin will arrange that as soon as possible."

"What of her family and friends?"

"No one has visited her yet to my knowledge, but I'm sure someone will soon. I don't really know what friends and family she has."

"What will happen to her next?"

"She'll be up in front of the magistrates at Southwark Police Court next week."

"Poor Sally." I couldn't imagine the childlike woman coping with the formality of a court.

"Remember that she is a murderer, Penny. She has admitted to the crimes and we have found evidence to corroborate her confession."

"And Catherine?"

"We have received reports of more sightings in Rotherhithe, and I believe Parish Constable Lopes is finally putting some of the necessary legwork in now. She can't stay hidden for much longer. We almost got her a few days ago, didn't we? Our chance will come very soon, I feel sure of it."

I glanced down at the steps in front of us, enjoying this rare moment in the sunshine with James.

"It's rather different today compared with that cold, foggy day we first met here last October," I said. "Do you remember it?"

"I remember it well," he said with a smile. "The body of poor Lizzie Dixie had been found in Highgate Cemetery and I was told that I urgently needed to speak to a news reporter called Miss Green who had been a friend of hers."

"And you waited for me here."

"I did! Having called at your office I was told that you spent a lot of your time in the reading room. I waited for about five minutes, wondering whether I should go in and disturb you. I was quite nervous, because I'd only heard about you from Chief Inspector Cullen and he'd just had you dismissed from your job. I understood why you had no wish to be bothered by anyone from Scotland Yard. But when I set eyes on you, I saw that you weren't what I had expected at all."

"What had you expected?"

"Someone rather austere and serious. Trout-faced, perhaps."

I laughed. "Trout-faced?!"

"Yes!" He grinned. "I wasn't expecting someone so…" His words trailed away, but his eyes remained on mine.

"What?" I asked quietly.

He looked away and scratched at his chin. "Well-favoured, I suppose. I can't say any more than that; it wouldn't be appropriate."

"I see."

I looked in the direction of the Museum Tavern across the road. I recalled our first drink in there together as clearly as if it had occurred the previous day. I thought of Charlotte and anger balled in my stomach.

"You were quite serious, though," said James, turning to face me again. "And rather abrupt, if I may say so. But you had lost your job because of the actions of my superior, so I suppose it was justified."

"It was *all* justified," I said, looking back at him with a smile. "I apologise for my grumpiness. I didn't immediately realise you were a decent person, but I recognised it soon after you bought me a sherry at the Museum Tavern." I looked back at the pub again and added. "I recognised it quite quickly."

"So did I, Penny," he replied. "But as I have already said, this marriage was first considered long ago."

"Yes, you've already said that," I snapped, standing to my feet. "I must return to my work."

CHAPTER 20

D*earest Penny and Eliza,*

Monday 25th August 1884

I hope this letter finds you both well. I have successfully reached the Azores Islands! Not due to any effort of my own, of course, but by the sterling work of the captain and crew of the Pampero. We are currently moored at Terceira, a coaling station for transatlantic steamships. Terceira is one of the islands in this delightful archipelago, which belongs to Portugal. Much of the land here is divided by low walls into little squares, within which the inhabitants grow oranges, passion fruit, tea, tobacco and a number of other crops. The early settlers brought sheep and cattle here. Mark Twain visited these islands seventeen years ago, so I have been enjoyed reading about his experiences here in his fine work, The Innocents Abroad.

To date, the crossing has been calm, with only one night bumpy enough to require me to cling to the sides of my bunk bed. The *company on board is most pleasant, and conversation with my fellow travellers is helping to pass the time. I am also now well acquainted with my Spanish translator, Anselmo. He is a good-humoured fellow with a grasp of the English language more impressive than some who speak it as their native tongue!*

Despite the new sights and sounds around me, my thoughts often turn to you both and the great city I call home.

I shall write again once I reach the shores of Colombia.

Ever your friend,
  Francis Edwards

"What a lovely letter," said Eliza, dabbing at her eyes. "I haven't read anything so wonderful in months."

"Really?" I replied.

"You must excuse me, Penelope. My emotions are running rather high at the present time.'

We sat together in Eliza's drawing room, where several piles of papers were laid out on the hearthrug. Eliza had been sorting through them when I arrived.

"This letter is dated the twenty-fifth of August," she said. "Do you think Francis might have reached Colombia by now?"

"He'll probably arrive there in a day or two. I think he said that the crossing would take almost two weeks."

"Oh, I do hope his efforts won't be in vain. How wonderful it would be if he found Father!"

"I can't imagine how I will feel if that happens. But I don't want to raise my hopes too much. There's as much chance of him discovering bad news about Father as there is of him receiving good news."

"Oh no, Penelope. Do you really think so?"

Eliza began to cry again, and I wrapped my arm around her shoulders.

"I'm sorry, Ellie, I didn't mean to upset you. I must resolve to be more optimistic."

"Yes, you should," said Eliza, dabbing at her face. "And I'm sorry for getting upset again, but this business with George is affecting me so. I've spent much of the day trying to separate my papers from his, and one of his friends is visiting me later to collect his pile."

"Which friend?"

"Mr Bertrand Butler. Odd man. I can't bring myself to look at his horrible teeth."

"What's wrong with them?"

"It's the manner in which they protrude. I know the chap can't help it, but I worry that one or more of them may fall out while he's talking to me."

"What does he talk about when he visits you?"

"He uses words such as *peace parley* and *negotiation* with regard to discussions between George and myself. He comes here to collect something and then embarks on a great speech about something or other. He's an incredibly irritating man."

"Why bother with him, in that case? Why not speak to George yourself?"

"Because the mere sight of him makes me livid, Penelope!"

"That's understandable. Does he wish to be reconciled?"

"Yes, I believe so, but the trouble is that I don't feel as though I know him at all now."

"Of course you do."

"I don't! I had no idea that he would get himself caught up in an illegal scheme with a dubious customer."

"The world he inhabits can be morally questionable at times."

"But it's the law, Penelope!"

"Exactly."

"I don't share your scepticism about the justice system, and I wish you'd be a little more sympathetic. We're talking about my husband here! He is the father of my children! If we remain estranged people will talk, and I'm quite sure I will never be able to tell mother about it."

"Then perhaps you could find a way to reconcile."

"I'm not sure there is any way back. I feel... an intense disapproval for the manner in which he has conducted himself."

"Do you still love him, Ellie?"

We paused while a maid brought in a tea tray and placed it on the low table in front of us. Eliza waited for the maid to leave before replying.

"That is an interesting question," she said. "What is love, exactly?"

"I thought you knew."

"And so did I. But I'm beginning to wonder whether I might have been mistaken."

I thought about all the times Eliza had lectured me on love and marriage, and I bit down firmly on my lip to stop myself commenting on the irony of the situation. I didn't wish to cause further upset while her nerves were so fragile.

"I'm sorry to hear it, Ellie," I said softly. "It must be extremely difficult to have to consider whether you still love your husband or not."

"It's awful!" my sister replied as fresh tears flowed down her face. "I never expected to be presented with such agonising emotions. Ever! I made my marriage vows in the presence of God. How on earth can I start questioning them now?"

"Questioning them isn't necessarily a bad thing. These are merely thoughts you are entertaining at the present time because you're angry with your husband. Thinking in such a way doesn't mean that your marriage is doomed; in fact, it may help you view matters in a different, and perhaps even a better, way. This period of reflection may eventually help your marriage, and once the anger has subsided you might be able to discern the best means of reconciling with George. You may have many more years of happiness together."

Eliza's face brightened a little. "For a woman who has never married, Penelope, you can be very wise about these things."

"There is no need to be married to understand love, Ellie."

"Perhaps not. Your rather complicated affection for Inspector Blakely has taught you that, no doubt."

"There is nothing complicated about my affection for him," I replied.

"But he is to marry someone else!"

"Yes," I sighed, "and I wish that had changed how I feel about him, but unfortunately it has made no difference at all."

"It can't be long now," ventured Eliza.

"Two weeks today," I replied curtly. "Though I prefer not to dwell on it."

"You cannot pretend that it isn't happening."

"I'm not! But there is nothing I can do about it."

"You could try to change his mind."

"And how would I go about that? He knows how I feel about him, yet he persists in this marriage with Charlotte. I can only imagine that he cares for her more than he cares for me. Why else would he allow the wedding to go ahead?"

"Perhaps he does," said Eliza, "but perhaps he doesn't. I think you should remind him of your affection for him one last time."

"He won't change his mind, regardless of what I say."

"He just might."

"Weren't we just talking about the sanctity of marriage?"

"Yes, we were. And I think it is incredibly important to marry the right person. There is nothing worse than realising you've made a mistake once it is already too late."

CHAPTER 21

"The chemist at the Royal Institution has graciously worked through the weekend and completed his tests on the remains of Thomas Burrell and Francis Peel," said Sergeant Richards. "He has concluded that they were both poisoned with large quantities of arsenic."

"As we suspected," said James.

He and I stood with the sergeant in the parade room at Bermondsey police station. Today was Monday the first of September, and only twelve days remained until James' wedding. I tried not to dwell on this dispiriting fact and instead concentrated on what Sergeant Richards was telling us.

"The chemist has also examined the bottles and fly papers we removed from Miss Chadwick's home," continued the sergeant, "and he found a quantity of arsenic in the solution inside the bottles. Each fly paper has been confirmed to contain a grain of arsenic in soluble form."

"Then the chemist's findings support everything Miss Chadwick has told us!" said James.

"I still cannot believe that she did it," I said.

"It's rather difficult to argue with the evidence," said James. "And she has also confessed to it all. It makes our work much easier when we have a confession."

"But something isn't quite right about it," I said. "I don't think the case is as simple as it seems."

"You're right, Penny," said James. "Catherine Curran is still evading us, and we have a good few questions to ask her."

"Where is Inspector Martin?" I asked.

"Unfortunately, he has been taken ill," replied Sergeant Richards. "Hopefully he'll be fully recovered and back with us soon."

"Let's hope so," said James. "We've a lot to do." He removed his notebook from his pocket and looked something up in it.

I watched him and thought about my conversation with Eliza at the weekend. *Might it really be worth my while trying to remind him of my affection for him? Was there any chance that he would cancel his wedding if he knew how I truly felt?* I thought I had already made my feelings clear, but perhaps I hadn't spoken directly enough.

"I'll have another conversation with Miss Chadwick shortly," said Sergeant Richards. "She'll be brought up in front of the magistrates on Wednesday."

"Does she have a solicitor?" I asked.

"She told Inspector Martin she didn't want one."

"Oh dear. She needs one!" I said. "She can't represent herself. I don't think she will be able to understand anything that is happening inside the courtroom."

"I don't think she really understands what a solicitor is," said the sergeant.

"James," I pleaded, "can we do something about this?"

"She has been asked if she would like a solicitor and she refused," he said. "We cannot simply force one upon her."

I sighed. "There must be someone who knows her who

could give her some advice," I said. "She can't cope with this ordeal all by herself. Did anyone visit her over the weekend?"

Sergeant Richards shook his head. "I don't think so."

"Can I see her?" I asked.

"Why?"

"Because I feel sorry for her. She's shut up in a cell and has had no visitors to speak of."

"She has confessed to multiple murders, Miss Green."

"I realise that. But does she really know what she's caught up in, or what the consequences might be? I don't believe she does."

"Penny, I understand why you feel some sympathy toward Miss Chadwick," said James, "but you're a news reporter. The well-being of a prisoner is not something you need worry yourself about."

"But I *do* worry," I retorted. "She approached me in the street and confessed to me. It was my idea to bring her here, and now I feel partly responsible for her unfortunate predicament."

"You're not responsible for it at all, Penny! She has murdered three men, and with all the bottles of arsenic-laced water we found in her home I'm amazed she hasn't poisoned herself in the meantime! Your work has been of huge value to us, but her predicament is entirely of her own making. Please don't feel any responsibility for her."

"Someone needs to."

"But not you."

"Can I see her for just a few moments?" I asked. "It may help her a little to see a friendly face. A female face."

James gave an exasperated laugh. "I know that you won't give up on this idea until we agree, so yes, I don't see what harm it could do. I'm assuming that Sergeant Richards will accompany you."

The sergeant nodded and indicated for me to follow him

down the stone steps to the gaoler's office. The gaoler was a hatchet-faced man of few words. He led us along a damp, brick corridor to the three cells reserved for female prisoners. Croaky strains of 'Champagne Charlie' were blaring out of one of them.

"Shaddap!" yelled the gaoler, thumping the door of the cell.

A torrent of curse words was hurled at him in response.

The gaoler opened the door of the next cell, where Sally sat on a thin mattress atop a small wooden bedstead. She wore the same scruffy dress and apron she had been wearing the last time I saw her. Her dirty, straw-coloured hair was even more unkempt.

"Good morning, Miss Chadwick," said Sergeant Richards. "I've brought Miss Penny Green with me this time. Do you remember her?"

She gave me a broad, lopsided smile.

"How are you, Sally?" I asked, stepping into the cell. The air was stale and smelled of unwashed bodies.

She nodded and smiled again.

"You're to appear in court in two days' time," I said. "You should agree to have a solicitor go with you."

"Don't want one," she replied cheerfully.

"But the solicitor will explain to you what's happening and will help you answer any questions the magistrates might want to ask you."

Sally shrugged nonchalantly and began to hum a quiet tune.

I glanced at Sergeant Richards, who gave me a look that suggested I should give up all attempts to reason with her.

The woman in the neighbouring cell began to sing again.

"Are you happy here, Sally?" I asked.

She stopped humming and looked up at me. "Yes!" She grinned.

"Did Catherine Curran tell you to poison those three men?" I asked.

Sally's face fell at the mention of Catherine's name.

"Miss Green, I must ask you to leave," said Sergeant Richards sternly. "That's the sort of question that must be left to the police."

I took a step back. "I'm sorry, I shouldn't have asked that," I said. "It was foolish of me."

"Please step out of the cell now, Miss Green," said the sergeant firmly.

"I will visit you again soon, Sally," I said with a smile in a desperate attempt to cheer her up again.

She gave me a faint smile in return.

"Not if you're going to ask her questions like that one, you won't," said Sergeant Richards.

"I won't, I promise," I replied as I left the cell. "It's just that I'm sure she must know—"

"We'll get it out of her before long," he said, nodding to the gaoler, who closed and locked the door. "You do your job, Miss Green, and leave us to do ours."

CHAPTER 22

As I climbed the steps up to the police station I felt angry with myself for asking Sally Chadwick about Catherine Curran. I had spoken without giving my actions proper thought, and I knew it was borne out of the frustration of being certain that Catherine must have had something to do with her husbands' deaths. Sally was the only person who could confirm this for us. However, I knew this was no excuse for taking matters into my own hands.

We found James in the waiting room talking to a tall, thin man with red hair and whiskers. He wore a rough woollen suit and held his cap in one hand.

"You believe that someone poisoned you, do you?" James asked the man.

"Aye, but I lived ter tell the tale. That's why I'm 'ere!" He grinned.

"This is Mr Benjamin Taylor," James told me and Sergeant Richards. He introduced us to the man, who gave us a genial nod.

"And who do you believe it was that tried to poison you?" James asked him.

"I reckon it were the missis what done it." His brown eyes were wide and earnest-looking.

"Your wife?"

"Aye."

"Why would you think that?"

"Whenever I was at 'ome I was tooken ill, and whenever I went away I got better again. I remember jokin' wiv 'er that it were being at 'ome what made me ill."

"Did you stay away from home regularly, Mr Taylor?" asked James.

"Yeah, I was doin' buildin' work, and when it were far away I stayed elsewhere. Sometimes fer a few weeks or more. I don't do it no more. I work at Doulton's now."

"The pottery?" asked James.

"That's the one. Like I say, I was workin' away and whenever I went 'ome I got ill again. I joked that it were summink in the water. Then a friend o' mine said as I was bein' poisoned, and 'e was jokin' an' all, but I got ter thinkin' 'bout it 'cause I knowed she took out the insurance. We 'ad no money for insurance, but she was quick ter do it anyways, and when I asked 'er did she want me dead she jus' laughed. Then when I asked 'er was she poisonin' me, she didn't take kindly to it. I only said it as a joke, like, but she took it bad and was shoutin' at me 'bout what sort of wife did I think she was."

"How long ago was this?" asked James.

"We was married in '75 and I ain't seen 'er since '78. We're still married, but I ain't seen 'er this last six years."

"And what was your wife's name?"

"Jane Vincent."

James and I exchanged a glance.

"And you have no idea what became of her?" asked Sergeant Richards.

"Not an inklin'."

"Did you know her family?"

"They lived in Kent's what she told me. I met 'em once or twice, but I couldn't tell yer where they lives now. Wouldn't recognise 'em if I fell over 'em these days."

"And how do you think your wife was attempting to poison you?" asked James.

"Puttin' it in me food, I reckon. And I got sick; so sick I couldn't work no more, and then no money was comin' in. So she got a job down the leather market."

"Which one?"

"Lambeth."

"Can you describe your wife for me?"

"Yellow 'air, small. Brown eyes. Pretty, she were. That's what drew me to 'er in the first place."

"And how old was she when you were married?"

"'Bout twenny."

"You married nine years ago, which means she would be round twenty-nine years old now. Is that right?"

"Dunno. Summat like that."

"And you say that you joked about her poisoning you and that she didn't find it funny?" asked James.

"She didn't. She took it bad."

"Do you think she continued to poison you after that?"

"Aye, and that was the worst one! Nearly died, I did! Doctor told me I was lucky ter survive it. Couldn't stop with it, all the vomitin' an' that. She was nursin' me, but I told 'er I wanted 'er away from me. I told 'er she were a witch. She didn't like that, and I told 'er ter get outta the 'ouse else I'd kick 'er out. So she went back down ter Kent and I ain't never seen 'er again."

"Did you report your suspicions to the police?"

"I never did, 'cause I weren't sure of it meself. I thought it must of been 'er makin' me sick, but I couldn't prove nothin'. The police wouldn't of believed me."

"And this was when, exactly?"

"It were in '78."

"You lived in Lambeth together, you say?"

"That we did."

"Do you spend much time in Bermondsey as a general rule?"

"Not likely. I just come 'ere 'cause I 'eard about these 'ere poisonin's."

"Does the name Sally Chadwick mean anything to you?"

"No, it don't."

"She lives in Grange Walk. Are you sure you have never come across her?"

"Name don't ring a bell. Might know 'er by sight, I s'pose."

"She has confessed to committing the three poisonings we are already investigating."

"That's the myst'ry solved then!"

"Only partly," said James. "We are still looking for Catherine Curran, who was married to the three men who appear to have died in suspicious circumstances. We believe she is travelling to be reunited with her family in Kent."

James asked Sergeant Richards to fetch the photographs and we waited a moment while he did so.

"News reporter, yer say?" Mr Taylor said to me.

"That's right, for the *Morning Express*," I replied.

He gave me an appreciative nod and I smiled. I hoped we would be able to confirm that his wife was indeed Catherine Curran.

The sergeant returned with the photographs and James showed them to Mr Taylor.

"Does the lady in these pictures look familiar to you?"

Mr Taylor studied them carefully, squinting slightly to ensure that his eyes were properly focused.

I saw his mouth slowly open. "That's 'er all right!"

"Are you sure?" asked James.

"Yep! In ev'ry one of 'em! It's 'er each time over."

"We believe it to be Catherine Curran in each of these pictures. However, you gave us a different name: Jane Vincent."

"Aye. I always knew 'er by that name."

"Do you believe it to be her true name?"

"Aye."

"In that case she may have changed her first name to Catherine."

"S'pose she mighta done. Who's the men she's with?"

"The men she has married since she married you," replied James.

"That's bigamy, that is!"

"It is if she's still legally married to you," said James." Do you have a copy of the marriage certificate?"

"Not no more."

"Which church did you marry in? We can check the records there."

"St Mary's in Lambeth. By Lambeth Palace, it is."

"Excellent. Thank you very much for your help, Mr Taylor. We now have further cause to arrest Catherine Curran. Or Jane Vincent. Presumably she called herself Jane Taylor after she married you."

"Aye. By rights that's what 'er name should still be now."

I gave James a nod. We both knew that Jane Taylor was the name Catherine had been using during her time on the run.

Mr Taylor rubbed his brow, his jaw still hanging open in amazement. "I never would 'ave thought it of 'er. Three more 'usbands!"

"And all dead," added James. "It seems you had a lucky escape, Mr Taylor."

"Four husbands now," I said once Benjamin Taylor had departed. "How many more could there possibly be?"

"She was twenty when she married Mr Taylor," said James. "Let's just hope she didn't find the time for any marriages before that. I shall ask L Division in Lambeth to obtain the records for her marriage to Mr Taylor. Then we will be able to prosecute her for bigamy."

"If we can find her, that is," I said.

"There is that challenge, of course. Sergeant, have any men been dispatched to Kent yet in a bid to locate Catherine Curran's family?"

"Yes, to the Orpington area. That's what you were told, wasn't it?"

"Yes, Miss Burrell, the sister of Thomas, told us Catherine had family in Orpington," replied James. "And fortunately the town is not too far from here."

"So after Mr Taylor left his wife she changed her first name to Catherine and retained the name we suspect is her maiden name, Vincent," I said.

"It certainly seems that way," replied James. "When she married Francis Peel she recorded herself as a spinster, which we now know to be untrue."

"Benjamin Taylor asked her to leave and she moved to Bermondsey, where presumably no one would know her. Once there she changed her name from Jane Taylor to Catherine Vincent and no one was any the wiser," I said. "She must have been disappointed that her plan to murder Benjamin Taylor had failed."

"If that was her plan," said James. "We still can't be certain that Catherine, or Jane Taylor as she was then, is the person responsible."

"It had to have been her!" I said. "Or do you think Sally Chadwick was somehow involved from the start? Mr Taylor claimed that Sally's name was unfamiliar."

"He and Catherine, I mean Jane, were married more than six years ago," said James. "Perhaps he has forgotten Sally Chadwick's name. It may turn out that he knows her after all."

"I am convinced that Catherine poisoned him," I said. "And the fact that he escaped with his life suggests she wasn't using such a large dose back then. I suppose there is bound to be at least one person she practised her technique upon, and it explains how she went on to poison three other men so effectively. At the moment it's hard to believe that Sally had a hand in Mr Taylor's poisoning."

"Perhaps Catherine enlisted Sally's help after failing to poison her first husband," suggested James.

"It's possible," I said. "But how I desperately wish that Sally would tell us the truth."

CHAPTER 23

I left James and Sergeant Richards at the police station and made my way down Bermondsey Street toward St Mary Magdalen's church. I had remembered something from Sally Chadwick's confession which I hoped might lead me to someone who could help her.

The church's tranquil interior offered respite from the heat and noise of the street outside. My eye was drawn to the stained-glass window at the far end of the aisle, and once I had become accustomed to the gloom I saw rows of pews either side of me and an elegant arched ceiling supported by two rows of columns.

My footsteps echoed along the aisle and I noticed a few people sitting quietly in the pews. Not wishing to disturb them, I looked around for anyone else who might be able to help me.

An old man rose from a pew at the front of the church and began to walk toward me.

"I'm looking for a lady named Maggie," I whispered. "Do you know who she is?"

He seemed not to hear me properly, giving me a fierce scowl as he continued on his way.

I went out into the churchyard, hopeful that I might find someone more obliging there. I blinked in the bright sunshine, looking for anyone I could ask about the woman Sally had mentioned.

As I walked through the churchyard I passed a recently dug mound of earth. I paused to look at the tombstone and shuddered when I saw the inscription.

Francis Peel
1849 - 1880

Further along the path I came across a man sawing a low-hanging branch from a yew tree.

"She'll be around somewhere," he replied when I asked him about Maggie.

"Do you know exactly where?" I asked.

He stared at me as if I had asked a foolish question.

"Just keep lookin'," he responded.

I took this to mean that she couldn't be too far away. I began to walk slowly back toward the church, and as I did so I noticed a small door beneath an arched window. Unsure whether I was permitted to use this door I decided to give it a try.

It creaked open, and once again my eyes had to adjust to the gloom.

"Hullo!"

I jumped as a wizened face loomed into view. I saw that it belonged to a lady who was exceptionally small in stature.

"I'm sorry to disturb you," I said. "I'm looking for Maggie."

"You just found 'er," she replied. "What d'yer want?"

I stepped inside and found myself inside a narrow, high-ceilinged room with a red velvet curtain draped along one wall.

"I should like to speak to you about Miss Sally Chadwick," I said.

"Oh, 'er." Maggie pursed her lips. She wore a long, dark dress which was buttoned up to her throat. A dark shawl hung around her shoulders and her grey hair was pinned up in curls on top of her head as if she were trying to gain a little extra height.

"Do you know her?"

"Who are you?"

I apologised for not having introduced myself and explained who I was.

"Sally confessed to me that she had poisoned three men," I said.

"I 'eard about that."

"She's being held in a cell down at the police station and she doesn't seem to understand the severity of her situation. She appears to have no family or friends, either; no one has visited her there. During a conversation I had with her she mentioned that Maggie from the church had taught her to read and write. Might that have been you?"

"Yes, I done that."

"Have you known one another for a long time?"

"She was one o' the horphans down the horphanage. I used ter go there and teach 'em their letters an' numbers."

"Does that mean she has no family?"

"She was a horphan."

"Have you spoken to her recently?"

"Not too recent, no."

"She seems like a nice girl."

"Yes, *girl*. That's the word. She'll always stay a girl, she will. Simple-minded, like. I thought she were nice till all this murderin' business come up."

"I cannot believe that she did it."

"Me neither, but if she said she done it she must of done it."

"Did you ever see her with Catherine Curran?"

"She knows 'er, I can say that fer sure. Ev'ryone knows Sally."

"But no one has visited her since she was arrested."

"That's 'cause she murdered John Curran! An' Tom Burrell an' Francis Peel. No one wants ter be 'sociated with 'er."

"But if she's *simple-minded*, as you described her, could it be possible that she didn't fully understand what she was doing?"

Maggie gave this some thought. "I s'pose so. If she's got a child's mind she wouldn't 'ave thought it through proper."

"Especially if someone had told her to do it."

"Like who?"

"Catherine Curran, perhaps."

Maggie shook her head. "I can't see that 'appenin'."

"Why not?"

"Catherine wouldn't do nothin' like that."

"She has three dead husbands whose lives she had taken life insurance policies out on, and she is now evading the police."

"So'd you be if they was after you."

"Not if I were innocent."

"Police don't always care if yer hinnocent or not. They goes harrestin' yer just so they got someone ter blame for it all."

I realised that Sally Chadwick's arrest must have been the subject of much local gossip. Maggie's mind was probably as convinced as everyone else's that Sally was guilty of all three murders.

"I'm worried about Sally," I said. "If she is not of sound mind and carried out these poisonings without really realising what she was doing, is it fair for her to be punished in the same way as if she were an evil, calculating killer?"

"Murder's murder in the eyes o' God."

"I can understand that sentiment, but wouldn't God show some small mercy toward an unfortunate young lady with the mind of a child?"

Maggie pondered this. "What yer sayin'?"

"I think Sally needs some help. She's to appear in front of the magistrates this Wednesday and she'll have little idea of what is happening to her. She says she doesn't want a solicitor, but I think it's because she doesn't know what a solicitor is. I realise that she appears to have done something terrible, but she has the right to defend herself and I don't think she can manage it alone."

"Yer want me ter 'elp 'er, do yer?"

"It doesn't have to be you. I came to speak to you because you're the only person I have been able to find so far who knows her reasonably well. Perhaps you know of someone who could persuade her that she needs a solicitor. I suppose I'm just looking for someone who can show her a little compassion. I'm worried about her."

"About a murd'ress?"

"So she claims. But I think we are agreed that her mind is unsound. Perhaps she just says things she thinks people wish to hear. Perhaps she has been told to say them."

"I'll think on it," said Maggie, "but I've got a lot ter do 'ere. I 'elps the churchwarden, and between you and me 'e needs a lot of 'elp."

"Thank you for giving me your time," I said. I rummaged about in my bag and found one of my cards to give her. "This is where you can find me if you wish to discuss the matter further. I'm spending quite a bit of time in Bermondsey at the moment as I am reporting on the case."

"Yer a news reporter and yer frettin' about some girl down the police station?"

"I can't help it, I'm afraid. I know it's not really my job to get involved, but I have to worry about her because no one else seems to be."

CHAPTER 24

"I hope you don't mind me saying this, but you look a little down in the mouth, Miss Green," said Edgar when I arrived at the newsroom the following morning. "And I can't say that I'm surprised with all this poisoning business taking place. I think you need a jollier story to be getting on with. Can you think of a jolly story for Miss Green, Frederick?"

"Not offhand, but I'm sure there must be one." Frederick scratched his curly-haired head with the end of a pencil. "There must be some amusing anecdotes from a society bean-feast that would be worth a mention."

"Lord Routledge often holds such parties, doesn't he?" said Edgar. "I'm sure Lord Routledge has some amusing antics for us to report on."

"I couldn't give a fig for Lord Routledge's antics," I commented.

Edgar gasped. "Miss Green! I fear you will never be invited to one of his parties after saying such a thing."

The door of the newsroom opened and pale-faced Mr Childers entered.

"Oh, there you are, Miss Green. How nice it is to finally see you here first thing in the morning. It's usually quite difficult to keep track of your movements."

"I've been spending quite a bit of time in Bermondsey, Mr Childers. It has been confirmed that three of Catherine Curran's husbands have died from arsenic poisoning, and now a fourth husband has come forward to say that she also attempted to poison him."

"Goodness! Have the police caught her yet?"

"No, and as you know the case has been complicated further by a woman coming forward who claims to have poisoned the men herself. I shall write an update on the story now."

"Only a brief update is required, thank you. The case appears to have been solved."

"It's far from being solved, Mr Childers! Sally Chadwick has confessed to the three murders, but her motive remains unclear. Catherine Curran must have been involved in some way, and she is still on the run."

"Surely it is solved in the eyes of the law. Three men have died and a woman has confessed. Is there sufficient evidence to back up her confession?"

"Bottles of poison were found at her home."

"There you are, then. The case is complete and there is no longer any danger to anyone. We can publish a story about the trial when it takes place, but I shouldn't think there will be much to report given that this woman has confessed. Your time would be better spent on other stories from now on, Miss Green."

"I've already told her she needs to get writing about a jolly beanfeast, sir," Edgar chipped in.

Mr Childers gave him a blank stare. "Beanfeasts are not news, Mr Fish."

"Their inclusion in a newspaper lightens the mood a little,

sir. Reading about nothing other than parliament, stocks and shares, and coroner's inquests can become a rather dreary affair."

"Perhaps you would be better suited to working for a publication which features irreverent stories," Mr Childers said. "My uncle gave me the impression that his staff at the *Morning Express* took their jobs seriously. I think there must have been a misunderstanding."

"Allow me to reassure you that we are all thoroughly professional, sir," retorted Edgar. "However, the *Morning Express* newspaper has always included news stories of a lighter nature."

"I shall consult my uncle on the matter. In the meantime, Mr Fish, I am awaiting your article on the smallpox epidemic. Mr Potter, I need your parliamentary report. Miss Green, I would like a story from you on the Belgian elections."

We remained silent as Mr Childers left the room.

"Blimpy's been out of sorts ever since Fish left that tack on his chair," grumbled Frederick.

"Did he sit on it?" I asked.

"Yes," said Edgar with a chuckle. "You should have heard the screech from the editor's office!"

"Does he realise that you put it there?"

"I hope not. I shouldn't think he has any idea. He's the sort of chap who would never comprehend that another person might wish to cause him any mischief."

"It must have been quite painful," I said with a wince.

Edgar gave another quiet laugh. "I'll say! That'll teach him, won't it?"

"Not really," said Frederick, "because he doesn't realise we did it, and all it's served to do is put him in an even fouler temper than he was in before."

"It's funny though, isn't it, Potter?"

"I'd say that it was rather counterproductive."

"Why are you so serious all of a sudden?"

"We need to stop Blimpy making our lives such a misery."

"Be pleasant to him, you mean?"

"Yes, I think we will have to be."

Edgar snorted. "I won't hear of it! The day I'm pleasant to Blimpy is the day I rest in my grave!"

"What a sombre thought," I said, sitting down at the typewriter.

"I know what I'm going to do," said Edgar. "I'm going to include the word beanfeast in my article about smallpox and see if Blimpy notices."

"Of course he'll notice," said Potter.

"Ah, but I don't think he will. Have you noticed how rigid the man's neck is? That's a clear indication of panic. He struggles so much to maintain a calm demeanour that he can barely move his head. Behind that icy stare is a man who is frantic with worry that he's not up to the job. His eyes are likely to be darting all over the place as he edits, completely uncontrolled and filled with angst. He's so busy worrying about how to impress Uncle Conway that he won't even be concentrating on the words in front of him. I'm right, you know. Just wait and see. The word beanfeast will appear in my article tomorrow, and if it doesn't I shall eat my pencil."

"If only Mr Sherman were still here," I said sadly.

"I attempted to visit him yesterday," said Edgar.

"You *attempted* to?" I asked.

"Yes. He stood at the door and told me he didn't want any visitors."

"Oh dear. It doesn't sound as though he's coping very well."

"He's getting by. He says he can't stand anyone visiting and feeling sorry for him. Sympathetic faces cause him to fly into a rage."

"Perhaps he just didn't want *you* visiting him, Fish," said Frederick.

"Understandable that you might say that, Potter," replied Edgar, "but I'm afraid the same rebuff applies to everyone."

"I am sorry to hear that," I said.

We were interrupted by a knock at the door, and moments later James stepped in. His expression was sombre and he held his bowler hat in his hands.

"Inspector Blakely!" said Edgar. "It's been a while since we last saw you here. How are you? Goodness, is everything all right? You look as miserable as Miss Green did when she arrived this morning. The pair of you haven't fallen out, have you?"

"Not at all," replied James, giving me a weak smile. "Penny, I bring some sad news."

"What is it?"

I rose to my feet, but he gestured for me to return to my seat.

"Inspector Charles Martin has died."

I felt my mouth open then close again.

"Oh goodness, James, I'm so sorry to hear it," I said. "He had been unwell, hadn't he? I didn't realise his condition was so serious."

"Neither did I. He died yesterday evening."

"How awful," said Edgar quietly.

A heavy, sinking sensation lurched in my stomach.

"What was his illness?" I asked. "He seemed perfectly well when we saw him last week. Thursday, wasn't it? That was only a few days ago."

"Apparently, he was taken violently ill on Thursday evening. We think his death may be suspicious."

"Not poison?"

"His death was considered so irregular that an autopsy was conducted late last night. The police surgeon says there are clear indications that Charles had consumed a toxic substance."

"It is poison, then," I said, staring at the floorboards beneath my boots. I felt as though someone had just knocked me over. I pictured Inspector Martin's young, pleasant face. *How could he be dead?*

"Did Sally poison him?" I asked.

"She must have done somehow. She must have been carrying the poison on her person. No one thought to determine whether she might have been in possession of anything hazardous on the day she was arrested. It is an extremely unfortunate situation."

"He visited her home, didn't he?"

"Later that same day, yes."

"Perhaps he was poisoned while he was there. He may have handled the bottles or the fly papers."

"He may well have done, but none of the other constables were affected and I think they had more contact with the paraphernalia than he did. Besides, Dr Grant believes that Charles ingested a large dose of the poison. We know that he drank some tea while interviewing Miss Chadwick. Somehow, by sleight of hand, she must have been able to tip the poison into his cup without him noticing."

"But that's so very brazen!" I exclaimed. "I cannot believe she would have been able to do such a thing without anyone noticing! She doesn't even strike me as someone who is clever enough to do it."

"Perhaps she is adept at ensuring that people underestimate her. She may simply be a good actress; in fact, I'm sure that she is. To get away with all that she has done so far is quite impressive when you consider it. She has been fooling all of us."

"I still can't quite believe it," I said. "When she approached me in Grange Walk that day it was my suggestion that we went to the police station. She didn't even have time to prepare herself."

"Perhaps she was planning to go to the police station and carry out her attack all the while. It just so happened that you suggested taking her there."

I shook my head. "I still cannot comprehend it. Why would she admit to having poisoned three men and then go on to poison the investigating officer while she was in custody? Everyone knows that she has confessed. What would she stand to gain by murdering him?"

"What did she stand to gain by murdering any of them? We have already established that her motive remains unclear. I think we are dealing with a lunatic."

"A lunatic clever enough to poison a police officer while he was sitting in the room with her?"

"This one seems to be, Penny. I can't think of any other explanation."

"Me neither. What a terrible tragedy! This sort of thing shouldn't happen to a police officer while he goes about his daily duties."

I held James' gaze and felt a sickening twinge of worry in my stomach as the thought crossed my mind that the same thing could happen to him.

"It's a sober reminder of the danger we put ourselves in sometimes," he said. "At least the suspect is already in custody. We must make sure that she has no opportunity to harm anyone else."

"The men at Bermondsey station must be finding it extremely difficult to go about their work," I said.

"They are, but Sergeant Richards is managing the situation well. He's a good officer. The purpose of our work now is to ensure that Miss Chadwick faces trial and is convicted for her actions."

CHAPTER 25

The shock of hearing about Inspector Martin's death remained with me as I walked along Borough High Street to Southwark Police Court the following day. The time had come for Sally Chadwick to appear in front of the magistrates and I still couldn't make my mind up about her.

Was it possible that Sally's childlike manner was nothing but a clever act? If it was, she had fooled a great number of people for a very long time. But if she was genuinely of unsound mind, how had she managed to poison four men without detection? And why had she suddenly confessed to her crimes?

It was early September and the weather was mild, despite the light drizzle. The warm damp encouraged foul odours to rise from the gutters at the side of the road. I walked beneath my umbrella past the many inns which had welcomed stage-coach travellers to London before the advent of the railways.

A crowd had gathered outside the courthouse. There was no doubt that the case of the Bermondsey poisoner had roused a substantial amount of public interest.

The courtroom was busy by the time I made my way inside. Every seat was taken and there was barely enough space to stand. I joined the other reporters and wiped my spectacles so that I could survey the public benches clearly. I immediately spotted fair-haired William Curran, the brother of John. I also recognised the scarred face of Florence Burrell, the sister of Thomas. A tall, red-haired man managed to find space to sit at the back of the room, and I realised it was Benjamin Taylor.

The room fell quiet as three magistrates walked in and seated themselves behind the highly polished desk. The chief magistrate, Mr Sidney Parnell, sat at the centre in a large leather chair. He had a hooked nose and a mane of white hair with matching whiskers.

Silence descended as a police officer escorted Sally Chadwick into the dock. Everyone turned to look at the woman, who bowed her head as she walked. Her straw-like hair had been pinned to the nape of her neck and she wore a shabby brown dress. Walking behind her was a diminutive grey-haired figure wearing a black hat and a smart, dark dress. I smiled to myself as I realised it was Maggie. Although I felt pleased that my words had encouraged her to help Sally, I felt fearful as to what her reaction might be when she discovered that Sally had possibly murdered a fourth man.

Mr Parnell opened the proceedings by inviting James to step forward and speak. He looked smart in his dark suit and I felt proud of him as he addressed the courtroom.

"I became engaged in this investigation nine days ago on Monday the twenty-fifth of August, when the body of Thomas Burrell was exhumed from the churchyard of St Mary Magdalen in Bermondsey. M Division requested my assistance because there was a suspicion that Mr Burrell's death had been caused by poisoning. The cause of this suspicion was the death of Mr John Curran from arsenic poisoning on the seventeenth of August. His wife, Catherine Curran, is currently evading capture. She had been married to Thomas Burrell from 1880 until 1882. Naturally, my suspicions were firmly on Catherine Curran being the culprit to begin with.

"However, on Thursday the twenty-eighth of August, the prisoner, Miss Sally Chadwick, confessed to Inspector Martin and myself at Bermondsey police station that she had poisoned John Curran and Thomas Burrell, along with a third victim whose name she could not recall. I believe this third victim to be Mr Francis Peel, another husband of Catherine Curran's, who died in 1880. His remains have since been exhumed and scientific analysis has confirmed that all three men – Mr John Curran, Mr Thomas Burrell and Mr Francis Peel – died as a result of arsenic poisoning. In addition to the prisoner's confession, we found evidence of arsenic both in the form of fly papers and a bottled solution at the prisoner's home."

"Very good, Inspector Blakely," said Mr Parnell. "A succinct and informative statement." He placed an antiquated pair of spectacles on his nose. "I shall now read out the prisoner's signed confession to the court. 'I, Sally Chadwick, have murdered three men. The first, Francis Peel, died on the ninth of February 1880. The second, Thomas Burrell, died on the eighteenth of May 1882. The third, John Curran, died on the seventeenth of August 1884. Each of these deaths was caused by me giving these men bottles of beer which I had poisoned with arsenic. In each case I acted alone, and no one knew of my intent or my guilt.'"

He removed his spectacles and nodded at Sally. "May I confirm, Miss Chadwick, that this statement was made by you, and of your own free will?"

"Yes." She nodded sadly.

Mr Parnell addressed James again. "Inspector Blakely, I am sure you are aware that I must ask you whether any inducement has been made to the prisoner in order to extract this confession?"

"No, Your Honour. This confession has been made voluntarily by the prisoner. She attended Bermondsey police station on Thursday the twenty-eighth of August in the company of Miss Penny Green, who informed me and the other police officers present that Miss Chadwick had confessed to the three murders."

"Then let us hear from Miss Green."

I had not expected to be called upon as a witness.

All eyes turned on me as I stepped out into the centre of the courtroom, and my knees suddenly felt weak. James caught my eye and gave me an almost imperceptible nod.

"Please introduce yourself to the court," ordered Mr Parnell.

"My name is Miss Penelope Green." My voice sounded small and timorous in the large courtroom. "I'm a reporter for the *Morning Express* newspaper."

"Can you please explain, Miss Green, how the confession from Miss Chadwick came about?"

I told the magistrates about my encounter with Sally in Grange Walk and how I had then accompanied her to Bermondsey Street police station.

"During your time with the prisoner, was any inducement made by you, or by anyone else, to extract her confession?" asked Mr Parnell.

"No, Your Honour."

"None at all?" His unblinking eyes bored into mine. "I must stress the importance of this point, Miss Green. I'm sure everyone in the court is aware that news reporters often use persuasive tactics in the pursuit of a story."

"Your Honour, I did not coerce Miss Chadwick into making a confession. In fact, I was extremely surprised and slightly disbelieving of it, if the truth be told." I felt a trickle of nervous perspiration run down between my shoulder blades.

Mr Parnell scowled at me. "Feeling surprise and disbelief does not mean that you are innocent of inducing the confession, Miss Green."

My heart was thudding so heavily I felt as though it must have been audible in the silent room. *Was the chief magistrate putting me on trial?* My work had been helpful to the investigation, yet I was beginning to feel as though I had done something wrong. I didn't wish anyone to think that I had persuaded Sally to confess for the sake of writing a gripping news story.

"Your Honour." I spoke loudly in an attempt to hide the tremor in my voice. "I wish to reassure you and the court that I gave Miss Chadwick no inducement whatsoever to make her confession. I know that doing so would not only bring my own profession into disrepute but would also be considered an attempt to pervert the course of justice, which is a most serious offence."

There was a pause as Mr Parnell regarded me. "It is indeed, Miss Green," he said finally. "And I am reassured to hear that you understand the responsibilities of your profession."

The magistrate turned his attention away from me. Shaking with relief, I resumed my position as an observer at the back of the room.

Mr Parnell asked the clerk to read Sally's confession to the court once again.

"Can you confirm that this is the statement you wrote, Miss Chadwick?" asked Mr Parnell.

"Yes." Her voice was barely audible.

"Once again, I must ask you to confirm that you have made this confession by your own free will and have received no inducement or persuasion from anyone else."

"Yes."

"*Your Honour*," Maggie whispered to her.

"Your Honour," repeated Sally.

The magistrate asked the clerk to copy Miss Chadwick's confession onto the charge sheet and then asked her to sign it.

"The serious nature of these crimes demands that the prisoner must attend the Central Criminal Court," said Mr Parnell. "I request that the prisoner be confined within the House of Detention until the next session is called."

James stepped forward. "Your Honour, I would like to request that a fourth murder be added to the list of charges."

There were gasps from the public benches and Mr Parnell raised an eyebrow, clearly displeased by this interruption to the proceedings.

"Has the prisoner confessed to the crime?" he asked.

"No. She denies it, Your Honour."

"Please explain the circumstances to the court as succinctly as possible."

"My much-respected colleague, Inspector Charles Martin, died of suspected arsenic poisoning two days ago on Monday the first of September," said James. "He interviewed and arrested Miss Chadwick on the day she confessed to the three murders, and it is my belief that she put poison into his tea during their encounter, which led to the violent illness that ultimately claimed his life."

Heads started shaking and there were several stifled mutters around the room. Maggie's eyes were fixed on Sally, as if looking for some sign of guilt.

"The inquest into Inspector Martin's death will be opened tomorrow," added James.

"What evidence do you have that the prisoner committed this crime?"

"It is purely circumstantial at present, Your Honour.

However, I suspect her involvement given that the cause of Inspector Martin's death appears to match that of the men she has already admitted to murdering."

"How much time do you need to gather further evidence?"

"I should like to request the remand of the prisoner for a week. This will enable me to search for evidence that she committed this dreadful crime against Inspector Martin and will also allow time for the inquest into his death to run its course, and for the chemical analysis required when poisoning is suspected to be carried out."

Mr Parnell conferred with his fellow magistrates in hushed whispers. Several minutes elapsed before he addressed James again.

"Very well, Inspector Blakely. The prisoner is to return here at ten o'clock next Wednesday to hear this new charge against her. Miss Chadwick, there is no need for you to make a statement at this time, but is there anything you wish to say?"

She glanced around the courtroom, then gave Mr Parnell a nervous smile. "It weren't me what murdered the policeman, sir."

I noticed a few heads shaking sadly.

Why would Sally confess to the murders of three men, yet deny the murder of Inspector Martin?

It made no sense.

CHAPTER 26

A police carriage with blackened windows took Sally Chadwick to the House of Detention in Clerkenwell. A crowd followed behind in the rain as it made its way up Borough High Street toward London Bridge. I wondered how Sally would fare in a gaol which housed some of the country's most dangerous criminals.

I noticed a small figure watching the carriage as it departed.

"Thank you for coming, Maggie," I said.

She spun around, startled by my words. "Oh, 'ello, Miss Green."

She turned to watch the carriage again and I noticed the fine quality of her dark dress and wondered how she had been able to afford it.

"I didn't know nothin' about a fourth one," she added. "A police officer, 'e said?"

"He died on Monday evening," I said. "And it appears that Sally poisoned him. We don't know how she managed it, and I am struggling to believe that she is capable of doing such a thing. Is it possible that she pretends to be simple-minded in order to fool everyone?"

"Pretendin'?" Maggie turned to face me again. "That ain't our Sally. Always been like it, she 'as. Like I says, she's always been a child and always will be."

"You've known her since she was a girl, haven't you?"

"I met 'er in the horphanage," she replied. "I dunno what's made her so bad as all this. I don't understand it."

"Did you find much opportunity to speak to her before the court hearing this morning?" I asked.

"Not much. She don't understand what's 'appenin' to 'er, do she?"

"Is she still refusing to receive any help from a solicitor?"

"Yep. I dunno what good 'e'd be, anyway."

"A solicitor would help to explain what's happening to her. And he might be able to persuade her to implicate Catherine Curran in the murders rather than taking all of the blame herself."

"This ain't nothin' ter do wiv Catherine."

"How can you be so sure of that?"

"'Cause she jus' wouldn't of done it. Sally's a lunatic, but I always thought she was a nice, kind lunatic. But now we're seein' what she's really like and folk ain't safe around 'er." I noticed that her eyes were damp. "It makes me sad ter say it, but she'll 'ave ter be in gaol for the good of everyone."

"I think a doctor needs to examine her."

Maggie shrugged. "Maybe, but what can 'e do now? 'E can't change what's 'appened. None of us can. It's a sad endin' to the 'ole thing."

She nodded farewell and walked away down the street.

I turned back toward the courthouse with a heavy heart, realising that Sally Chadwick had lost her only possible ally.

James found me lingering outside.

"Well done in that courtroom, Penny." He smiled, but I

could see signs of strain in his eyes. Inspector Martin's death had obviously affected him deeply. "Mr Parnell can be rather intimidating."

"For a moment I feared he was convinced that I had encouraged Sally to make her confession."

"It's his duty to ensure that she did so under her own free will," said James. "But he can make you feel rather uncomfortable, can't he?"

"Sally needs to be examined by a physician," I said. "Surely if her mind is greatly affected she cannot be held entirely responsible for her actions."

"We can request that she is visited by a doctor."

"I think the request should be made as a matter of urgency. If a physician confirms that her mind is unstable she may avoid appearing at the Old Bailey."

"Possibly. At the present time I find myself struggling to find any sympathy for the woman who appears to have murdered a man who was both my colleague and my friend."

"But if her mind isn't sane she may not have been able to help herself!"

"Perhaps."

"You mustn't allow your sadness for a deceased colleague to colour your view of the case, James."

"I realise that," he snapped, "but Charles' death has come as a great shock to everyone. I know I will soon be able to resume my investigations in the same calm, detached manner I am accustomed to. But at the moment I am finding it difficult, and I only have a week to ensure that Sally is charged for his murder."

I wasn't convinced that it was right for James to be involved in a case in which the victim was a friend of his, but I knew that it would only antagonise him further if I mentioned it. I reluctantly bit my lip and silently assured myself that I would do whatever I could to ensure that Sally Chadwick was assessed by a doctor.

William Curran approached us. "She'll 'ang for it, won't she?"

There was a flash of vitriol in his dark eyes and his words left a bitter taste in my mouth.

"We cannot predict what the judge at the Old Bailey will decide," said James.

"She certainly *should* hang for it!" added Florence Burrell, who had also joined us, spots of rain covering her headscarf and spectacle lenses. "She's confessed to three murders. *Three!*"

"She may not have known exactly what she was doing," I said defensively.

"What are you talking about?" Florence responded angrily. "She's poisoned four men! And using such a cold method of murder. No argument or anger; instead, she calmly planned it all and stood back to let them die!"

"It is horrible," I agreed. "And it is certainly not the work of a sane mind."

"What makes yer say that?" asked William.

"Because she seems to be such a simple, ordinary girl," I replied. "I just cannot imagine her plotting to do something like this."

"You don't even know 'er!" said William. I noticed his right hand had clenched into a fist.

"No, I don't," I replied as calmly as I could. "And I'm not saying that she didn't do it. I'm simply saying that I don't think she can be fully in control of her actions."

"She knew what she was doing all right," said Florence. "My brother was taken from us because of her! At least she's going to prison now, I'm pleased about that. I shall write my family and tell them. They'll be happy to hear it."

"What about Catherine?" I asked her. "Do you think she could have been partially responsible?"

"Catherine can't have had nothing do with it."

"Then why has she run away?"

Florence shrugged. "I don't know. Maybe she feared everyone would blame her."

"Mebbe she's upset," suggested William. "Mebbe she weren't in control of 'er actions neither. She weren't 'erself when John got taken sick. Wouldn't even let me in the 'ouse! It must 'ave been too much for her after seein' the other ones dyin' an' all."

"Sally propositioned my brother," said Florence "and she's killed him because he turned her down. She must have propositioned your brother as well," she said to William.

"'E never mentioned nuffink, but she mighta done," replied William.

"Well, I think she must have done it. I reckon she must have tried it on with all of Catherine's husbands and each of them has turned her away. That's why she's poisoned them," said Florence.

"We may never know for sure," said James. "She has confessed to these crimes, but we shall have to wait and see whether she decides to give us any further information about her motives for committing them."

"From the sounds of it I reckon it's gotta be summink ter do wiv Caffrine. She was jealous of 'er," said William. "She wanted to do summink to hurt 'er. She's tried ter take 'er 'usbands away, and then she's poisoned 'em. I was feelin' angry wiv Caffrine, but now I know what Sally's done I feels sorry for 'er. Caffrine needs ter be found and brought back 'ere just so she knows as no one blames 'er and so's she can see justice bein' done down the Old Bailey."

"Catherine's first husband claimed that she had tried to poison him as well," I said.

My comment was met with a pause as William and Florence considered this new piece of information.

"He must have heard about the other murders and decided to make a tall tale out of it," said Florence. "If he was telling the truth he'd have said something at the time."

"He says that he didn't fully realise it at the time. He joked about it but hadn't completely accepted the idea until he read the recent reports in the newspapers."

"There you 'ave it!" said William. "He's read the papers and they've put ideas in 'is 'ead."

"When was this?" asked Florence.

"A little over six years ago."

"Long enough ago so as nuffink can be proved now," added William.

"You have a point," said James. "We have nothing to prove that the man is telling the truth."

"And nothing to disprove it either," I added. "Perhaps it might be worth interviewing his family and friends, James, and finding out what they can remember about the incident. He was in the courtroom this morning." I glanced around to see if I could spot him among the people still gathered outside the court.

"There he is," I said, pointing him out to William and Florence. Benjamin Taylor was smoking a clay pipe and speaking to one of the police constables.

"I'll suggest to M Division that they attempt to verify his claims somehow," said James. "But they probably won't make it a priority at the moment. Most pressing of all is ensuring that we have enough evidence to charge Miss Chadwick with the murder of Inspector Martin." James checked his watch. "I must get down to The Five Bells now. The inquest into John Curran's death resumes today. Are you coming along, Mr Curran?"

"I surely am." His dark eyes remained on Benjamin Taylor.

"I need to start writing my article about Sally's court appearance," I said. "I shall see you soon, James. Goodbye, Mr Curran. Farewell, Miss Burrell."

CHAPTER 27

"Thank you, Miss Green, but there was no need for you to bring me anything. I'm not an invalid."

Mr Sherman placed the box of Rowntree's Chocolate Cream Cigars on his writing desk. His face looked thinner than usual and there was a hint of grey at his temples that I had never noticed before. A pipe was lodged in his mouth and he wore a paisley smoking jacket made from velvet. We sat in his study, which was decorated with crimson wallpaper and looked as untidy as his office at the *Morning Express*.

"Sherry?" he asked, picking up the decanter from his desk.

I nodded. "Thank you."

"East India, of course," he said as he filled a glass and passed it to me.

I took a sip and it immediately warmed my throat.

Mr Sherman inhaled deeply on his pipe, sat back in his chair and blew out a cloud of smoke.

"Why are you here?" he asked. "I said I didn't want any visitors. I thought I'd made that abundantly clear to Fish."

"I've come to ask you something."

"I don't know why. I'm no use to anyone at the moment. I hear Conway's brought Childers in." Sherman smiled. "That boy is a waste of space."

"He's hopeless," I said, "and we all want you to come back as soon as possible."

"Is that so? I can't imagine Fish and Potter are clamouring for my return."

"Of course they are!"

"You misunderstand the situation, Miss Green. Now that they have learnt something more of my character they will no longer care to have me there."

"You might be surprised, sir."

"I doubt it." Sherman smiled again. "How's the case of the Bermondsey poisoner progressing? I read that there has been a confession."

"There has, although I'm not sure the supposed culprit has committed the crimes."

Sherman laughed. "You are never simply content to report on a story, are you, Miss Green? You must always question every incident and decision. It must take up an enormous amount of your time and energy. How do you manage to fit in anything else?"

"I do very little else, sir," I replied. "And who will hold the real culprits to account if I don't investigate these matters properly?"

"It's a fair point. Not many people have the tenacity to pursue stories in the way that you do. You're like a bloodhound. You don't look like one, I should add, but you remind me of one in every other way."

I smiled. "I'll take that as a compliment, sir."

"Please do. Now you should probably be getting back to work. I've already told you that I don't want any visitors."

I drained my sherry and remained in my chair.

"Sir, I should like to ask you a favour."

"A favour? From a man with a criminal charge hanging over his head?"

"You're not a criminal, Mr Sheridan."

"In the eyes of the law and the church I am."

"You have not been found guilty of any crime."

"Not yet I haven't. What's the favour?"

"I believe the woman who has confessed to these poisonings—"

"The Bermondsey poisoner, you mean?"

"She hasn't been found guilty of any crime yet, so I would hesitate to refer to her in that way."

"But she has confessed."

"Yes, but I don't think she is of sound mind. I cannot understand why she has confessed. The suggested motive for her crimes makes little sense to me. Besides, she doesn't seem the type to commit such a calculating act. She is currently being held at the House of Detention, and you know the sort of criminals they hold there. I cannot imagine how awful it must be for her!"

"She has poisoned three men, and most likely a police inspector as well."

"But has she really? And even if she has, surely some sympathy should be shown to her on account of her feeble mind."

"You consider her a lunatic?"

"I believe she may be. And if she's hanged as a result of her lunacy that would be a terrible injustice."

"She should be sent to an asylum."

"That would be a fairer punishment than hanging."

"Has she been seen by a physician?"

"I don't think she has so far. There was no physician present at the police court and she has no legal representation whatsoever. I'm quite worried for her."

"And you would like a physician to visit her... That's why you're here?"

"Yes, I wondered if you could—?"

"Ask my brother?"

"Yes please, Mr Sherman. Could you?"

Mr Sherman sighed. "I can try. I should add that my recent arrest has come as quite a shock to my family. I'm not sure how amenable he'll be."

"But this isn't about you; it's about a young woman with a fragile mind who has been caught up in the legal system."

"Hasn't your friend Inspector Blakely shown her any compassion?"

"He realises she's vulnerable; however, Inspector Martin was a good friend of his and James is extremely upset about his death. I'm certain that he will form a more balanced view of the case in due course."

"He shouldn't be investigating his friend's death."

"I agree with you, sir, and I plan to tell him that when he is a little more recovered."

"I'll speak to Henry. She's at the House of Detention in Clerkenwell, you say?"

"Yes. Her name is Sally Chadwick."

"I recall it now from your reports. I can't promise that he will be able to help, but I'll see what I can do."

"Thank you, sir. I hope to see you back at the office soon."

"I doubt that very much, Miss Green. Mr Conway's found me a lawyer, who he assures me is the best in London. He must be costing a pretty penny too, but I don't think he's ever had to defend a charge like this before."

CHAPTER 28

"I stand by what I've said, Miss Green. She was poisonin' me. I ain't never felt that bad afore and I ain't never felt that bad since. I ain't the sort to get sick, an' that was the last time!"

"I believe you, Mr Taylor, and that's why I should like to interview you for the *Morning Express* newspaper. I think it's important that people have a chance to hear what has happened to you. It's possible that she may have poisoned someone else, and if that someone was to read your story he or she might also come forward."

"That's what's made me go ter the police! I saw it in the papers meself. Only no one seems ter believe me."

We had agreed to meet at The Royal Vauxhall Tavern in Lambeth. It was gloomy inside, with only a few gaslights burning. The smell of stale beer and tobacco smoke lingered in the air. I had last visited the tavern with James while investigating the death of a young maid named Elizabeth Wiggins.

"I'm afraid the timing of all this is most unfortunate, Mr Taylor," I said. "A Bermondsey police officer has been murdered and the investigation into his death has left little time to look into your case. And because your poisoning occurred six years ago it is rather difficult to collect any evidence that might help to support your words."

"But it's the truth, I'm tellin' yer!"

"You don't have to convince me, Mr Taylor, I believe you. That's why I wish to write about what happened. But you must surely agree that it would be rather difficult for the police to find any evidence of poisoning in your case after all this time."

"Yep, I 'ear yer." He sighed and took a long slurp from his mug of beer.

"Did you ever find the poison she was using?"

"Nope, I didn't find nuffink."

"Apparently, Sally Chadwick extracted arsenic from some fly papers. Were there any fly papers in the home you shared with Catherine?"

"Jane, yer mean."

"Sorry, Jane."

"Yeah, there must've been. Most 'omes have 'em, don't they?"

"Did she purchase a large amount of them?"

"I dunno."

"You didn't come across fly papers being soaked in water at all?"

He gave a hollow laugh. "Is that 'ow you get the poison out, then? Nope, I never seen that."

"Did you ever see her pouring what appeared to be water into bottles? Or see bottles stored on a shelf or in a cupboard and wonder what was in them?"

Benjamin gave this some thought. "I remember bottles, but anyfink could 'ave been in 'em. Syrup and medicines an' that sorta thing."

"And you believe she put the poison in your food?"

"She must've done. Can't think 'ow else she mighta done it."

"In your drink perhaps?"

"Yep, I reckon she could've put it in me drinks."

"What do you like to drink?"

"Beer. Whiskey."

"Sally Chadwick claims to have poisoned the other three men by putting arsenic into their beer."

"Maybe Jane done that an' all. You're tellin' me the two women done it the same way?"

"I suspect Jane, whom I know as Catherine Curran, had something to do with the murders of her other husbands. Can you think of anyone who might have witnessed Catherine, I mean Jane, doing anything suspicious like this?"

"The neighbours, mebbe. But that were six or seven years ago. We lived in Lollard Street back then, but folk move in an' out all the time."

"Do you remember anyone else who lived there at the same time as you?"

"Can't fink of no one."

I sighed. It was proving difficult to find any evidence to back up this particular case.

"Did you see a doctor when you were ill?"

"Yep."

"Can you remember his name?"

Benjamin took another long sip of beer as he gave this some thought. I prayed he would come up with a name so I had someone with whom I could follow up his story.

"Doctor Townley." A grin spread across his face. "Dunno 'ow I've remembered that. I just do!"

"Do you remember his first name?"

"Nope, jus' Townley. An' 'e was on Lambeth Walk."

"And he treated you while you were ill?"

"Yep, 'e come and seen me, 'e did."

"More than once?"

"A few times, I reckon."

"You're asking me about a man I treated six years ago?"

Dr Townley was a grey-haired man with a large nose and a wide, bushy moustache. I had been relieved to discover that he still occupied the rooms on Lambeth Walk.

"I don't expect you to recall him specifically, but I was hoping you might have kept a record of the treatment you provided."

Dr Townley sighed. "Miss Woburn!" he called toward the door of his office, which stood ajar.

A silver-haired lady in a dark blouse and skirt peered through the gap.

"Bring in the diary for '78, would you please?"

The secretary nodded and disappeared for a short while before returning with a large, leather-bound volume. She placed it on his desk.

"Very good. Thank you, Miss Woburn. Now then, Miss Green, what was the chap's name again?"

"Benjamin Taylor."

He began to leaf through the diary. "And what month would it have been?"

"Oh, I'm not entirely sure." I paused to consult my notebook, in which I had recorded all the relevant dates. "Here we are. His wife married again in November 1878, so it must have occurred a little before then."

"Did I hear you correctly? His wife remarried?"

"He asked her to leave, so she married someone else."

"Bigamy, eh? Was she prosecuted for that?"

"No."

"Interesting. So, before November 1878, you say? That gives me ten months to search through."

"I should think it more likely that he saw you earlier in the year. If his wife was ready to marry someone else by November she must presumably have met him by the summer at least."

Dr Townley gave me a bemused nod. "Possibly, but what if there was some overlap between the two?"

"I don't know enough to say either way, I'm afraid."

Dr Townley sighed again and began to look through the January entries, examining the appointments recorded there in a small, slanting hand. "Benjamin Taylor... Where did he live?"

I consulted my notebook again. "Lollard Street."

"I know it well. What symptoms did he present with?"

"Vomiting, and most likely diarrhoea as well. His symptoms would have been quite severe, I imagine. You apparently told him he was lucky to be alive."

"Did I indeed?" The doctor reached the end of January and began to skim through February. "He must have been taken quite unwell in that case."

I prayed that something would jog the doctor's memory or that he would come across the notes he had written about Benjamin's illness.

"He may have joked with you that he was being poisoned."

"Really? Can you describe him to me?"

He would have been a young man; about twenty-three or twenty-four at the time. Tall, with red hair and whiskers. He previously worked as a builder and is now employed at the Doulton Pottery."

"I see. Poisoned, you say?"

"That's what he now believes."

"This doesn't have anything to do with this Bermondsey poisoner business, does it?"

"It might do. That's what I'm trying to find out."

The doctor closed his eyes in concentration, as if trying to recall a patient named Benjamin Taylor.

"I think I do remember a chap who was quite fearfully unwell. Red hair. Pleasant wife, who was extremely attentive."

I smiled. "Jane?"

"Was that her name?"

"It's what she called herself at the time."

"It might have been Jane, but I don't remember. However, I'm sure I recall a young, fit man who was most distressed by his debilitating symptoms. I would have suggested milk and lime water, along with castor oil. I'd also have told him to remain in bed. I wish I could remember what time of year it happened." The doctor continued leafing through his diary.

"What did you suspect was the cause of his symptoms?" I asked.

"It was difficult to suspect anything, really," he replied. "The reasons for vomiting and diarrhoea are many and varied. It could be something carried in the air or in food which disagrees with a person. It could be an indicator of another disease one is suffering from. Fortunately, he doesn't appear to have been too seriously affected as he has made a full recovery. Otherwise he would have been unable to tell you all about it."

"You didn't suspect that he had been poisoned?"

"No, I can't say that it would have crossed my mind in this case, given that there were many other more likely causes. And different poisons affect the body in different ways. Some symptoms provide quite an obvious sign of poisoning, while others provide none at all."

"How about arsenic poisoning?"

"Arsenic poisoning causes gastrointestinal upset, and that

may have been the cause of Mr Taylor's symptoms. However, I still think it highly unlikely."

"Unless he was married to the Bermondsey poisoner, that is."

Dr Townley gave a hearty laugh. "Indeed! In which case I suppose you might consider it. Reporters are always looking for an interesting angle on a story." He laughed again and then stopped when he noticed that I did not share his mirth. "You're serious about this, aren't you, Miss Green?"

"Yes, I am."

"You think that pretty young woman he was married to was poisoning him?"

"That's what he thinks. But seeing as it was more than six years ago, few people are prepared to listen to him."

"I see."

Dr Townley began leafing through his diary more earnestly. "Let's just confirm that I saw this same chap and am not mistakenly thinking of someone else."

I waited patiently.

"Here we are," he said eventually. "Monday the eighteenth of March. I attended to a Mr Benjamin Taylor at twenty-one Lollard Street. Does that sound right to you?"

"It does." I smiled. "Thank you, Dr Townley."

"And I made a note of his symptoms here. Lethargy... abdominal pain... vomiting... Yes, this ties in with what we've been discussing."

"Thank you, Dr Townley. I think Scotland Yard will be very interested to hear of your visit to Mr Taylor."

"The Yard?" The doctor's face fell. "I don't have anything to tell the police, Miss Green. I visited Mr Taylor when he was unwell, but I certainly couldn't confirm whether he was poisoned or not. I couldn't even speculate on it all these years later. I have a vague recollection of his illness and a record in my diary that I visited him. However, I refuse to be dragged through the courts and—"

"I'm sure it won't come to that. My conversation with you serves to confirm Mr Taylor's story, and that's the only important matter here. Up to this moment we only had his word for it, but now we have evidence that he was seriously unwell, as he has claimed."

"But we cannot surmise that it was due to arsenic poisoning. I must make that abundantly clear."

"No, I realise that. You have made yourself clear, Doctor."

"Miss Green, I really would prefer not to have the Yard sniffing around here if possible. I've been dragged into police investigations before and it isn't something I enjoy. What's important is that Mr Taylor is alive and well today. He has survived his ordeal."

"His account, and perhaps also yours, implies a pattern of behaviour which Jane Taylor, as she was called back then, began to adopt. Thank you for your time, Doctor, and I hope not to have to bother you again. I will simply inform the Yard that you have confirmed Mr Taylor's claim that he consulted you regarding his illness."

Dr Townley closed his diary. "Very well, but I refuse to be drawn on any speculation whatsoever. Please inform the Yard of that."

"I will. Thank you."

CHAPTER 29

"That was not a particularly satisfactory hearing," said James as we left The Five Bells pub, where the inquest into Inspector Martin's death had been swiftly opened and adjourned by the coroner, Mr Osborne. "It raised more questions than it answered."

"The adjournment gives you two weeks to find sufficient evidence to prove that Sally Chadwick poisoned Inspector Martin," I said.

"I have less time than that, Penny. Sally is only being held on remand for that charge until next Wednesday. I have six days, and if I can't provide the evidence in time she will face trial for three murders instead of four. I can't understand it. Bermondsey Street police station has been thoroughly searched three times over and there is still no sign of the poison she used in Inspector Martin's murder."

We walked up Bermondsey Street toward the police station. The warm drizzle which had begun the day before continued to fall. I surveyed the heavy grey above our heads and wondered whether we had seen the last of the summer.

"Did you check Sally Chadwick's clothing for any sign of the poison she used?" I asked.

"We did, but only once she had become a suspect, which wasn't until Monday evening. Inspector Martin was poisoned last Thursday, which means she had almost four days to dispose of the bottle. That sounds like a long time, but given that she was in the cell for most of it she had rather limited opportunity to dispose of anything."

"Perhaps she consumed the rest," I suggested.

"She shows no signs of having poisoned herself."

"Perhaps there was very little poison left and she had been practising Mithridatism?"

"Practising what now?" James gave a slight laugh.

"Consuming small amounts of poison on a regular basis, which builds a greater tolerance to it."

"Perhaps she had." He gave me a sceptical look. "Though Miss Chadwick doesn't seem the sort to practise something of that kind, does she?"

"She doesn't seem the sort to plan and execute the deaths of four men either."

"You think she's innocent, don't you? Despite the over-whelming evidence against her."

"I don't know whether she is innocent or not, but I think she has been coerced."

"How might you explain Charles Martin's death, in that case?"

"She must have done it, there's no doubt about that. But I still believe it was carried out on someone else's orders. And perhaps she used up all of the remaining poison when she did it?"

"Then where is the bottle?"

"It has to be somewhere. Or perhaps there wasn't one."

"What would the poison have been stored in, then?"

"I don't know. How else can arsenic be obtained?"

"I'm not sure, but I know that it is obtained with great difficulty. Its availability has been well regulated for more than thirty years."

"She must have found an inventive way of storing and administering it. Perhaps she used a packet of rat poison."

"In which case you'd think we would have found the packet somewhere, but we have found nothing. Nothing at all."

James' brow had worn a perpetual scowl ever since he had told me the news of Inspector Martin's death. I didn't like to see him so dejected.

Was he giving his impending wedding much thought? I wondered. *Had Charlotte been of any comfort to him during this difficult time?*

These were questions I wished to ask him but didn't dare to as I knew he already had so much on his mind.

"There appear to have been some genuine sightings of the elusive Catherine Curran in Orpington," he said. "Some constables from M Division are working alongside the local constabulary to find her. Hopefully we shall soon receive the good news that she has been apprehended."

"She must have been pleased to hear that Sally Chadwick has been arrested. She's probably hoping that no one will come looking for her now."

"Which is where she's quite wrong. We still need to speak to her, regardless of whether she's innocent or not. And there is also a charge of bigamy for her to answer to."

"Don't you feel that you could do with some rest, James?" I asked.

He stopped and stared at me, his bowler hat sparkling with spots of drizzle.

"What on earth are you talking about, Penny? Some *rest*? We're in the middle of an important investigation!"

"You have just lost your friend," I said. "Perhaps you need

to take a quiet moment and give yourself a chance to accustom yourself to this tragic event."

"I shan't ever accustom myself to it, no matter how much *rest* I have. I will only rest when those responsible are brought to justice. Does that sound reasonable to you?"

"Yes, it does. It's just that..."

"Just what?"

"I don't like seeing you so down, James."

His face softened and he gave a sigh. "I don't like being so down," he said quietly. "It's been a dreadful week, but I must get on with my job."

I nodded. "I understand that."

"Of course you do. You're as bad as I am for getting embroiled in a case and working relentlessly until a satisfactory conclusion is reached." He held my gaze, then added with a smile, "We're like two peas in a pod, you and I."

❧

"I don't recall asking you to write about another supposed poisoning victim, Miss Green," said Mr Childers. "Where's your article on the purchase of Raphael's *Ansidei Madonna* for the National Gallery?"

"It's here, Mr Childers, and I have typewritten it for you," I replied, handing the article to him.

"Good. I am very much looking forward to seeing the painting once it's in situ. I should imagine the great and good of Fleet Street will be invited to the preview."

"Sir, would you please print the interview with Benjamin Taylor?" I asked. "It's important because it suggests that the Bermondsey poisoner attempted her first murder six years ago."

"Is it the same woman who has confessed?"

"No, that's Sally Chadwick, who is currently awaiting trial."

"Then who is the Bermondsey poisoner?"

"Some believe it is Sally Chadwick, though others suspect Catherine Curran, who was once called Jane Taylor."

"So there are two Bermondsey poisoners?"

"Two *suspects*," I said.

"Or even three," Edgar piped up.

"Three?" I questioned.

"Sally Chadwick, Catherine Curran and Jane Taylor."

"Catherine Curran and Jane Taylor are one and the same person," I corrected. "She was forced to change her name because she had committed bigamy."

"Goodness, what a confusing case," said Edgar. "I'm relieved not to be the one who is working on it."

"You will publish Benjamin Taylor's interview, won't you?" I urged Mr Childers.

"How do you know this Taylor chap is telling the truth?" he asked.

"Because the doctor who treated him confirmed his story to me. The article is currently four hundred words, sir. I can shorten it a little if you are struggling to find space in tomorrow's edition."

"Even if you shortened it to ten words I'm not sure there would be any space, Miss Green. We're already catering for the prime minister's visit to Scotland and important developments in Egypt and Sudan. Those are the stories our readers wish to read, and my uncle is rather concerned about our circulation figures at the present time."

"Please, Mr Childers," I continued. "This is a complicated case, which has taken an even more tragic turn with the death of a police officer in Bermondsey. I'm certain that our readers will be most interested to read this interview with Mr

Taylor, which will not be printed in any other newspaper. It's an exclusive story."

The editor held out a limp hand for the interview script and I passed it to him.

"I'll find out where the compositors have got to and see what I can do."

I watched him leave the room, then walked over to the typewriter.

"Have you heard the good news about our circulation figures, Miss Green?" asked Edgar.

"No, what of them?"

"They've fallen by ten percent."

"Well, that's just awful. Why on earth should that be good news?"

"Because it means Blimpy's on his way out. Conway won't stand for it. You know how important circulation figures are to him."

"Blimpy is his nephew. Mr Conway would never dismiss him."

"He'd better do, otherwise Potter and I are leaving."

"Oh no, you mustn't do that. I don't want to have to face Blimpy all on my own!"

"Then we must all pray that he gets the old heave-ho."

CHAPTER 30

"I think it's downright dreadful what she did to him," said Mrs Garnett as she removed her reading glasses and handed back my copy of the *Morning Express*.

I felt rather pleased that Mr Childers had decided to print my interview with Benjamin Taylor.

"I don't know how she wasn't arrested at the time," my landlady added.

"I don't think he suspected that it was a poisoning at the time," I replied. "I don't think anyone did."

We were seated in my room. Mrs Garnett had made herself comfortable at my desk, while I perched on the edge of my bed. Tiger had been patting a balled-up piece of paper along the floor, but she was now eyeing my landlady warily from the top of my chest of drawers.

"And the woman who tried to poison him is the same woman Mrs Wilkinson and I were looking for?"

"I believe so. It's thought that she's in Orpington as she has family there."

"In Kent?"

"Yes."

"It's a nice place, Kent. Hercules and I used to take the train from Charing Cross down to Margate. Terribly sad that the Assembly Rooms burnt down. We used to take tea there on a Thursday and listen to the band play on a Sunday. The Oriental Music Hall was another favourite of ours, and the Royal Theatre too. And then there's the sea air, of course. In fact, it makes me wonder why I'm living in London instead of there. Why am I living here, Miss Green?"

"Because you're a Londoner?"

"I feel like a Londoner, though I was born in Africa. But I think I could happily be a Margater. I hear there's good money to be made in the hotel business there."

"I should think there is. Hopefully Catherine Curran hasn't made it as far as Margate and will soon be found in Orpington."

"But she's not the poisoner, is she? It was that other woman who's admitted to it."

"I don't think anyone is entirely sure just yet."

"And then there's that poor policeman who got poisoned as well." Mrs Garnett shook her head. "Why do people do these things to each other? There's so much poisoning going on these days."

"It probably happens no more frequently than in the past, only these days we find it easier to prove through autopsies and chemical analysis."

"I don't want to hear that word."

"Which one?"

"I'm not repeating it. The one where they do things to folk after they're dead."

"An autopsy is sometimes necessary to establish the cause of death."

"It's ungodly."

"But necessary."

"Says who?"

"The legal and medical professions. An autopsy confirmed that Thomas Burrell's death was caused by poisoning. It would otherwise have been assumed that he died of a natural illness, and that no one was to blame for it. But by exhuming—"

"That's enough!" Mrs Garnett flung her hands over her ears. "I won't hear any more of it!"

"Let's change the subject, Mrs Garnett."

"Thank you." She removed her hands from her ears and glanced over at Tiger. "That cat has only been in my parlour once this week."

"That's good to hear."

"She hates lemons. I cut two lemons open and put them both in saucers. I put one by the window and one by the door, and now she has no desire to come in."

"Poor Tiger."

"You don't feel sorry for me with my sneezing?"

"Yes, I do. It's a sad situation for both of you, Mrs Garnett. If only cat and landlady could get along."

"Life's not always so simple, Miss Green. She's not a bad cat. I quite like her, in fact. But it's the sneezing that's the problem. How's that lovesick librarian doing on his boat to South America, by the way?"

"Mr Edwards, you mean? I should hope he has arrived there by now. He's not a librarian any more, and I shouldn't think he's lovesick either. He never really was."

"Oh, he *was*." A wide grin spread across Mrs Garnett's face. "I remember him coming to the door here under some pretence, using any excuse he could come up with to visit you. I miss him, poor man."

"Don't feel sorry for him, Mrs Garnett. He is no doubt enjoying himself immensely in South America by now."

"And now the inspector's married I don't suppose there are any potential suitors left."

"He's not married yet, Mrs Garnett."

"Is he not?"

"No."

"It seems as though we've been waiting for his wedding for years."

"Yes, it does."

"So when is it?"

"In a week's time."

"A week today?"

My stomach gave an uncomfortable flip. "Yes."

"It's almost upon us, then. Have you been invited?"

"No."

I felt relieved to be interrupted from this line of conversation by a voice calling up from downstairs.

"Good mornin', Mrs Garrrrr-nett!"

"There's only one person with a voice that loud," said my landlady, "and that's Mrs Wilkinson. Something interesting must have happened."

She left my room and made her way downstairs. I followed a little way behind, hoping to eavesdrop. Mrs Wilkinson was often the first person in the vicinity to pass on newsworthy gossip.

I heard the two ladies talking in the hallway, and when I heard the words *Morning Express* mentioned I hurried down the wide staircase.

"Hello, Mrs Wilkinson. Is there any news?" I asked.

She turned to face me. Mrs Wilkinson was a short, stout woman of around sixty with sharp eyes and artificially darkened hair.

"There's been a murder!" she announced gleefully. "A man in Vauxhall, and what's more he was in the newspaper. *Your* newspaper!" She grinned, displaying a number of yellow teeth.

I felt a sudden coldness grip my chest.

"Who is it?"

"Taylor, they say. I heard it from a cabbie who's just driven up from that way."

I leaned up against the wall, fearing my knees would give way beneath me.

"Benjamin Taylor," I said quietly. "The man I interviewed."

"It was in the newspaper, wasn't it?" said Mrs Wilkinson.

"The man I was reading about just now?" said Mrs Garnett in a shrill, excitable voice.

"Yes." I removed my spectacles and rubbed at my eyes, as if doing so would help me comprehend what had happened.

"So the man who was poisoned has now been murdered," continued Mrs Garnett. "The things that are happening in this city these days." She sucked her lip in dismay. "It's dreadful. I really should move to Kent."

"It's not much better there," said Mrs Wilkinson. "They had a murder in Maidstone just the other week. A man had a knife put in his back while he was out buying sausages. *In broad daylight.*"

"Someone must have read my piece," I muttered. "They read the interview and went to see him. But who? I don't understand."

"Come into the parlour and have a sit down, Miss Green," my landlady suggested. "I can give you a spoonful of Dr Cobbold's—"

"Thank you, Mrs Garnett, but no thank you. I must make my way over there." I turned and ran up the stairs, two at a time, to fetch my carpet bag from my room.

CHAPTER 31

I hailed a cab at the end of Milton Street. The journey to Vauxhall took half an hour, which gave me time to think about my interview with Benjamin Taylor. *Could its publication have prompted his death? Had someone read it and felt compelled to silence him?*

The person he had implicated in the interview was Catherine Curran, whom he had referred to as Jane Taylor. *Had she travelled back from Kent to track him down?*

My stomach kept turning over as I became increasingly concerned that I was in some way responsible for the poor man's death.

We passed Lambeth Workhouse and entered a maze of terraced streets.

"Are yer wantin' ter see where this murder's 'appened?" the cabman called through the hatch in the roof.

"Yes, thank you," I replied. "I'm a news reporter!" I added, in an attempt to explain that my interest was not merely morbid curiosity.

We turned into Tyers Street, which was lined with small

terraced houses. It ran for some length until we reached a crowd of onlookers. I paid the cabman and walked up to the narrow three-storey house that appeared to be holding everyone's interest. I felt my throat tighten as I saw a coffin shell being loaded into a black carriage. It was extremely difficult for me to accept that the coffin contained the body of the same man I had spoken to at The Royal Vauxhall Tavern just two days previously.

A number of constables held the crowd back as the doors to the coffin carriage were closed and the carriage pulled away.

I introduced myself to one of the constables. "Who's in charge here?" I asked him.

He nodded at the house. "They're inside."

"And the victim is Benjamin Taylor, is that right?"

"You'll have to ask the inspector," he replied. "I ain't s'posed to be speakin' to the press."

I loitered for a short while, hoping the departure of the carriage meant that the inspector would soon step out of the house, having done all he could at the property.

"Did you know Mr Taylor?" I asked a man in a flat cap standing nearby. He puffed on a pipe and kept his hands in his pockets.

"Aye."

"For how long?"

"Two years or so."

"Do you know what happened to him?"

The man shrugged. "Found dead this mornin', he was."

"Do you know how it happened?"

The man shrugged again and blew out a puff of smoke. "No idea."

"Did anyone see or hear anything suspicious either this morning or last night?"

The man took his pipe out of his mouth and stared at me. "'Ow would I know that?"

"I just wondered if you'd heard any rumours about what has happened to Mr Taylor."

"All I knows is what I've told yer."

"Thank you."

A police officer wearing a chief inspector's uniform stepped out of the house, and my heart skipped when I saw James following closely behind him. I dashed over to them.

"Penny," said James, giving me a subdued smile. I understood that the gravity of the situation prevented any warmer greeting.

He introduced me to Chief Inspector Austen of Lambeth L Division, who had a large red face and brown whiskers.

"Do you have any idea what happened to him?" I asked.

"Little idea yet, I'm afraid," replied the chief inspector. "He appears to have been taken unwell."

"Poison?" I ventured.

James gave an exasperated sigh.

"We can't rule it out. The usual examination will take place, of course, and if he has been poisoned we clearly have a significant problem on our hands. I think it's obvious these murders are the work of more than one person, but as for who, and how many, I really couldn't say at the moment."

"Was he found this morning?" I asked.

"Yes, and he was last seen when he arrived home from work at the Doulton Pottery at five o'clock yesterday evening," said James. "He ate with his landlady and another lodger as usual, and then the landlady went out for the evening. We haven't found the other lodger yet, but we're looking for him. The landlady said she returned to the house late last night and all was quiet. When Taylor didn't make an appearance for breakfast this morning she grew concerned and went to his room. The door was locked, and she had to ask a neighbour to help her force it open. Once inside they found Taylor lying on the bed, quite clearly dead."

I shook my head. "I only saw him two days ago. I am struggling to believe it."

"Your interview with him was published just yesterday, wasn't it?"

"Yes. I'm concerned that the murderer might have read the interview and decided that Mr Taylor needed to be silenced!"

"I'm sure that's not the case."

"But it has to be linked to the fact that he was telling everyone who would listen that he believed Catherine Curran had poisoned him. And she finally has! Somehow she must have returned from Kent and finished the job. We need to find her, James! She must be hiding somewhere near here. And someone must know something they're not telling us!"

"You saw the deceased just two days ago, Miss Green?" asked Inspector Austen.

"Yes. I interviewed him at The Royal Vauxhall Tavern."

"In which case you can most likely provide us with some useful testimony."

"I don't know about that. A lot may have happened after I met with him."

"All the same, Miss Green, I think you will be a useful person to speak to. I'd like you to come and speak with us at the police station on Lower Kennington Lane."

A police sergeant beckoned the chief inspector over and I shook my head in dismay.

"I feel responsible," I said to James.

"How so?"

"Perhaps if I hadn't interviewed him for the *Morning Express* he would not have been targeted."

"You can't blame yourself, Penny. The man told lots of people that he suspected his wife had poisoned him; something we will never be able to prove."

"But she achieved it in the end, didn't she?"

"We don't know who has done it, Penny."

"But it has to be Catherine, doesn't it? She was probably disappointed that she hadn't succeeded in murdering her husband six years ago. She finally finished what she had set out to do, though I don't understand how she managed to get back from Kent so swiftly."

"Orpington isn't far from here by train," said James. "But I'm beginning to feel certain now that there is more than one poisoner. We already have Sally under arrest, and she cannot possibly have been involved in Mr Taylor's death given that she is being held in the House of Detention. Now there is another person involved. It may be Catherine, or it may be someone else."

"Perhaps the same person who poisoned Inspector Martin?"

"No, that could only have been Sally."

"It might have been another police officer."

James' face fell. "You don't think a police officer would do such a thing, do you?"

"Possibly. Another officer would have been present when Sally was interviewed by Inspector Martin. What about Sergeant Richards?"

"Oh Penny, that's ridiculous. He would never do such a thing."

"You have convinced yourself of that with other police officers in the past, remember?"

"Yes, I remember, though I prefer not to. I suppose you're right, Penny. When a situation like this arises everyone must be considered a suspect."

Chief Inspector Austen approached us. "Are you ready, Miss Green?" he asked, gesturing toward a nearby blue police carriage. It had the letters VR and a crown painted in gold on the side.

"Of course, Inspector."

I bade James farewell and climbed into the carriage.

CHAPTER 32

I thought Inspector Austen might ask me about Benjamin Taylor during our short carriage ride to Lower Kennington Lane, but instead he spent the time making copious notes in his notebook. He wasn't interested in anything I had to say until we were seated at a table in a small interview room within the police station.

He sat opposite me with a pile of papers between us, and he was accompanied by a young freckle-faced sergeant with wispy auburn whiskers. The sergeant asked me for my name, age and address, painstakingly filling the details in on his form. I began to grow impatient, wishing I could tell them what I knew and then be on my way.

"You saw Benjamin Taylor on Thursday the fourth of September, is that right?" asked Inspector Austen. He had small, steely eyes set deep into his red face.

"Yes, that's right," I replied.

"And you instigated this meeting with him because you wished to interview him for your newspaper, the *Morning Express?*"

"Yes."

"Where did you meet?"

"At The Royal Vauxhall Tavern."

"Who suggested the venue?"

"Mr Taylor did."

The inspector indicated to the sergeant that he should write this down.

"I take it you both had something to drink while you were there?"

"Yes."

"May I ask what you had?"

"I had an East India sherry and Mr Taylor had a mug of beer."

"Just the one?"

"I seem to recall that he had two."

"You must have turned a few heads at The Royal Vauxhall Tavern, Miss Green. Ladies such as yourself are not frequently seen in public houses."

"My profession takes me to all sorts of places, Inspector, and I have interviewed a fair number of people in pubs and taverns."

"Were you aware of having drawn the attention of anyone else in the tavern that day?"

"Not particularly. I think a few people may have glanced over and been vaguely surprised to see me there, but I'm not aware of anyone making a big fuss about it."

"How long did it take you to conduct the interview with Mr Taylor?"

"About an hour."

"Did anyone approach you while you were with him?"

"No."

"Did anyone within or outside The Royal Vauxhall Tavern speak to either you or Mr Taylor before, during or after your interview with him?"

"We spoke to the bar tender, but that was all."

"Did you see Mr Taylor acknowledge anyone else during your meeting with him? It might have been a subtle acknowledgement, such as a slight nod of the head or a wink."

"No. Why are you asking me all these questions, Inspector? Surely it would be easier for me to make a formal statement? I could even write it down for you if you would like me to. It would save your sergeant here having to do it."

"It's part of his job; don't you go worrying about him. This case is an extraordinary one, Miss Green, and by asking the right questions I'll be able to get to the bottom of what has really happened here rather than accepting an embellished version of events."

I began to feel wary. "I have no intention of embellishing anything, Inspector. I have been reporting on this case for more than two weeks, and I can assure you that I wish to do everything possible to ensure that the poisoner is caught. My account will be honest and purely based on fact."

"I should hope so, Miss Green."

More seemingly irrelevant questions followed and then the questioning became quite antagonistic.

"Did Mr Taylor leave his tankard unattended at any time while you were with him?"

"No, I don't think so."

"Was he sufficiently distracted at any point to allow someone enough time to interfere with his drink?"

"Not that I remember."

"It could have been a simple distraction, such as a communication from another person in the public house or Mr Taylor stooping to pick something up which had dropped to the floor."

"No, I don't remember anything of that sort happening."

"So it may have happened but you just don't recall it?"

"I'm certain that it didn't happen."

"Did you deliberately distract him at any point so that his drink could be interfered with?"

"No, Inspector! I would never do such a thing!"

"Did you administer a poison to his drink while he was distracted from it?"

"No!" My heart began to pound. "Why should I wish to do something like that?" I said, worried that my expression would somehow convey a guilt which wasn't there. "I was interviewing him for my newspaper, and I have already told you that I cannot recall him being distracted."

"There's no need to raise your voice, Miss Green. I appreciate the fact that these are searching questions, but you will do yourself an injustice if you fail to remain calm while I question you."

I felt my blood run cold. "Are you treating me as a suspect, Inspector?"

"No, Miss Green, but I must ask you some direct questions so that I can be quite certain. I take the same approach with everyone I interview."

"There is no need to ask me whether or not I poisoned Mr Taylor. I would never do that to anyone. I wouldn't even know how to go about it! Your time would be better spent locating Catherine Curran. She is the key suspect in this case, and she must be close by! You need men on the ground searching for her, Inspector."

"They already are, Miss Green," he replied icily, "and you will continue to answer my questions until I'm satisfied that you have told me everything you know."

CHAPTER 33

It was mid-afternoon by the time I was finally permitted to leave the police interview room. The anger I had felt about the incessant questioning had dulled to a vague sense of relief that I hadn't been arrested.

"Penny!" James' voice stopped me mid-stride just as I was leaving the police station.

"James." I managed a smile. "You haven't been waiting here for me, have you?"

"No, I've only just called in. I need to have a brief conversation with Inspector Austen and then I'll be calling in at Bermondsey police station. Are you heading in that direction?"

I wasn't sure which direction I planned to head in, so I nodded my head.

I waited for James outside the police station, not wishing to spend any more time within its walls. The air felt warm, and bright sunlight streamed through occasional gaps between the grey overhead. A steady rumble from a nearby printing works had an almost soothing tone to it.

I watched people pass me and wondered where Catherine was now. She had to be close by. *Could she be watching the police station at this very moment?* I surveyed each person who walked along the street, looking for someone who resembled the pretty, fair-haired woman from the photographs.

James joined me moments later.

"Thank you for waiting, Penny. I've just spoken to Inspector Austen about the work we need to do next on this case."

"I don't like that man," I replied as we began to walk.

"He's rather serious, isn't he?"

"He made me feel as though I had done something wrong! I agreed to answer his questions in the hope that I'd be helping his investigation, but instead he seemed intent on trying to trip me up and somehow making me admit that I had poisoned Mr Taylor. How could he even think such a thing?"

"I'm sure he doesn't. He will no doubt question everyone in the same manner. I'm sorry he was rude to you."

"I suppose he has a job to do. I like to think that our professions can work well together, but he doesn't seem to share the sentiment."

"Well I do, Penny."

"Thank you, James."

We climbed on board the horse tram beside the church-yard in Newington Butts.

"We received some exciting news while you were being interviewed by Inspector Austen," said James. "Catherine Curran has been arrested."

"That is excellent news!" I said. "You have finally found her!"

I sank into a seat on the tram with a grin on my face.

"Where was she?" I asked.

"Kent. Chislehurst, I hear... not far from Orpington."

"Kent? So she made a quick visit to Lambeth yesterday evening to poison her first husband, then swiftly returned?"

"No. She wasn't in Lambeth at all. She was arrested yesterday evening in Chislehurst."

I paused for a moment while I considered this. "So while Benjamin Taylor was being poisoned Catherine Curran was being arrested in Chislehurst?"

"Yes. Catherine couldn't have poisoned him."

"Then the culprit must be this other person we have discussed. Someone else is doing this and we have no idea who it is!"

"Exactly. And we have very little evidence that Catherine Curran has poisoned anyone at all."

I closed my eyes and tried to reorganise the jigsaw puzzle in my mind. "It's no good," I said, opening them again. "I'm baffled."

"Only because you have always felt so certain that Catherine Curran is behind all this."

"We have all been certain, haven't we? And by running away as she did she appeared to have confirmed her guilt."

"She was found close to Chislehurst Caves. There is some speculation that she had been planning to hide in there."

"The ancient mines?" I shuddered. "I shouldn't like to be down there on my own. But what is she hiding from if she's innocent?"

"Hopefully we'll find out now that we've got her. She has been arrested on the charge of bigamy."

"Perhaps that is all she's guilty of," I said resignedly.

For so long I had been sure that Catherine was behind the poisoning of all her husbands. Even though Sally Chadwick had confessed I had still believed that Catherine was somehow involved.

"And don't forget we are making the assumption that Benjamin Taylor was poisoned," said James. "We cannot be sure until the autopsy and chemical analysis are carried out. It's possible the cause of death may have been something altogether different."

"Perhaps the other lodger had something to do with it."

"L Division are still searching for him. I have no doubt that Austen will question him thoroughly once they find him."

"Yes, it's reassuring to know that he will do that conscientiously," I added with a faint laugh.

"I'm looking forward to meeting Catherine Curran," said James. "She'll be brought up to Bermondsey by train."

After disembarking from the horse tram we walked up Bermondsey Street toward the police station.

"I'll update Sergeant Richards and check that everyone is feeling prepared for Inspector Martin's funeral tomorrow," said James.

"It will be a truly sad day," I said.

"It will indeed." His blue eyes dampened.

While James was speaking to Sergeant Richards, I sat in the waiting room and wrote a rough draft of an article about Benjamin Taylor's murder and Catherine Curran's arrest in my notebook. I hoped Mr Childers would consider the news important enough to publish in Monday's edition.

Once James had finished at the police station we walked in the direction of the river, moving past the stinking railway arches, beneath the railway lines and up toward the Tower Subway.

"How is your sister faring?" asked James as our footsteps echoed on the spiral staircase down to the tunnel. "Has she reconciled with her husband?"

"Not yet. She's struggling to forgive him. I think he made the wrong decision out of stupidity rather than malice; I don't believe him to be an unpleasant person. But he has been foolish, and I can't see how she will ever be happy with him again."

"It may take her some time to forgive."

"Perhaps she never will. They're quite different from one another. George is rather stuffy and old-fashioned, as you no doubt recall. Eliza is modern in her thinking; much more so than many other people. She campaigns for rational dress and women's suffrage. The ideal wife for George would be someone who enjoys being the lady of the house while never questioning anything about her position, and never wanting anything more. Eliza wants more, you see. She wishes to work, but George forbids her from doing so."

"It's not something married women usually do."

"But why shouldn't they?"

"It's a fair question."

"For some reason Eliza has listened to her husband and not sought employment," I said. "I think she now has the perfect opportunity to take on some form of profession."

"Presumably there are children to be looked after, are there not?"

"There are, and she has a nanny who costs money, of course. If she were to divorce George she would no doubt have to move out of her home, and she would need to earn enough money to pay for a home and to have someone care for the children. In the past I have found myself envying her lifestyle; however, I have since realised how constrained it is. With George being the sole source of household income she has no independence."

"Polite society would argue that she doesn't need independence, since everything is provided for her."

"And in theory she should be happy. Yet she possesses a spirit which yearns for freedom and choice, much like mine."

James smiled.

"And I suppose it is difficult to feel sympathy for my sister when she has such a fine home as a result of her husband's good salary," I continued. "I have encountered enough poverty and destitution during the course of my work to know that she is well positioned in life. But the reality is that she married the wrong person. The repercussions of that may not always be immediate, but they will manifest sooner or later. I think she pretended to be in love with George because, sadly for my sister, even now at the age of thirty-two, I don't think she understands what real love feels like."

There was a long pause as we continued walking.

"That's a pity," James said quietly.

The silence grew as we continued walking and I wondered whether James was considering his own situation in the light of my words. His wedding to Charlotte was just a week away and I was trying my hardest not to dwell on it, hoping in vain that ignoring the event might somehow prevent it from happening.

But there was no preventing the image of a smiling, apple-cheeked Charlotte in her wedding dress leaping into my mind. It hung there so clearly that it almost floated before me in that miserable, dingy tunnel.

"Don't do it!" I exclaimed, stopping and turning to face James. "Don't marry her!"

CHAPTER 34

J ames stopped walking and turned to face me. I held his gaze, hoping beyond hope that my eyes would implore him to do the right thing.

"Don't you see why Eliza is so unhappy now?" I asked. "She married a fool. I know there are times in many marriages when husbands and wives fall out, but George has always been a fool. He was a fool when they courted and a fool the day they married. I don't believe she was completely blind to it, but she married him because she felt she should.

"If you marry Charlotte, James, you will likely be perfectly happy together during your honeymoon. Perhaps you will be happy for a few months as you set up home together. You may even be happy for a year or two. But will you be happy together for the rest of your lives?"

He opened his mouth to speak, then seemed to think better of it.

"No, you won't," I continued. "I know this because of the manner in which you kissed me as we stood in Eliza's hallway. A man who is happily engaged does not kiss another woman in such a way!"

James stood quite still, his eyes intently searching my face.

"I don't want you to make a mistake that you will regret for the rest of your life," I said quietly.

He took a step forward, bent his head toward mine and kissed me gently. I closed my eyes and breathed in his scent, praying that my words had changed his mind.

Then he took a step back again. "I wish I could tell you how much I care about you, Penny, but it wouldn't be fair."

"What do you mean?"

"It wouldn't be fair for you or for me."

"You still intend to marry her?" I asked, my heart sinking into the pit of my stomach.

He began to walk slowly along the tunnel again. "I have to, as I've explained before. I can't tell you how many people have been invited to this wedding. My parents... particularly my father. He has been suffering with ill health for some time. For a while he doubted whether he would still be alive when the marriage took place. And he is so excited about the wedding, Penny. My parents are overjoyed. If I change my mind about it they will be heartbroken!"

"But this isn't about your parents," I said. "It's about you."

"It's partly about me, but marriage is also the union of two families. I think of all the siblings, the aunts and uncles, the cousins and so on. I'd have to do a terrific amount of explaining to them all if I called it off. My brother and his wife are travelling all the way from Scotland to attend."

There was a thud of anger in my chest. "So you are marrying Charlotte out of obligation to your family?"

"I suppose that's partly it, especially this close to the event. You can't just call off a wedding with a week to go."

"You can if you think you're making a terrible mistake."

"She would sue me, Penny."

"That would be unreasonable of her."

"Would it? I'm not sure that it would. She has already threatened to sue me for breach of promise once."

I gave a hollow laugh. "She has already *threatened* you with it?"

He stopped again and turned to face me. "A lot of conversations have been had about you, Penny. If truth be told, Charlotte suspects that I hold some affection for you. It's why she prevented us from meeting at the Museum Tavern."

"Just imagine what she would say if she knew that you had kissed me! Twice!"

James sighed. "I cannot even begin to consider what she would say. She'd be angry, that's for sure. She has been angry in the past, and that's when the threat came. Women are perfectly entitled to sue, of course. The law is there to protect them. I simply cannot imagine how my father's health would cope with the wedding being cancelled or by the ugly scene with my former fiancée in the courts. I couldn't do that to him, Penny."

"You're not saying anything about you or what you want, James."

"It's too late for that now. The wheels were set in motion a long time ago. If I change my mind now I'll be letting down the people who matter most to me."

"Your parents."

"Yes, my parents. And Charlotte, in some respects."

"Do you love her?"

He scratched at his temple. "I have a good deal of affection for her. I've known her for a long time, and our families are close."

"So you love her as if she were a cousin or a friend?"

"I think you have described it very well, Penny." He smiled.

"That is not sufficient reason to marry someone."

"I'm sure you're right, but at this stage I can see no other option. Everything is ready for next Saturday, and my father is in the best spirits I've seen him in for a long time. To call it off... I honestly don't know how I could do it, Penny."

"I should think it would be quite simple. You inform Charlotte that you no longer wish to marry her and then cover your ears as the world crashes down around you. People will be upset and disappointed, but the uproar won't last forever. It will probably be quite short-lived, I should think. Anyone who knows you well, and cares about you, will want you to make the right decision. They will forgive you for disappointing them in time."

"If only it were that simple."

"But it is!" I snapped. "The problem is that you're afraid of letting people down. But if I explain to you now that I love you, and wish nothing more than for us to be married, might that cause you to reconsider?"

James stepped toward me, as if he wished to kiss me again. I felt my face grow hot as my declaration of love hung heavily in the air. I had said everything I was capable of saying. It felt as though my heart was in his hands.

I waited, hoping there would be a declaration of love from him in return. *If my words hadn't changed his mind, surely nothing would.*

I heard footsteps behind me and turned to see two young men walking toward us. I recalled, to my great horror, how easily voices carried along the tunnel.

James and I stood back from one another and the men grinned at us as they approached.

"Oy, oy," said one of them as he doffed his hat. "Fair brings a tear to yer eye. Are yer goin' ter reconsider, mister?"

James glared at him. "I would ask you to mind your own business!" he retorted.

"Aye," replied the man with a smirk as he placed his hat back on his head and they walked on.

Another couple was approaching from behind them and I felt irritated that we were no longer alone.

James and I walked on.

I didn't know what else to say. Any words we spoke would be overheard by the other people walking nearby.

I felt embarrassed and ashamed, but I had done all I could.

If James went ahead with his wedding despite my impassioned pleas I would have to do something else with my life. I couldn't bear to remain in London, continuing with my work and constantly worrying that I might bump into him. How could I ever work with him while he was married to another woman? It would be too upsetting. I would have to leave London and my job and my home to go and make a life for myself elsewhere.

I felt a strong temptation to follow Francis out to Colombia to help him search for my father. I needed to do something, anything, that could make me forget about James' wedding.

We climbed the stairs at the far end of the tunnel and emerged, blinking, into the bright daylight.

We stood for a moment, taking in the view of the Tower of London.

"I need to give the situation a great deal of thought," said James. "I have never felt so much conflict in my mind before."

"Surely my feelings for you do not come as a surprise," I said.

"To hear you express them as you did is a surprise to me indeed. Until now I had suspected... Well, I suppose I knew. But it was easier to continue as we were and not go upsetting anyone. That's changed now and... It's certainly regretful that we are now so close to the wedding day. I keep picturing my parents' faces if I were to tell them the bad news, and Charlotte's face as well... not to mention her parents. And then there's my sister to consider, and my little nephew, who I'm told is extremely excited about attending his first ever wedding. There is so much to consider."

I gritted my teeth. I had heard enough. "Well, I know where I shall be a week from today," I said. "Drowning my sorrows at the Museum Tavern!"

CHAPTER 35

I woke early the following morning, still turning the exchange with James over in my mind. I realised that he hadn't said that he loved Charlotte during our conversation.

Had he omitted to do so to avoid offending me? Was a concern for his family the only reason he was continuing with the marriage, or did he feel something deeper for her after all?

I pictured the vicar asking whether anyone knew of any lawful reason why James and Charlotte should not be married. That would be the perfect moment to stand up and declare my love for him.

I knew that it wasn't a lawful reason for them not to marry, and that James would never forgive me for ruining his wedding. No one would. My actions would be unpopular with everyone present, and doing such a thing would be the act of a truly desperate woman. Although I felt suitably desperate about the situation I was too proud to plead with James at the altar. If his mind was made up there was little more I could do about it.

Inspector Martin's funeral was held at St Matthew's Church in Brixton. The church was filled with police officers proudly wearing their blue Metropolitan Police uniforms, though I also noticed the black uniforms of some City of London Police officers among them. I saw James among the mourners, busy comforting his colleagues and Inspector Martin's widow. My heart ached when I saw the young Martin children dressed in their mourning clothes. The littlest was just a baby.

My conversation with James after the funeral service was brief. He was accompanied by Charlotte, who wore a black veil and sniffed constantly into a black handkerchief. I expressed my commiserations and quickly moved away. Even if Charlotte hadn't been there I wasn't sure what I could have said to him after our conversation in the subway. The wedding was just six days away now and I was beginning to wonder what I could possibly do with myself once James was married.

I spoke with William Curran for a while in the churchyard.

"Hangin's too good for Sally Chadwick," he fumed.

"If we can be sure she was responsible, that is," I said. "It seems there is another poisoner at work."

William's dark eyes bored into mine. "Who?"

I told him about the death of Benjamin Taylor, and while I was still speaking Florence Burrell joined us.

"Benjamin Taylor's dead?" she asked, her eyes wide behind her thick-lensed spectacles.

"Yes," I replied, trying hard to stop my eyes being drawn to the angry red scar. "The police think he was also poisoned, though we must wait for the results of the autopsy to be certain."

"I feel sad for him," said Florence. "He said he'd been poisoned by his wife, didn't he?"

"And he was telling the truth," I added. "I confirmed it with a doctor who treated him at the time."

"'E were married to Caffrine, weren't 'e?" said William. "'E said as Caffrine 'ad poisoned 'im. Although 'e called 'er a different name, didn't 'e?"

"Jane," I replied. "And she has just been arrested in Kent."

"So they've got 'er?"

I nodded.

"But she ain't done nuffink wrong, 'as she?"

"We don't know," I replied. "She faces a charge of bigamy at the very least."

"But Taylor's dead now," said William. "It can't be bigamy no more. All 'er 'usbands are dead. They should leave 'er alone."

"She could have helped herself by not running away," I said. "She was found close to Chislehurst Caves, which suggests that she was planning to hide herself there. Her behaviour is rather suspicious."

"Surely she couldn't have been planning to hide in the caves?" said Florence. "How long was she going to stay there?"

"I don't know," I replied. "She's up to something, and I can only hope the police solve this case very soon. Inspector Martin's death is a terrible tragedy, and with Mr Taylor also dying in suspicious circumstances I'm extremely worried that we shall have another death on our hands before long."

CHAPTER 36

Benjamin Taylor's inquest was held at The Crown Tavern, a four-storey public house which sat on Albert Embankment between the railway lines and the River Thames. Autumn seemed to be on its way as a brisk wind blew leaves and spots of rain along the street.

I fastened a few more buttons on my jacket and looked out over the river as I waited for the inquest to begin. Cranes rose from the wharves further downstream, and across the water lay the grey, forbidding walls of Millbank Prison. I thought about Catherine Curran and hoped she had been brought to London by now. I also hoped there would somehow be an opportunity for me to be present during her questioning, as I desperately wanted to hear what she had to say for herself. I was intrigued to meet the woman I knew only from the three oddly posed photographs with her deceased husbands.

I turned back toward the Crown and saw Inspector Austen arriving with his freckle-faced sergeant. I bid them good morning, then followed them into the pub and climbed a wooden staircase to an upstairs room.

The Lambeth coroner began the proceedings and I looked around for James, assuming I had missed him as he entered the room. There was no sign of him. I took out my notebook and prepared myself to make detailed notes.

Benjamin Taylor's landlady spoke first and described, through stifled sobs, how she had found him dead in his bed on the Saturday morning. During the night she had heard him go out to the lavatory in the yard a few times but had otherwise noticed nothing unusual.

Next to speak was the other lodger. The coroner asked him to introduce himself.

"I'm George Goodin' and I lives at an 'undred an' twenny-seven Tyers Street, Lambeth. I works at Doulton's."

"You lodged at the same address as the deceased, Mr Gooding?"

"Yes, sir."

"And when did you last see Mr Taylor?"

"Friday ev'nin'."

"And where was he when you saw him on the Friday evening?"

"At 'ome."

"At one hundred and twenty-seven Tyers Street?"

"Yeah, that's me 'ome."

"And at what time did you see him?"

"I seen 'im twice. I seen 'im at 'alf past six, then 'e wen' out and I saw 'im again at ten o'clock."

"And do you know where he went?"

"Proberly the Vauxhall Tavern."

"The Royal Vauxhall Tavern close to Vauxhall Station?"

"Yes, sir."

"Do you know for certain that he went there?"

"'E always did, so I reckons 'e musta done."

"But you can't be completely certain?"

"'E wouldn't of gone nowhere else."

The coroner gave a slight grimace of exasperation. "Did the deceased seem to be in a state of inebriation when he returned home?"

"A what now?"

"Do you think that Mr Taylor may have been drunk when he returned home?"

"Oh no, 'e never got too bad wiv the drink. 'E'd 'ave 'ad a few, but 'e never got bad wiv it."

"By use of the word *bad*, do you mean *drunk*?"

"Yes, sir. 'E weren't drunk."

"But you suspect that he had consumed a quantity of alcohol on Friday evening?"

"Yes, sir, on account of 'e'd been to The Vauxhall Tavern."

"Did you have a conversation with Mr Taylor on his return?"

"Not much. Jus' the usual."

"What is *the usual*?"

"Just 'ello an' that. An' 'e said he was goin' up ter get some kip."

"Did he tell you anything about his evening?"

"No, sir."

"Did he mention anyone he had met with or spoken to that evening?"

"No, sir."

"And he went up to his room shortly after arriving home?"

"Yes, sir."

"Did he mention that he felt unwell at all?"

"No, sir."

"Did he seem unwell to you?"

"No, but 'e looked a bit pale. 'E never usually looked pale."

"Did that observation lead you to suspect that he was feeling unwell?"

"No, sir. I didn't know 'e was sick or nuffink. It was only when I thought of it later that I thought as 'e'd looked pale."

"In summary, then, you last saw the deceased at about ten o'clock on Friday evening just before he retired for the night?"

"Yes, sir."

The next witness was the landlord of The Royal Vauxhall Tavern. I recognised him from several months earlier when James had spoken to him about the murder of Elizabeth Wiggins. He was a broad man and he wore a tight-fitting jacket.

"Me name's Gerald Smith and I'm the landlord of The Royal Vauxhall Tavern."

"Did you see the deceased at your public house on the evening of Friday the fifth of September?"

"Yes, sir."

"Did you speak to him?"

"Yes, sir. He said 'ello."

"Did he seem his usual self to you?"

"Yes, sir."

"He didn't seem unwell at all?"

"No, sir."

"Can you recall what he drank?"

"Beer. Just 'is usual, sir."

"Can you recall how many mugs of beer he consumed?"

"Difficult ter say. I must've served 'im two or three, and 'e proberly 'ad one or two more than that, like 'e usually did. 'E was proberly served 'em by Forbes, who works behind the bar with me."

"Can you tell us who Mr Taylor was with?"

"Yes, sir. He was with the regulars."

"And who are they?"

"Friends of 'is."

"Do you know these men well?"

"I've known 'em all for years."

Once Mr Smith had finished speaking a succession of

Benjamin Taylor's friends appeared as witnesses. Each of them deposed that they had drunk with him at The Royal Vauxhall Tavern that evening, and that he had seemed his usual self.

Everyone gathered at the inquest suddenly became more attentive when two of Taylor's friends mentioned that a woman had approached him toward the end of his time there. Neither was able to identify this woman, but she was described as slightly built with dark hair, and both men reported that Taylor seemed to know her. After conversing with her in a corner, they had left the pub together at about half past eight.

Once the last of Taylor's friends had finished giving his testimony, the police surgeon was summoned. He described how he had carried out an autopsy on Benjamin Taylor. The room collectively held its breath as he described what he had found.

"I examined tissue samples from the stomach and intestine, and I found them to be ulcerated and inflamed."

"Which is an indicator of what?"

"That the deceased consumed a large volume of irritant."

"Poison?"

The police surgeon ignored the gasps. "Yes, poison could certainly cause this sort of damage."

"I must bear in mind the recent incidence of poisonings in this area as I ask the next question," said the coroner. "Might arsenic have caused the sort of ulceration and inflammation you have witnessed?"

"It would indeed, sir. I suspect arsenic poisoning to be the cause of death, and to that end I have sent samples of the viscera off for chemical analysis."

I sighed. This inquest was remarkably similar to the others I had reported on in recent weeks. But who was the woman Benjamin Taylor had left the pub with? I would have assumed that it was Catherine Curran had she not been arrested twelve miles away in Chislehurst at around the same time.

Inspector Austen took the witness stand and the coroner asked him whether he had succeeded in finding the woman who Taylor had left the pub with that evening.

"None yet, sir. L Division is working day and night to track her down."

"Have you any idea as to her identity?"

"None whatsoever, sir."

"Do you suspect that she may have had a hand in his poisoning?"

"On the face of it, sir, I would say that any of the people Mr Taylor spent his last evening with could have had a hand in his poisoning. However, my suspicions rest on the anonymous woman because Mr Taylor claimed that his wife had once attempted to poison him."

"And when was this?"

"Six years ago, sir."

"And Mr Taylor was estranged from his wife?"

"Yes, sir. They separated six years ago but remained legally married."

"Had he seen her since their separation?"

"Not to my knowledge."

"Could his wife have been the woman he left the public house with on Friday evening?"

"It could have been her. However, I hear that the lady in question, who goes by the name of Catherine Curran these days, was arrested in Chislehurst, Kent, the very same evening. So it seems unlikely."

"Why was his wife arrested?"

"I understand that a charge of bigamy is to be brought against her, sir. I would also like to add, though the relevance cannot fully be determined yet, that Catherine Curran's three other husbands died from poisoning."

"Another woman has already confessed to those poisonings, has she not?"

"Yes. And while there is no conclusive evidence that Catherine Curran was involved in the poisonings, the fact that her husband Benjamin Taylor also appears to have died of arsenic poisoning cannot be ignored."

"I am aware of the Bermondsey poisoner case, and also of the suspected poisoning of the respected serving police officer, Inspector Martin," said the coroner. "I understand that Scotland Yard is involved with what has become an increasingly complex investigation, and the unfortunate death of Mr Taylor may form part of that. Is there a Scotland Yard detective present this morning?"

"Detective Inspector James Blakely of the Yard was due to attend this morning, sir, but he has been taken unwell," replied Inspector Austen.

I felt my heart leap into my throat. I had never known James to be unwell.

"I suggest an adjournment of this inquest for a period of two weeks," said the coroner. "That will allow time for chemical analysis to confirm the cause of death in this case, and hopefully Inspector Blakely will have recovered by then and will update us on Scotland Yard's investigation into the poisonings. In the meantime, Inspector Austen, I'm quite sure that you don't need me to tell you to find the woman who was with Mr Taylor on the night he died as a matter of extreme urgency."

CHAPTER 37

With the inquest adjourned I decided to go and find James. I needed to reassure myself that he hadn't been taken seriously ill the way that Inspector Martin had.

He lived in St John's Wood, which lay on the north-west side of London. It would be a long, frustrating journey from Lambeth. I took a horse tram down to Vauxhall Bridge and crossed the bridge on foot. From there I took another horse tram to Victoria Station, where I was able to take the underground railway to Baker Street station. From Baker Street I travelled by the Metropolitan Railway to St John's Wood Road. I managed to find time during the tram and train rides to draft my report on Benjamin Taylor's inquest.

James lived at Henstridge Place. One side of the street was lined with large stuccoed buildings, and his home was one of the smart terraced houses on the opposite side.

I hammered at the door, hoping James would be well enough to answer. It was opened a short way by a fair, broad-faced woman with blue eyes.

Charlotte.

I smiled as best I could and greeted her politely. Her expression was cool.

"I heard that James is unwell," I said. "How is he?"

"He's quite weak, but in good spirits."

"Has a doctor examined him?"

"Not yet."

"Do you intend to send for one? I think it's quite important. I'm worried it may be linked to the other poisonings."

Charlotte gave a dry laugh. "James hasn't been poisoned!"

"How do you know? Arsenic poisoning presents with common gastric problems, meaning that people often put the symptoms down to other causes."

Charlotte frowned. "How do you know that James has been poisoned by arsenic?"

"I don't, but I'm worried that he might have been, especially after the poisoning of his friend Inspector Martin."

Charlotte's face fell even further. "Yes, that was terribly sad. But James couldn't have been poisoned. No one would have done that to him."

"I hope they haven't, but I feel worried just the same."

"Oh dear, I do too now. He won't let a doctor anywhere near him. He says that it's nothing to worry about."

"That sounds typical of James, putting on a brave face. Is he well enough to receive visitors?"

"No." Charlotte pushed against the door so that it was almost closed. "He needs to rest," she said through the gap between the door and the frame. "He needs to recover in time for our wedding. Doesn't life play mean tricks? I have never known James to be unwell in all the time I've known him, then five days before we're due to be married he's laid up in bed. I've a good mind to ensure that he stays there until the morning of the wedding! Hopefully he'll be well recovered before then, but I think he could do with a proper rest. This job is simply too much for him."

"No, it's not. He loves his work."

"He has an obsession with his work, and as we see now it's not good for his health. You should see the state he's in."

"You will make sure that a doctor examines him to rule out poisoning, won't you?"

"I'll ask him first. I don't know how on earth he would have managed to get himself poisoned. That would be even worse, wouldn't it? Poisoned just days before his marriage!"

I began to wish that someone would poison Charlotte. Just the sight of her before me made my teeth clench with anger.

"You'll let him know I called, won't you?" I said. "Could you tell him that I attended the inquest into Benjamin Taylor's death this morning, and that arsenic poisoning is suspected?"

"I shan't bother him with work matters at the moment. It's important that he devotes his energies to making a full recovery."

"Indeed. Well, I'm certain your tender-hearted nursing skills will ensure that he makes a quick recovery, Charlotte." I wondered if she had noticed the tone of irony in my voice as I forced a smile.

I bid her farewell and descended the steps of James' home with a heavy heart. I prayed fervently that he hadn't been poisoned and that he would soon be better again. I also prayed that he wouldn't permit Charlotte to keep him prisoner in his own home until the day of their marriage. I couldn't bear the thought of not seeing him again until after they were married.

Our conversation in the Tower Subway had not been fully resolved, and the only comfort I had was that he had kissed me again.

I called in at the newsroom on my way to Bermondsey.

"Fifteen percent now, Miss Green," said Edgar, rubbing his hands together with glee.

"That's how much the circulation figures have fallen?" I asked.

"Exactly right! You're sharp-minded. Isn't Miss Green sharp-minded, Potter?"

"Extremely sharp-minded," agreed Frederick.

"Blimpy's not going to get away with a fifteen percent drop," continued Edgar. "It's bound to set Uncle Conway on the war path."

"I hope so," I said.

"My father frequents the same gentleman's club as Mr Conway," said Edgar. "I've asked him to have a quiet word in the proprietor's ear."

"He's influential enough, is he?" I asked.

"I can't tell you exactly what my father does, but whatever it is he's a master at string-pulling. Do you remember when he had my reading ticket reinstated at the British Library?"

"I do remember. That was after you were thrown out for fighting in the reading room."

"Tom Clifford started it."

"He always does."

"That business is all water under the bridge now, and I feel sure that old pater will help out again. Never doubt a Fish, Miss Green."

"I'd be foolish to do so, I'm sure," I replied.

Pale-faced Mr Childers quietly entered the room.

"Cholera, Miss Green," he said.

"I'm sorry?"

"In Naples. I need four hundred words from you on the subject."

"Terrible shame," said Edgar. "I visited Naples when I did the Grand Tour."

"You did the Grand Tour?" asked Frederick.

"Doesn't every chap do the Grand Tour?" replied Edgar.

"Only the chaps with plenty of money and time on their hands," said Frederick. "Where did you go?"

"Oh, the usual places. Paris, Geneva, Turin, Venice, Florence, Rome and then Naples, of course. Naples is the traditional terminus, but I hopped over to Sicily and Malta and did a little bit of Greece. Then I travelled back via Vienna, Munich, Dresden and Berlin. Oh, and Innsbruck too, I think. Remind me to tell you about the ladies in Naples next time we're in Ye Olde Cheshire Cheese, Potter. I can't go into detail about it in polite company."

"Have you quite finished, Mr Fish?" asked Mr Childers.

"Sorry, sir. I didn't realise you were still in the room."

"Can't Edgar write the article about Naples?" I asked the editor, mindful of the reporting I needed to do in Bermondsey. "By all accounts he has experience of the city and its peoples."

"*Female* peoples," added Frederick.

"Absolutely not!" bellowed Mr Childers. "Your deadline is tomorrow."

CHAPTER 38

I returned to Bermondsey to find out if there was any news from the interrogation of Catherine Curran. Maggie was leaving the police station as I arrived.

"Is everything all right?" I asked her.

"Oh 'ello, Miss Green. It is indeed. Why d'yer ask?"

"I wasn't expecting to see you here."

"Oh I 'elps out 'ere from time ter time. I does a bit o' cleanin' an' that."

"You help at the police station as well as the church?"

"Yeah, keeps me outta trouble!" She gave me a wink and continued on her way. She wore an apron, but the dress she wore beneath it appeared rather smart for cleaning work.

Sergeant Richards seemed perplexed when I reached his desk.

"She's been here almost a day, but she won't talk at all. She's sitting in the cell downstairs refusing to say anything to anyone."

"Who has tried speaking to her?"

"Me, Sergeant Grimes and some of the constables. Inspector Wallis from Blackman Street station in Southwark has also tried. He's stepped in to help with the case as we're becoming rather short of men. We've lost Inspector Martin and now Inspector Blakely—"

"You won't lose him," I said determinedly. "He'll be back."

"I hope so."

"I think you've done a fine job of finding Catherine Curran. I hear she was planning to hide out in the caves at Chislehurst."

"Yes, we believe so. The men had been concentrating on searching Orpington, but then she caught the eye of a Chislehurst constable while she was walking along the high street there. She was unaccompanied and looking about her as if she were unfamiliar with the place.

"Toward the end of the afternoon he saw her again, this time loitering near the caves, which is an odd location for a lady to be standing around on her own. She told him she was waiting to meet someone. He replied that he'd heard reports of a woman matching her description who was on the run in Kent, and that his colleagues in nearby Orpington would be particularly interested to meet her. She refused to tell him her name, but she went with him quietly. She's quite thin and seems to be lacking in nourishment. She was probably too weak and tired to put up much resistance once she was found."

"Did she have any belongings with her?"

"Yes, she was carrying a bag with some clothes in, so there is no doubt that she was on her travels. A search of her person revealed a second-class train ticket from London Bridge station, so we know that she has travelled down to Kent from London in recent days. She was also carrying a significant amount of money on her person; about forty pounds. That's what you might expect to find on a woman who has recently claimed against a life insurance policy.

"We've shown her the photographs she had taken with her deceased husbands, but she has displayed no emotion. We asked her about Sally Chadwick and she has said nothing. It's most unusual. I'm beginning to wonder whether she has been rendered mute by the tragedy of losing three husbands. I think her mind has been disturbed by it all. I feel quite sorry for her. She faces the police court later this week on the charge of bigamy, but I don't think her nerves will stand it."

"Might I be permitted to see her?"

"I don't think so, Miss Green. You'll probably start asking inappropriate questions again."

"I won't this time, I promise. And I won't publish anything from my meeting with her."

Sergeant Richards shook his head.

"Please?" I begged. "As she's refusing to speak to you, I wonder whether the presence of another woman might help. She may feel quite intimidated at a police station surrounded by men."

He sighed. "Very well, though I don't know why I'm agreeing to it. Perhaps it's because I know that you won't leave me alone until I do. And maybe another woman is what she needs to get her talking. But you must be very careful with your line of questioning, Miss Green. And I shall accompany you, of course."

"Absolutely fine, Sergeant. Thank you."

We walked down to the cells and the gaoler opened the door of the cell that had previously accommodated Sally Chadwick.

"Good afternoon, Mrs Curran," said the sergeant. "I've brought Miss Penny Green with me this time. She's a news reporter for the *Morning Express*. Hopefully you'll feel a little more comfortable with a lady to talk to."

A quick glance at Catherine Curran's face made me doubt it. Her large, dark eyes stared at me coldly from her pale face. Her mood appeared hostile, but she wasn't at all intimidating. In fact, she looked much younger than her twenty-nine years.

"Good afternoon, Mrs Curran," I said, hoping to put her at ease. "Sergeant Richards has just been telling me how you were found in Chislehurst. Were you on your way to see members of your family in Orpington? I've heard that's where you come from."

There was no reply.

"A lot has happened since you've been away," I continued, hoping that she would begin to respond. "You'll be relieved to hear that someone has confessed to poisoning all of your husbands." I wondered whether anyone had told her about Benjamin Taylor yet. "You could come to court when she's there next and see her for yourself. I think you already know her quite well. Her name is Sally Chadwick."

Catherine gave me no response, and I wondered what she was thinking.

"Do you know Sally Chadwick?" I asked.

There was still no reply.

"Would you like something to eat?" I asked. "Or drink?"

Catherine looked away.

I caught Sergeant Richards' gaze and sighed.

"Well, I think I'll go now, Catherine, unless there's anything you'd like to tell me. As Sergeant Richards has already explained, I'm a reporter for the *Morning Express* newspaper. I won't publish anything you say without your permission, but I thought there might be something you would like people to hear?"

She looked down at her hands and I wondered whether she had even heard what I had just said to her.

"Thank you for your time, Catherine. I'll leave you be for now."

I turned to walk out of the cell.

"I want to go home," came a timorous voice from behind me.

I turned to look at her again. Her eyes were damp, and her lower lip quivered as if she were close to tears.

"I'm sure you do," I said. "Perhaps a bail agreement could be arranged with Sergeant Richards here."

I gave him a hopeful look, but he said nothing.

The charge of bigamy seemed unnecessary in my mind, having seen how small and vulnerable Catherine looked. Her husbands were all dead and I struggled to imagine that this frightened-looking woman could have done anything to harm them.

The gaoler closed the door on Catherine and locked it behind him.

Something still didn't feel right. Catherine was not what I had expected. I had anticipated a hard look in her eye and an air of defiance or argument in her tone. It seemed I had formed the wrong impression of her.

"May I look at those photographs of Catherine with her post-mortem husbands again?" I asked Sergeant Richards once we were upstairs in the parade room.

He walked over to a chest of drawers, pulled one of them open and retrieved a paper file. He placed it on a nearby desk and flicked through it until he found the photographs. Then he laid them out in front of us. This was the first time I had seen the three pictures side by side. I tried not to look at the glassy-eyed expression on each of the men. Their faces made me shiver.

I looked closely at Catherine's face in the three photographs. Each had been taken two years after the previous one. I particularly focused on the photographs taken in 1880 and 1884. There was no doubt that Catherine's face showed slight signs of ageing in the most recent picture. Her face was slightly plumper in the earlier picture and her skin was noticeably firmer around the eyes and chin.

"Are you sure that the woman you're holding downstairs is Catherine Curran?" I asked Sergeant Richards.

"Absolutely certain. She fits the description of Catherine and was found looking lost with a train ticket from London in her purse. Besides, she was carrying a large sum of money and a bag which contained clothing and a pair of shoes."

"Have you identified her by any other means?"

"There was nothing among her personal effects to identify her as Catherine Curran."

"Then how do you know for certain that it's her?"

"Who else could it be?"

"I don't know. But surely you need to be certain that the woman you are holding here is Catherine Curran. Have you asked her?"

Sergeant Richards gave a dry laugh. "Of course we've *asked* her. But you've seen how she refuses to talk to anyone."

"She spoke to me."

"She didn't deny that she was Catherine Curran, did she? You'd think that if she chose to say anything the first thing she'd say would be, 'You've apprehended the wrong person.' Then she would presumably go to some lengths to prove who she really was, and perhaps point us in the direction of a friend or family member who could identify her."

"Maybe she doesn't want anyone to know who she is."

"And why not?"

"I don't know. But I'm questioning whether you have arrested the right person, because the evidence you have to suggest that the woman downstairs is Catherine Curran is merely circumstantial. If you look at the photographs on the desk here you can see that the woman in the cell downstairs most closely resembles the Catherine we see in the first picture. However, the Catherine in the photograph taken this year looks much older than the woman in the cell downstairs. She didn't look twenty-nine to me."

"You can't always judge a person's age by their face, Miss Green."

"No, not always, but you can usually get a rough idea. Consider the life Catherine has led. I know nothing of her youth, but I do know that she has worked for most of her adult life in leather markets in Bermondsey and Lambeth. This type of employment is quite strenuous, and after some years it takes its toll on a person's appearance. Consider also that Catherine has been married four times and has endured the death of three of her husbands. Perhaps she had a hand in that, but we don't know for sure yet. I would therefore expect Catherine to look much as she does in this photograph." I pointed at the one which had been taken most recently. "This looks to be a woman of twenty-nine who has endured a certain amount of adversity. The woman you're holding downstairs does not appear that way to me."

"She may have suffered great adversity."

"But she looks much younger than the woman in the photograph. Could you arrange for someone to identify her?"

"Such as who?"

I wished James were present. I liked Sergeant Richards, but I was beginning to doubt his ability to handle such a complex case. I felt sympathy for him as he had recently lost his colleague in tragic circumstances, but I was finding the conversation increasingly frustrating and was beginning to worry about the impact this situation might have on the case.

"Someone who knows her! Florence Burrell or William Curran, for example. Catherine Curran was married to their brothers, after all. Or perhaps a neighbour, or someone she worked with at the leather market."

Sergeant Richards nodded. "We could ask Miss Burrell or Mr Curran, I suppose."

"Please do so, Sergeant, because if you're holding the wrong woman you know what that means, don't you? It means there is a possibility that Benjamin Taylor *was* poisoned by his wife on Friday evening. And it also means that she is still at liberty to poison someone else."

CHAPTER 39

I worked in the reading room the following day, developing my article about the cholera epidemic in Naples. It was difficult to concentrate. I couldn't help wondering whether Sergeant Richards had managed to confirm that the woman under arrest was indeed Catherine Curran. *If she wasn't Catherine, who was she? There was no doubt that the police investigation had been hampered by Inspector Martin's death. Had that been the poisoner's intention?*

I was deeply concerned that James was unwell for the same reason. What I wanted to do, more than anything else, was to visit his home again and find out whether he was beginning to recover. *Would Charlotte inform me if his condition worsened?*

Thoughts of James consumed my mind. *Would it really be so terrible if I called at his home again and inquired how he was?* I pictured Charlotte's stormy expression as she answered the door to me a second time. There was no doubt that another visit would antagonise her.

I sat back in my chair and sighed. I needed to know that he

was all right. I couldn't bear the not knowing. I wanted to be there beside him, and I wanted to ensure that he got better again. I began to think the best thing to do was send him a telegram.

As I pondered this, I became aware of a figure from the corner of my eye. I turned to see Mr Sherman walking toward me. I blinked, struggling to believe my eyes.

But it was him, and I felt a smile spread across my face.

"What are you doing here, sir?" I whispered once he had reached my side.

"Can we find somewhere to talk?"

I packed my papers away excitedly and we made our way outside.

"What's happening with your case, sir?" I asked as we descended the steps of the British Museum.

"We're all due back in court to face the charges this Thursday," he said glumly. "And no doubt all the luminaries of Fleet Street will be there to report on the former editor of the *Morning Express'* public downfall."

"Not *former*, surely?" I said. "You can return to your job once this has all blown over."

"After serving a jail term of four months? I doubt it very much."

"You haven't been found guilty yet, or even stood trial. Perhaps the charges against you will be dropped."

"That's what my supposedly brilliant lawyer is working toward, but I can't say that I'm terribly hopeful. Standing trial will mark the end of my career on Fleet Street whether I'm found guilty or not."

"That doesn't seem fair at all," I said. "You're so good at your job, Mr Sherman."

"Thank you, Miss Green. I'm not perfect, though; far from it. And I can't pretend that I didn't know what I was getting myself into. I knew the risks and I was foolish.

Anyway, that's by the by. I didn't come here to bemoan my situation."

"Shall we have a drink at the Museum Tavern?"

"That sounds like a good idea."

The cut-glass mirrors, flickering gas lamps and haze of tobacco smoke made me think of James again. I glanced over at our usual table and saw a man seated there reading *The Times*. Would *James and I ever meet in this place again?* It seemed unlikely.

I shivered as a fresh wave of concern that he was suffering from the effects of poison flashed into my mind. I knew that arsenic didn't always kill people immediately; poor Inspector Martin's death was proof of that. He had been poisoned on a Thursday but had died the following Monday, having endured four days of agony.

"Are you all right, Miss Green?" asked Mr Sherman as he handed me a glass of sherry.

"I am. Thank you, sir."

He gave me a look which suggested that he didn't quite believe me as we sat down at a table. He wore a suit that I had often seen him wear at the office, though it wasn't as tight-fitting as it had been before.

"This confusing case must be creating a lot of work for you," he said.

"It is, sir. As soon as I begin to think that a conclusion has been reached something else occurs to complicate matters."

He took a sip of his sherry. "My brother paid a visit to Miss Chadwick."

"Did he?" I smiled. "Thank you. What did he think of her?"

"The gaol is a rather difficult place to get into."

"I suppose it would be. It's the House of Detention, after all."

He gave a feeble laugh. "Yes, Henry was quite surprised by it all. He probably thought it would be as straightforward as walking into the Peter Jones department store in Sloane Square. Fortunately, he persevered. He managed to convince the authorities that he had been instructed to visit Miss Chadwick by an eminent London lawyer. Henry knows a few prominent lawyers socially, and he can put on quite an intimidating display when required. If he hadn't become a doctor he could easily have been an actor."

"And how did Sally seem when Dr Sherman saw her?"

Mr Sherman's brow furrowed. "He was concerned. So concerned that he has visited her again since then."

I felt a chill in my stomach. "Goodness, really?"

"She's quite distressed, apparently, which I suppose is to be expected in a young woman being held in such a gaol. She has been causing herself some harm."

"Doing what?"

"She has terrible scratches on her arms and legs, and she is eating very little."

"I knew she would struggle to cope in there."

"In theory she's a murderess awaiting trial. Many would say that she deserves to be there."

"And what does your brother think?"

"Henry is of the opinion that she should be in a lunatic asylum instead. He doesn't believe that she should appear at the Central Criminal Court. The stress of the situation would be too much for her."

"I agree that it would, though I think an asylum might be almost as bad as the House of Detention. It doesn't seem fair when her mind is clearly affected. Surely there must be another way."

Mr Sherman shrugged. "Such as what? She has confessed

to three murders and must be detained somewhere." He drained his glass and lit his pipe.

"Does Dr Sherman believe she is guilty?"

"He seems rather surprised that she managed to carry out three poisonings without being detected. The murders would have required a significant degree of planning and stealth, which he does not believe her capable of."

"So he thinks she is innocent?"

"I think it would be difficult to proclaim that. After all, many crimes surprise us. The evidence against her is overwhelming, isn't it? They found all those bottles of poison in her home. Henry thinks she carried out her crimes without considering the severity of them due to the weakness of her mind. She was incapable of realising the seriousness of what she was doing."

"But if her mind was too weak to consider the severity of her crimes, how could it possess the strength to plan and execute them so efficiently? It's a paradox."

"Yes, it is. Henry believes she was coerced."

"By another person. I knew it! Catherine Curran must have made her do it."

"She's been arrested as well, hasn't she? It shouldn't be too difficult to charge her in connection with the murders."

"I'm afraid not, Mr Sherman. I think they have arrested the wrong woman and that the real Catherine Curran is still out there."

CHAPTER 40

Mr Sherman bought another round of sherries and took a large sip from his glass. I told him about my meeting with the young woman in the police cell the previous day.

"What does Inspector Blakely of Scotland Yard make of all this?" he asked.

"I don't know because he's currently unwell at home. I tried to visit him yesterday but his fiancée wouldn't let me see him."

Mr Sherman gave a knowing smile.

"I'm worried that he has been poisoned just as Inspector Martin was," I continued. "This is a complex case and the people who are best-placed to solve it are being targeted."

"It sounds like a coordinated plan."

"It is. And Sally Chadwick has very little to do with it, I feel sure of that."

"So apart from the sergeant at Bermondsey, who else is working on the case?"

"There's an Inspector Wallis at the Blackman Street station in Southwark. I'm not quite sure what he's doing. And there's a rather annoying chief inspector from L Division who is investigating Benjamin Taylor's death. Personally, I think the police are being outwitted. I suspect that Catherine Curran is behind the whole thing, but she seems to have other people helping her. How could one woman outwit the combined efforts of the Metropolitan Police?"

"By killing one of their officers, it seems. And you think she may be trying to do the same thing to Blakely?"

"I truly hope not. But he's rarely unwell and I'm desperately worried about him." I took a sip of my sherry. "He's due to be married this weekend, and his fiancée is concerned that he won't be well enough to attend the wedding."

"Is he indeed?" Mr Sherman raised an eyebrow. "In which case his illness is unfortunate indeed."

He watched my face as if waiting for me to say something further. I tried not to give anything away.

"I think you should send him a telegram as soon as we're finished here," he said.

"Do you think I'm right to be worried about him?"

"It's natural to be concerned, especially if it's unusual for him to be taken ill. And in light of the other poisoning I can certainly understand your concern. Let's hope he makes a swift recovery. He's generally fit and well, isn't he? And it sounds as though he is being well looked after."

"I'm sure he is." I felt my stomach turn.

"How is Mr Childers faring?"

"Circulation figures have already fallen."

"Oh dear, really?"

"I wish you could come back, sir. It's not the same without you."

"You know that won't be possible."

"But you've been at the *Morning Express* for so long. It's not fair!"

"Perhaps it's time for a change, anyhow. Perhaps I should

be doing something different. It may be best for me and the newspaper."

"I don't see how."

"I couldn't be the editor forever, Miss Green. Perhaps twelve years is long enough."

"Perhaps it is long enough for you, but if the newspaper is to survive it will require a better editor than Mr Childers."

"You're right, it will. If circulation figures are already down he won't last long. Mr Conway values the numbers above all else, so he'll soon be rid of Childers, nephew or not."

"I hope so. That's what we are all hoping. Please pass on my gratitude to your brother. I'm grateful to him for taking the time to visit Miss Chadwick. I'll tell the police about his concerns."

"He told me he would write up a report for them."

"Really? That's very helpful of him."

"He is concerned about her, just as you are. It sounds as though she needs help rather than punishment. Perhaps someone could be persuaded that she shouldn't have to face the Central Criminal Court."

I left the Museum Tavern feeling pleased that Mr Sherman and his brother had been so helpful. A report from Dr Sherman would presumably prevent Sally Chadwick from having to face a courtroom at the Old Bailey: a court where only the most serious criminal cases were heard. I remained concerned, however, about her future. If she was deemed unfit for prison her confession would undoubtedly lead to her confinement in a lunatic asylum; an institution which was probably little better than gaol.

I sent a note to James from the telegram office on Great Russell Street. Feeling certain that Charlotte would read it I kept the wording polite and simple, choosing not to mention any developments in the case. I then made my way down to Bermondsey, keen to find out whether Sergeant Richards had found anyone who could positively identify the woman he believed to be Catherine Curran.

⚜

Inspector Wallis from Blackman Street station was at the Bermondsey station when I arrived. He was a tall man with grey whiskers, and he walked with a limp.

"It's rather queer," he said when I asked about recent progress. "We have one person who has confirmed that the woman is Mrs Curran and another who claims she isn't."

My heart sank. This felt like the worst possible outcome.

"Two people have seen her?" I asked.

"Yes. Remind me who they are again, Sergeant," said Inspector Wallis.

"Mr Curran and Miss Burrell," said Sergeant Richards.

"And which of them said that it was her?"

"Miss Burrell," replied Sergeant Richards. "But Mr Curran says that it isn't."

"And is the woman saying anything herself?"

Sergeant Richards shook his head. "Nothing, I'm afraid."

"Why not? Why does she not wish to defend herself?"

"It's a mystery," said Inspector Wallis. "Her mind must be extremely muddled."

I sighed. "I suppose it makes sense to listen to Mr Curran given that he has seen her more recently than Miss Burrell. Thomas Burrell died two years ago, so Miss Burrell presumably hasn't seen Catherine Curran for at least that length of time. Mr Curran saw her shortly before his brother died two weeks ago, so I think we should listen to him."

"That means the search for Catherine Curran must be resumed," said Inspector Wallis.

"Only if we are assuming that the woman in the cell is not her," said Sergeant Richards.

"I think we have to, don't we?" replied the inspector. "There is reasonable doubt over her identity, so we should carry on looking for the woman."

"I'm so pleased you've said that, Inspector," I said. "Because this development makes it far more probable that Catherine Curran has murdered her first husband. It seems she attempted to do so six years ago and came back to finish the job. And because his poisoning happened in Lambeth you can also draw on the help of L Division. If everyone starts looking for her again she will surely be found soon."

CHAPTER 41

A telegram was waiting for me on the hallway table the following morning. I hurriedly opened it, hoping it would bring news of James.

James is recovering.
  Charlotte Jenkins

She had used few words, but I still felt relieved to read them. Then I began to doubt the good news. I thought of the effects of arsenic on the body once again and how the suffering could be prolonged.

James obviously wasn't well enough to write a telegram himself. Was he really recovering or was Charlotte just saying that so I'd stay away? Could she be certain that he was recovering?

Even if Charlotte was correct in her assessment of James' condition I didn't hold out much hope of seeing him before his wedding, which was only three days away.

"Oh dear, what's happened?" asked Mrs Garnett as she arrived in the hallway with a feather duster in her hand.

"Good morning. Nothing has happened."

"Then why does your face look so terrible?"

"Regrettably, this is my usual face, Mrs Garnett."

"No, it's not. You look like you've just received bad news."

"The only news I have is that Inspector Blakely is recovering."

"So why aren't you happy about that?"

"I am. Anyway, I need to head off to Southwark Police Court, Mrs Garnett." I pinned my hat to my head.

"Whatever for?"

"Sally Chadwick, the woman who has confessed to three of the poisonings, is back in front of the magistrates again today."

"Oh, *her*. The poisoning murderess."

"The case isn't quite as straightforward as that, Mrs Garnett. I'll explain it all to you when I have a little more time."

I took the omnibus in the direction of London Bridge and pondered the impending court appearance. It had been arranged so that James could find sufficient evidence to add Inspector Martin's murder to the existing charges against Sally Chadwick. However, he had found no compelling evidence and still wasn't well enough to attend court. It meant that the morning's proceedings would most likely be a waste of time and that, for the time being at least, the mystery surrounding Inspector Martin's death remained unsolved.

The courtroom was busy, just as it had been a week previously. I stood with the other press reporters and wondered whether Inspector Wallis and Sergeant Richards had restarted their search for Catherine Curran. The inspector had seemed reasonably convinced that they were holding the wrong woman in custody, so I tried to remain hopeful that the search would soon be underway again.

The three magistrates entered the room. Among them was Mr Sidney Parnell with his familiar hooked nose and cloud of white hair. Sally Chadwick was brought into the dock and I stood on tiptoes to look at her, feeling saddened by the sight of her gaunt face and slumped shoulders. I was surprised to see that she was followed by Maggie once again, and felt a touch of relief knowing that someone was supporting her.

Mr Parnell opened the proceedings and went on to explain the reason for this second court session.

"A week ago, Detective Inspector Blakely of Scotland Yard requested some additional time to find evidence that the prisoner may have committed a fourth murder," he said. "Has any evidence been found?"

He looked around the silent courtroom but there was no response.

"Is Inspector Blakely present?" he asked.

More silence ensued and I felt a heavy weight in my stomach. This hearing was a waste of time and James would be sorely disappointed.

"Is there anyone here who can speak for him?" asked Mr Parnell with a hint of impatience in his voice.

Sergeant Richards hesitantly stepped forward. "He has been taken ill, Your Honour."

"I see. Are you able to speak for him, Sergeant Richards?"

"I can try." The young sergeant's voice was quiet, making it difficult to hear what he was saying.

"My question is this," continued Mr Parnell. "Has any evidence been found that would justify a charge being made against the prisoner for the murder of Inspector Charles Martin?"

Sergeant Richards was about to open his mouth when another man who had only just entered the courtroom stepped forward. He moved cautiously, as if nursing a strong headache.

It was James.

My heart skipped, and I suppressed the urge to dash over and embrace him. He looked pale and moved slowly, but I felt encouraged that he was well on the road to recovery. I realised there was a grin on my face, which must have looked quite out of place on such an occasion.

"Good morning, Your Honour," said James. "I apologise for my late arrival this morning. In the past week Bermondsey police station has been thoroughly searched for evidence to suggest that Miss Chadwick poisoned Inspector Martin. I regret to say that no such evidence has been found."

Mr Parnell asked the clerk to make a note of this.

"Very well," replied the chief magistrate. "Miss Chadwick, no charge will be brought against you for the murder of Inspector Martin. The charges against you remain the same as before for the murders of Mr Peel, Mr Burrell and Mr Curran, for which you have freely admitted your guilt. Now, before we finish I must mention a report which has been passed to me by a physician, Doctor Henry Sherman."

I felt myself smile once again. Mr Sherman's brother had not only written a report about Sally but had also given a copy to the magistrates.

"Did you commission this report, Inspector Blakely?" asked Mr Parnell.

"No." His brow furrowed. "I know nothing about it, Your Honour."

Mr Parnell scowled and muttered something to his colleagues. There was an uneasy silence before the chief magistrate addressed James again. "My understanding, Inspector, is that Dr Sherman was requested to visit the prisoner at the House of Detention. Did you not issue such a request?"

"No, Your Honour."

I bit my lip and felt rather sorry for James as he tried to comprehend this new piece of information. He gave Sergeant Richards a searching glance.

"Perhaps my colleague can enlighten you further, Your Honour."

Sergeant Richards shifted from one foot to another. "I think a copy of the report was handed in at the station, but I haven't had a chance to read it yet."

The chief magistrate frowned. "I see. Did you not commission the report yourself, Sergeant Richards?"

"No, Your Honour."

"Do you know who did?"

"I'm afraid not, Your Honour.'

"Didn't you seek to find out once a copy of the report had been handed in to Bermondsey police station?"

"It was something I intended to do, Your Honour, but I hadn't found an opportunity." His face began to redden.

The chief magistrate frowned again and examined the report in front of him. Then he lifted his head and addressed the court.

"May I ask if Dr Sherman is here?"

CHAPTER 42

Heads turned as a man in black-and-grey-striped trousers and a grey jacket stepped forward. He had a thick black moustache and his hair was parted to one side. I stared at him intently, convinced that my former editor, Mr Sherman, had just stepped forward.

"I'm Dr Henry Sherman, and I have been a practising physician for almost thirty years." His voice was also similar to Mr Sherman's, and I found myself rather bemused by his appearance. Not only was he Mr Sherman's brother; he appeared to be his twin. "I'm a medical registrar at St George's Hospital," he added.

"There appears to be some confusion over who asked you to visit the prisoner at the House of Detention," said Mr Parnell. "May I ask who it was?"

"A concerned member of the public."

James and Sergeant Richards exchanged a puzzled glance. I felt a surge of heat pass across my face and worried that my expression would give me away. *Surely Dr Sherman did not intend to name me?*

"Do you often respond to requests like this from concerned members of the public?"

"Not at all, Your Honour. But I received assurances that the request had come from a respected individual with a detailed knowledge of the case. Having assessed the situation myself I agreed that there might be cause for concern."

"Concern about what, sir?"

"Concern that the prisoner is of unsound mind but is to be tried as a common criminal, Your Honour."

"And the reason you have given for your concern is detailed in the report I have here in front of me, is it?"

"That's correct, Your Honour."

"And what leads you to believe that the prisoner is of unsound mind?"

"She is a woman of twenty-seven years of age, yet her mind is that of a young girl's," replied Dr Sherman. "I was able to converse with Miss Chadwick during my visits to the House of Detention, and I discovered that her view of the world is a very simple one. Though there is no denying that she possesses some intelligence, as she is able to both read and write."

I noticed Maggie giving Sally an encouraging smile.

"However, her nature is extremely trusting," continued the doctor. "And I would suggest that she lacks the capacity to judge the intentions and motives of others. To that end, I would call her suggestible. She seems keen to please and is easily intimidated by others. She lacks the ability to assert herself. Although she is in possession of some intelligence, I believe she is incapable of planning the poisoning of three men over a four-year period without assistance from someone else."

James watched Dr Sherman closely as he spoke.

"In addition to this, I don't believe the prisoner harbours malice toward anyone," continued the doctor. "In my view she probably poisoned those men because she was told to do so by another individual."

"Yet she denies that any other individual is involved," said Mr Parnell.

"I realise that, Your Honour, and I suspect this denial is borne out of two things. Firstly, a fear of the individual she is protecting, and secondly, a strong need to please that individual."

"You believe the prisoner would rather risk a sentence of death than name the individual who has coerced her?"

"Yes, I believe so. To the ordinary mind it sounds absurd, of course, but I should add that the prisoner is unable to fully comprehend the danger she has placed herself in by confessing to these crimes. I believe she is unable to understand the true implications of her actions. She has merely done what she was instructed to do by this other person."

The chief magistrate sighed. "You seem extremely convinced that there is another person involved, Dr Sherman. Do you share this hypothesis, Inspector Blakely?"

"While I respect Doctor Sherman's opinion, and am willing to believe that another person may be involved, I am yet to find any evidence to support the notion, Your Honour."

My eyes shifted to Sergeant Richards. This was his opportunity to admit that the wrong woman had been arrested in Kent, and that the real Catherine Curran was still at large. My heart pounded as I watched him, and I felt my teeth clench with frustration as I realised that he intended to remain silent.

"This lack of evidence is proving problematic, isn't it, Inspector Blakely?" said Mr Parnell. "There is no evidence to suggest that the prisoner murdered Inspector Martin, and no evidence to confirm that anyone else was involved in the three murders to which the prisoner has confessed."

He paused to have another whispered conversation with his fellow magistrates.

James surveyed the courtroom while they spoke, and we caught each other's eye. I smiled, and he nodded in return. He didn't look particularly well, and although I was pleased that Dr Sherman had turned up I felt sorry that James had only received news of the report while he was standing in front of the magistrates.

The magistrates finished their conversation and looked up. Then Mr Parnell cleared his throat and prepared to address the court.

"We are agreed that the work of the police on this case has not been particularly thorough," he said. "Although the prisoner has confessed to her crimes, many unanswered questions remain. I refer to the deaths of Inspector Martin and Mr Benjamin Taylor, both of whom died in circumstances similar to the prisoner's victims. In the case of the latter, whose death occurred while the prisoner was already being detained, the crime may either have been perpetrated by someone imitating the infamous crimes or by the unnamed individual to whom Dr Sherman refers."

I looked over at Sergeant Richards again, hoping that he would clarify the situation regarding Catherine Curran. He remained silent and I muttered a curse beneath my breath. James probably had no idea that the wrong woman was being held in Bermondsey.

I wanted to cry out and tell the magistrates what was really happening. Instead, I had to bite my tongue and watch as Mr Parnell issued James and Sergeant Richards with a sharp rebuke.

"It is possible that this case is more complex than we have considered," said Mr Parnell. "For that reason I shall once again recommend a delay in referring it to the Central Criminal Court. May I urge you, Inspector Blakely, and all your colleagues in the Metropolitan Police, to establish, as a matter of urgency, whether or not a second person may have been involved in the three murders to which the prisoner has confessed. I would also ask you to consider whether this unknown person might have been involved in the two other fatal poisonings, as it seems wholly unlikely to me that they are not connected to this case."

"Of course, Your Honour," replied James. "It's something we have considered, and we—"

"Having to adjourn proceedings due to police incompetence is something which grieves me enormously," interrupted Mr Parnell. "It is both unnecessary and inconvenient."

James said nothing further, but I noticed his jaw clench.

Dr Sherman stepped forward again. "Your Honour, I wish to request that the prisoner is not returned to the House of Detention, but that she is housed in an asylum instead."

"We require the opinion of two physicians to confirm that the prisoner is of unsound mind," replied Mr Parnell. "The prisoner will return to the House of Detention for the next seven days, during which time I will request that she is visited by another physician who will provide a second opinion. We will reconvene here on Wednesday the seventeenth of September to hear from the second physician. This time-frame will also allow the police to prove whether a second culprit is involved or not. No more time-wasting please, gentlemen."

CHAPTER 43

"James!" I caught up with him as soon as he left the police court.

"Penny," he said with a smile, but his eyes were dark.

"Are you fully recovered?" I asked.

"Almost. It's been an unpleasant few days but I'm back on my feet, as you can see. I think Charlotte harboured the notion that I would stay in bed until our wedding day, but there was little chance of that!" He took out his handkerchief and wiped his brow. "What an embarrassing scene in that courtroom!" he said. "I don't think I've ever felt so humiliated before. Where did Dr Sherman come from? Are you sure he's not your editor in another guise?"

"They are twin brothers."

"That explains it! I've just had a brief conversation with him, but he had to dash off back to St George's. I was trying to tell Mr Parnell we had arrested Catherine Curran when he rudely interrupted me! Some of these magistrates don't give you a chance. They have no idea how much work is involved in a case like this. He accused us of incompetence, and I suppose I have to agree with him. We looked completely incompetent in there today. I've only been absent for a short while and the case has already gone to the dogs. Richards!" he barked.

"Yes, sir?" Sergeant Richards tentatively stepped toward us.

"What's been happening over the past few days?"

"Erm... I thought Inspector Wallis would be here to help us."

"He's not here, though, is he?"

I turned to face Sergeant Richards. "Why didn't you tell the magistrates you have been holding the wrong woman?" I asked.

"Because we haven't yet confirmed whether it's her or not," he replied.

"What's this?" asked James.

I told him about the mistaken identity of the woman in the cell.

"Good grief!" he said when I had finished. "Why didn't you tell me this, Richards?"

"You were unwell, sir."

"Yes, I was," said James through gritted teeth. "And what an enormous inconvenience it has been."

"There was no opportunity to tell you before the hearing this morning," said the sergeant. "In fact, I didn't realise you would be attending."

"Neither did I until three hours ago," said James. "The decision was made at the final moment."

The thunderous expression on his face made me wonder whether he had argued with Charlotte about his return to work that morning.

"It doesn't help when physicians compile reports about our prisoners without telling us," ventured Sergeant Richards.

"But he did tell us, didn't he? We just hadn't found the

time to read the report. And given that the doctor is the twin brother of the *Morning Express*' former editor, I think I know who the concerned member of the public might be." He gave me a reproachful look.

"Yes, it was me," I admitted.

James gave me an exasperated smile. "It would have been helpful if you'd told me."

"I didn't realise Dr Sherman had visited her until yesterday, and I would have told you, but you were—"

"Unwell. Yes."

"Did you receive my telegram?"

"Which telegram?"

"The one I sent you yesterday."

His face clouded. "No, I didn't see it."

"Did Charlotte tell you that I called for you on Monday?"

"Yes, she did mention that."

"I would have liked to have told you everything that was going on, but—"

"Let's leave all that for now," interrupted James. "We have plenty to be getting on with. Let's go back to the station, Richards, and get as many men working on this as possible. We need to find out who that woman in the cells is, and more importantly we need to find Catherine Curran. I'll get over to L Division and engender their help. This case has been stalled for long enough. We will not be made fools of again!"

CHAPTER 44

*C*atherine Curran is wanted in Bermondsey and Lambeth on suspicion of causing the deaths of four men by administering to each a fatal dose of arsenic. She is about thirty years of age and five feet four inches in height. She is slim-built with a fresh complexion, dark eyes and fair hair. She wears rings on her fingers and was last seen on the seventeenth of August dressed in a black dress, shawl and bonnet. She may also be known by the names: Jane Vincent, Jane Taylor, Catherine Peel and Catherine Burrell.

"I thought she had already been arrested," said Mr Childers.

"It was a case of mistaken identity," I replied.

"And she has murdered *four* men?"

"We think so, although there is also believed to be a fifth victim: Inspector Martin. She may not have poisoned him herself, but she might have instructed Sally Chadwick to do so."

"And Chadwick is the woman who has confessed?"

"That's right. She has admitted to three of the murders,

but we suspect that she was coerced. The physician who examined her is certain of it."

"I can't say that I would ever let anyone coerce me into murdering someone," said Edgar.

"That's because you are of sound mind," I replied.

Potter emitted a peal of laughter. "That half-wit has a sound mind, does he?"

"Watch yourself, Potter, or I'll be tipping arsenic into your tea next," retorted Edgar.

"I'm sure they'll catch the woman responsible very soon," said Mr Childers. "In the meantime, Miss Green, have a read of this and summarise it for tomorrow's edition."

He handed me a bound volume which declared itself to be the Annual Report of St Mary Abbot's, Kensington.

"It's an interesting read," he continued. "The population of the Kensington Borough has reached one hundred and sixty-eight thousand, which is about the same as the total population of Bristol."

"Must this be summarised for tomorrow's edition?" I asked. "Can it not wait until next week?"

"No, Miss Green, it cannot."

"But the Bermondsey poisoner case has reached a crucial stage. Everyone is out searching for Catherine Curran, and they may catch her at any moment!"

"You may report on it if and when they do catch her, but other things are going on in this city as well, you know."

"Such as the publication of annual reports?"

"Exactly."

He had failed to recognise the note of sarcasm in my voice.

I thought I heard the voice of Mr Conway beyond the newsroom door. Mr Childers glanced over at it, as if he had also heard his uncle speak.

Then he turned back to face me. "Once you've completed

Kensington I'd like you to précis a similar report on Fulham. It's the type of work you can do here at the typewriter. You'll be relieved to hear that there will be no further need for you to go gallivanting about London."

"But that's what proper news reporting is," I retorted.

"What do you mean?"

"Getting out and about. *Gallivanting* as you so condescendingly put it."

"I was not being condescending."

"I beg to differ, sir. The tone of your voice implied an accusation of flippancy about the manner in which I conduct my work. One of the biggest murder cases of the decade is ongoing and you wish me to remain at my desk summarising annual reports?"

"They contain facts and figures that would interest our readers greatly."

"I think our readers would be more interested to find out whether a prolific murderess has been apprehended or not."

"I find the public's appetite for murder stories quite tiresome."

"This is not just a story, sir. It's happening in south London. And five men have already lost their lives!"

"Tragic indeed. But there is only so much reporting one can do on these incidents before it becomes overly sensationalised."

"There's nothing wrong with a little sensation, sir," said Edgar. "It's what sells newspapers."

"Once again, I beg to differ."

"I know you do, and that's why our circulation figures have dropped by fifteen percent since you took the helm," Edgar continued.

A sneer began to spread across Mr Childers' face. "How dare you speak to your editor in such a manner, Mr Fish!"

"I'm merely stating a fact," said Edgar.

"Circulation figures are prone to fluctuation. You know that as well as I do."

"Fluctuation implies that something goes up as well as down, but in this case our circulation is only going down, sir."

"Why, you impertinent—"

We were interrupted by the newsroom door opening, and in strode the large frame of Mr Conway.

"Oh, there you are, Childers," he puffed. "I've just been looking for you in your office."

The proprietor was accompanied by the person he had presumably been speaking to in the corridor.

Entering the room just behind him, the second man allowed the door to slam behind him.

It was Mr Sherman.

Edgar and Frederick stood to their feet and greeted him with grins on their faces.

Mr Childers raised his eyebrows.

"How are you, Mr Sherman?" asked Edgar. "We've missed you!"

"I can't understand why, Fish. It's only been seventeen days."

"Is that all, sir? It seems much, much longer."

I had never seen Edgar so pleased to encounter Mr Sherman.

"The purpose of my visit here today," puffed Mr Conway, "is to inform you all that this gentleman here," he pointed at Mr Sherman, "was, this morning at Marlborough Street police court, cleared of all charges levelled against him."

"That's wonderful news!" I exclaimed, clapping with excitement.

Edgar and Frederick strode over to Mr Sherman and shook his hand. He nodded, embarrassed by all the attention.

Mr Childers said nothing.

"Now then, let it not be forgotten that whenever mud is

thrown it has a tendency to stick," continued Mr Conway in a loud voice as if he were addressing a large audience. "Some of our detractors will no doubt continue to believe that Mr Sherman is guilty of a serious offence. I care nothing for what they think. In my view this fine gentleman has been cleared of all wrongdoing in a court of law, so I therefore declare that this sorry business is completely behind us."

Mr Childers' lower lip began to protrude. "But Uncle..." he said tentatively.

"Thank you for all your help, boy," wheezed Mr Conway, patting him on the shoulder.

I was unable to suppress a smile at the proprietor's use of the word *boy*.

"You stepped in when it was needed, and I'm quite sure the staff at the *West London Mercury* will be pleased to have you back with them again."

I felt a warm flood of relief in my chest to hear that the *Morning Express* offices could finally return to normal.

Mr Childers glanced at each of us in turn. "I see. My return to the *Mercury* is immediate, is it?"

"Why not, Crispin? Today is as good as any other day."

"Well, it's been a pleasure working here," he said, giving each of us a nod.

"Don't forget your report," I said, handing it back to him. "It's probably quite interesting if you live in west London. I would say that it is of less interest to readers in the rest of the metropolis."

His lip rose in a sneer and everyone remained silent as he left the room.

"Cheerio, Mr Childers!" called Edgar as the door closed behind him.

Mr Conway sighed. "The boy's mother will no doubt be calling round this evening to box my ears. I'd better pre-empt the event with a telegram. I'll leave you in charge here, Sherman. Good to have you back. That lawyer's a fine chap, isn't he? Money well spent, I'd say."

"Thank you, sir."

Mr Sherman shook his head as Mr Conway left the room. "We've lost a lot of readers in just two weeks. We need to get them back again. You all know what to do, so let's get moving. Miss Green, go and find out what the hapless police are doing about the Bermondsey poisoner. Henry told me about the hotchpotch in court yesterday."

"It was far from perfect, sir. Please pass on my gratitude to your brother. Hopefully Miss Chadwick's predicament will be better understood now."

"I will do. Now get on with it."

"It's good to have you back—"

The door slammed closed behind him before I had finished my sentence.

CHAPTER 45

I travelled to Bermondsey police station, and when I stepped inside I found Maggie polishing the reception desk.

"Busy innit, Miss Green? They're so busy all the time these police officers. Everyone's been comin' an' goin' today."

"Is Inspector Blakely here, Maggie?" I asked.

"Gone down Lambeth station to see Inspector Austen, 'e 'as."

"Thank you. You're helping to keep track of everyone, are you?"

"I does what I can ter 'elp!" she said with a smile.

Sergeant Richards joined us. "It seems you were right about the woman we had in custody," he said. "Her name is Molly Coutts."

"Did she speak to you?"

"No, but her mother came down here yesterday. She was relieved to have finally found her; the poor woman had been worried silly."

"The mother travelled here from Chislehurst?"

"No, it turns out Molly and her family are from Bermondsey. Her mother had received word about a woman matching Molly's description being held here."

"Then Molly is from this area after all. Why didn't she speak up?"

Sergeant Richards shrugged. "I don't know. She seemed frightened to me."

"And she looked it. But even so you'd have thought the girl would have made some attempt to defend herself. At least she is safely home now, and hopefully recovering from her ordeal."

I remembered how fearful Molly had looked inside the police cell. We had five dreadful crimes on our hands and two young women who appeared to have been implicated and intimidated by a third party.

⚜

"There have been a number of supposed sightings of Catherine in the Vauxhall area," said James when I caught up with him at Lambeth police station.

He looked less pale than he had, but still appeared rather tired. I could tell that he had returned to work without giving himself enough time to recuperate, though I could understand why he had done so. He was as desperate as I was to have the case resolved.

"The difficulty we have is in deciding which sightings to follow up on," he added.

"There will no doubt be a number of time-wasters," added Inspector Austen, his face looking redder than ever, "but we have hundreds of men out on the streets, and we've drafted in help from Walworth, Clapham and Battersea."

"Surely it's only a matter of time before she's found," I said.

"We certainly hope so," said James. "I'm worried she may have run off to Kent again."

"How can you be sure that Catherine Curran ever ran off to Kent?" I asked. "The only evidence we have are the reported sightings."

"And that's all the evidence we can go on."

"But perhaps the sightings were incorrect?"

"Some will have been, but you spoke to a lady yourself on the Old Kent Road who said 'Jane Taylor' had stayed with her. And she stayed at that pub on the riverfront, didn't she?"

"*Someone* stayed at that pub."

"What are you suggesting, Penny?" asked James.

"What if it was Molly Coutts who stayed at that pub? Perhaps she also stayed at the lodgings on the Old Kent Road. Suppose Catherine Curran coerced Molly into pretending that she was Catherine on the run from the police? The two women bear a striking resemblance to one another, and it served as an extremely effective distraction. While everyone was chasing about after Molly, Catherine was able to concentrate on disrupting the inquiries being made in London."

"Namely the murders of Inspector Martin and Benjamin Taylor."

"Exactly!"

Inspector Austen shook his head. "I don't think she can have coerced anyone else to pretend to be her. After all, she must have known that the girl's true identity would eventually be discovered."

"She almost certainly knew that, but Molly has kept everyone off her trail for more than three weeks! And that allowed her to kill another two men."

"You may be right, Penny," said James, "but I wish I could understand what sort of hold Catherine has over Sally and Molly to make them agree to do her bidding."

"She chose meek, naive women; the sort who would be suggestible. She most likely intimidated them and perhaps even bribed them."

"She possibly used blackmail," added Inspector Austen. "In some cases the threat of telling someone else a piece of harmful information is enough to persuade the victim to do something they normally wouldn't do."

"That makes sense," said James. "And if it's true, Catherine Curran is even more scheming than we first thought."

I remained in Lambeth for a while to assist with the search. I called in at various shops and public houses, and wrote down the details of any possible sightings in my notebook. Many people claimed to have seen her, adding credence to Inspector Austen's theory that a significant number had to be time-wasters.

At the end of the afternoon, James and I travelled by horse tram up to Westminster Bridge. The tram stopped close to St Thomas' Hospital, and from there we walked across the bridge toward the Houses of Parliament. A warm wind blew upstream, carrying the smoke from the steamboats with it.

"I found your telegram," said James. "Charlotte apologised for not having shown it to me."

"I'm pleased that you received it in the end," I said. "Not that it was particularly interesting. I kept the wording simple as I suspected Charlotte would read it."

James smiled.

"I was quite worried about you," I continued. "I thought you might have been poisoned."

"So did I for a while!" He laughed. "I don't think I've ever been so sick in my life."

"Perhaps you were."

"Poisoned?"

"When did you first begin to feel unwell?"

"It was after Charles Martin's funeral. I assumed it was due to something I had eaten or drunk there."

"It may well have been," I said. "Did you leave your drink unattended at any time?"

"No," said James, before pausing to consider. "I don't think so, anyway. I did have a few drinks, and I have to say that everything was rather hazy by the end of the day. I suppose it is quite likely that I left my drink unattended at some point."

"So someone could possibly have tipped poison into it?"

"It's possible, but extremely unlikely. Are you suggesting that Catherine was there?"

"She might have been. How many people were at the wake?"

"Mostly those who attended the funeral service. Apart from you, Penny."

"I decided to leave you to spend time with your colleagues."

"Catherine couldn't possibly have been there," he said, "or someone would have noticed her. And surely she wouldn't have been so brazen, would she?"

"Possibly not in a room filled with police officers! Perhaps you weren't poisoned after all. I suppose I'm becoming rather preoccupied with arsenic."

"That's not so surprising, Penny."

He glanced behind him, as if looking for someone in particular.

"Is something the matter?" I asked.

"No, I just feel rather on edge, if truth be told. Ever since I returned to work I've had the odd sensation that I am being watched."

I looked behind us and then across the road to the other side of the bridge. I found myself looking for a petite, fair-haired woman, but I couldn't see anyone who matched Catherine's description.

"I still feel a bit odd from the illness," said James. "It's probably just my imagination playing tricks on me."

"I think you should trust your instincts," I said.

"I'm not quite sure what they're telling me at the moment. I feel as though two days of lying in bed unwell has robbed me of my senses."

"Being tended to by Charlotte."

"I detest being tended to! There is nothing worse than being reliant on another human being for your everyday needs."

"It can't be helped if you're unwell."

"I realise that, but I'm a terrible patient. Poor Charlotte has had to put up with quite a lot of nonsense from me."

"Perhaps that's why she hid the telegram I sent."

"She didn't hide it; she just didn't give it to me."

"It's almost the same thing."

"You're right. It's tantamount to the same thing, isn't it? It's no secret that she feels envious about our working relationship."

"And that's not really surprising."

"No, I suppose it's not."

"What do you think she would do if she knew?" I asked pausing beside one of the ornate gas lamps on the bridge.

"Knew about what?" He turned to face me.

"In the Tower Subway. The kiss."

"Oh, that." James scratched his temple.

"Do you think she would still agree to marry you in two days' time if she knew?"

"Oh goodness, I don't know." He looked down at the

ground. "Probably not, I suppose." He looked up at me. "And I wouldn't blame her."

"Me neither."

James' eyes widened. "You wouldn't *tell her*, would you?"

I laughed. "Of course not. Why should I do that?"

"To stop the wedding."

"I've done all I can on that front," I replied as I continued walking across the bridge. "I wouldn't stoop so low as to sabotage the day. There's only one person who can change what happens on Saturday, James, and that's you."

CHAPTER 46

"Oh, there you are," said my landlady, tying up her bonnet as I arrived home. "I'm just off out with Mrs Wilkinson. I've warmed up some pea soup for your tea. You'll find the pot on the stove."

"Thank you, Mrs Garnett. Where are you headed?"

"We're going out to look for that Curran woman! I can't believe she's on the run again after escaping from her police cell."

"She didn't escape."

"Then how did she get out again? Did they release her?"

"No, they haven't arrested her at all. They arrested the wrong person."

Mrs Garnett sucked her lip disapprovingly. "That's the problem with the police. They're getting worse and worse. It won't be long before it's down to normal, everyday citizens like you and me to keep the peace."

"Good luck with the search, Mrs Garnett."

"Do you want to come with us? I can wait five minutes while you have your soup."

"No, not this time. I have work to be getting on with."

"Work again, tsk. There will come a time when you realise you need to do something else to make a difference in this world. Life isn't just about work, you know."

I forced a smile. "Thank you for your advice, Mrs Garnett. Don't stay out too late."

"Mrs Wilkinson and I will stay together at all times. We'll be quite safe."

I sat in my room and tried not to think about James' impending wedding, but the more I tried to avoid these thoughts the more they invaded my mind. An image of Charlotte kept repeating itself in my mind. She was grinning from ear to ear while wearing her white wedding gown.

Perhaps I should tell her the truth after all, I mused. I had assured James that I wouldn't dream of ruining the wedding, but it was still within my power to do something to stop it.

The thought was extremely tempting, but I wanted him to be the one to call off the wedding. If not, I would have to accept the fact that he didn't care for me as much as I had hoped.

A letter arrived the following morning, and it provided a welcome distraction from my thoughts about James' wedding.

Dearest Penny and Eliza,

I have reached the shores of Colombia! I write this letter at a rudimentary train station in Salgar, from whence we are awaiting a train to Barranquilla. The train station consists of six simple mud huts and a number of pigs so lean that they resemble dogs. The natives are friendly, though clearly not accustomed to wearing much apparel. The heat in this part of the world is almost unbearable when wearing European fashion! There is some concern that air this warm may be infectious, so I shall take every precaution to ensure that I remain in good health.

We are waiting for our luggage to be inspected by customs officials, and I am told that the train journey will last an hour through the thick jungle. I'm looking forward to some respite from my travels in Barranquilla. I will be staying at a small French hotel, which is, by all accounts, a pleasant and inexpensive place.

From Barranquilla my journey will take me up the Magdalena River! I am enormously excited about the next stage of my expedition, when I shall begin to see more of this country your father clearly loved so much.

I shall endeavour to update you on my search as often as the capricious postal system allows.

I remain your loyal and trusting friend.
With fondest regards,
Francis Edwards

I felt immensely relieved that Francis had arrived safely, and that his search for Father could finally begin in earnest. I also felt envious of him. I wished that I could travel through the jungle on a train and take a boat up the River Magdalena. Life in London held little appeal for me now that James was on the cusp of being married.

Mrs Garnett joined me in the hallway.

"Mr Edwards has arrived in Colombia!" I said with a jubilant smile.

"Rather him than me," she replied, running her feather duster over the mirror by the stairs.

"You wouldn't like to see Colombia?"

"I'd like to see it, all right, but I don't like boats. I can't be doing with them. Even a steamboat on the Thames is too much for me."

"You travelled to Britain from Africa by boat, did you not?"

"That's what has put me off for life! I was seven years old and it terrified me. I don't like the sea, or anything in or on it."

"But you'd like to live in Margate, by the sea?"

"Oh, I can look at it, all right. I'm happy with just looking at it. But don't ask me to travel on it!"

"I won't, Mrs Garnett."

"So what does his letter say? Is he still lovesick?"

"No, and I don't think he ever was *lovesick*, as you describe it." I showed her the letter.

"Of course he was," she replied, sucking her lip again as she took the letter from my hand. "You should have seen his face whenever he visited you here."

"I *did* see his face!"

"Ah, but you didn't properly see it. You didn't notice the subtle expressions that dance across a man's face when he's in love."

"I didn't see those, no. How did you get on with your search for Catherine Curran?"

"No sign of her, but Mrs Wilkinson thinks she may be hiding out in some disused buildings close to the candle works in Lambeth. Do you know the ones I mean? Right by the railway arches and not far from Lambeth Palace. In fact, the Archbishop's Gardens would be a good hiding place, wouldn't they? She could probably find a way to get inside, and I shouldn't think many people would go searching for her there."

"Apart from you and Mrs Wilkinson."

"I suppose we would need permission from the archbishop, wouldn't we? Unless we were to sneak in. The gardens are so large he'd hardly notice us there. Mention it to the police, will you?"

"I will, Mrs Garnett."

CHAPTER 47

I walked along Fenchurch Street in the City with Francis'
letter in mind. Drizzle pattered onto my umbrella until
I eventually found the place I was looking for. A panel
above the polished wooden door was inscribed with 'Edward
Archdale and Co.' in gold lettering.

A young man who had been seated behind a shiny desk
rose to his feet and greeted me as I entered. An enormous
map of the Atlantic Ocean was mounted on the wall
behind him.

"Please could you tell me what a steamship ticket to
Colombia might cost?" I asked.

He seemed surprised by my question. I knew that
Colombia was probably one of the least-requested destinations.

"Of course." He gestured for me to take a seat opposite
him and opened one of the books on his desk. He leafed
through the pages.

"Carthagena, I presume?"

"Savanilla."

He raised an eyebrow. "Are you sure? I would strongly

recommend Carthagena. It is a civilised port town with proper accommodation, restaurants and the suchlike. Much more suitable for the lady traveller than Savanilla."

"But Savanilla is at the mouth of the Magdalena River."

"And that is important to you?"

"Yes, I wish to travel down the Magdalena."

"Will you be accompanied on your travels?"

"No, I haven't arranged for anyone to join me as such, although there is someone I hope to find once I'm there. Two people, in fact."

"You have acquaintances in Colombia?"

"Yes."

He ran his finger down the page which lay open in front of him. "Saloon is available from twelve pounds, and intermediate from nine pounds."

"Steerage?"

"I would strongly advise against travelling in steerage, madam."

"How much is it?"

The man sighed. "Six pounds. But a young lady like yourself would not wish to travel in steerage."

I thought this over. A steerage ticket would cost me a whole month's wages, and it would only get me as far as Savanilla. I would also need to fund my travel from the coastline to Bogotá.

"May I suggest Philadelphia, madam?" said the young man. "It's our most popular route at the present time. Steamships depart from Liverpool every Wednesday, and passengers are landed at the wharf of the Pennsylvania Railroad. From there you can travel on to Baltimore, Washington and New Jersey, among many other destinations. It is the fastest route to the West and I can offer you a competitively priced ticket at seven pounds. The accommodation is simply excellent."

I felt tempted by the idea. *Surely one of the many newspapers operating in these American cities would consider employing me as a reporter.*

"Thank you for your help," I said. "I shall think it over and return a little later."

CHAPTER 48

I had hoped there would be news of Catherine Curran's arrest by the time I arrived back at the newsroom, but there were no telegrams awaiting me.

I sat down at my desk, and for a rare moment felt rather at a loss as to what to do next.

"Miss Green, you look very despondent if you don't mind my saying so," said Edgar. "What's the matter?"

"I'm fine, thank you, Edgar."

"Are you sure?"

Frederick got up from his seat, stepped over to Edgar and whispered something in his ear.

"Oh, right, yes. Thank you, Potter," he muttered.

"Can't I hear whatever it is you have to say, Frederick?" I asked.

"It was nothing, Miss Green. I was just reminding Fish to use some tact."

"Why so?"

"Because he has none."

"Why does he need to use tact?"

The two men exchanged an awkward glance.

"Your feelings need to be considered, Miss Green," said Frederick.

"I wish I knew what on earth you were talking about. Besides, it's rude to whisper. You're making matters worse."

"Worse than what?" asked Edgar.

"Than they already are. If you feel there is a need to be tactful, why whisper something which I cannot hear?"

"There's no need to get upset, Miss G—"

"I'm not upset!" I snarled.

Edgar sat back in his chair with mock fright on his face. "I'm sorry, Miss Green. I won't say anything further."

"But that's ridiculous! Just speak normally without any whispered nonsense."

There was an uncomfortable pause, then Edgar spoke again. "Miss Green, I apologise if we upset you. I do try to be tactful, but I'm a straight-talking man, as you well know. I would rather not mince my words, so I shall say now that I realise the schoolboy inspector is to be married tomorrow and that you may not be exceedingly happy about it." He squirmed with discomfort as he delivered these solemn words.

"I find it amusing you still refer to him as the *schoolboy inspector*, Edgar," I said.

"The chap is undoubtedly youthful for an inspector of the Yard."

"So you have said in the past. Thank you for your statement, and I must say that it helps to hear the issue openly acknowledged."

"Well, we would be fools if we were to think that you weren't the slightest bit affected by it. If Mrs Fish were to marry someone else I would be most upset."

"But she couldn't," said Frederick. "She's already married to you."

"I meant if she had decided to marry someone else before she married me."

"But that didn't happen," said Frederick.

"Potter, you're confusing matters."

"You're confusing me."

The newsroom door slammed behind Mr Sherman as he marched into the room.

"Curious news from Falmouth," he said, reading from a piece of paper in his hand. "Three sailors have been arrested for eating a cabin boy."

"What?!" exclaimed Edgar.

"It's a Cornish story, but I think that a report on it would interest our readers. After almost three weeks drifting in a lifeboat on the South Atlantic they decided to kill the dying cabin boy for food, and this sustained them until they were rescued a week later. On arrival in Falmouth the three freely admitted to what they had done, believing they were protected by the Custom of the Sea. But the police and magistrates saw it differently, and it looks as though they may be charged with murder."

"Good," I said.

"But the boy was already dying," protested Edgar, "and he saved three lives! Presumably all four would have perished otherwise?"

"But you can't just decide to end someone else's life in order to save your own," I said.

"Those men may have wives and children," said Edgar. "How old was the boy?"

"Seventeen," replied Mr Sherman.

"There you are, you see. He's unlikely to have had a family waiting for him at home."

"What about his mother and father?" I said.

"Let's not argue about the rights and wrongs of the case," said Mr Sherman. "It has certainly caused a stir in Falmouth, and apparently public opinion is in support of these men. It's unlikely the boy would have survived anyway."

"I shall report on the case," said Edgar.

"Thank you, Fish."

"I think it's terribly sad," I said.

"That's because you're not cut out for sea voyaging, Miss Green," said Frederick. "It's a different life out there on the ocean."

"What do you know about the sea, Potter?" asked Mr Sherman.

"I have no personal experience, sir, but I know that it's a very different kettle of fish."

"Indeed. Any news on Catherine Curran, Miss Green?" asked Mr Sherman.

"None. I shall head down to Lambeth now and find out how the search is progressing."

"I thought she was from Bermondsey."

"She is, but with the most recent murder having occurred in Lambeth the search efforts are now being concentrated there."

"Well, good luck. Hopefully there'll be something to report on soon."

CHAPTER 49

The police station on Lower Kennington Lane was busy with constables filing their reports. A sergeant in the parade room had made notes of which areas had already been searched and which remained to be searched. I had a brief conversation with him, but he was too busy to talk for long. Members of the public loitered by the door, many keen to tell anyone who would listen that they had seen Catherine Curran.

An old man told me she had been seen laughing outside Mr Taylor's home on Tyers Street. A friend of his said she had been drinking in the Royal Vauxhall Tavern and joking about all the murders she had committed.

I waited outside the police station for a while hoping to catch sight of James, but he was nowhere to be seen. Deciding there was little left for me to do besides joining in with the search, I walked through a maze of streets lined with terraced houses. Beyond the roofs rose chimneys which filled the damp sky with clouds of smoke.

There was a small gathering of people outside what had until recently been Benjamin Taylor's home on Tyers Street.

Perhaps they believed local reports that the murderess had returned to the scene of the crime. I decided that Catherine would probably stay away from here, so I turned onto Broad Street and walked in the direction of the river. I passed beneath the railway arches and reached the red-brick buildings of Doulton's Pottery, where Benjamin Taylor had worked. The pottery buildings occupied a large area south of Lambeth Bridge. As I turned left onto the riverside Albert Embankment, I was greeted by the Doulton brick chimney, which rose to more than two hundred feet and was topped with a structure resembling a Romanesque bell tower. Beside it sat the six-storey pottery showrooms with countless arched windows, a steeply pitched roof, several spires and a beautiful terracotta and tile facade.

I paused by the river to admire these buildings and once again attempted to distract my thoughts from James' impending wedding. The drizzle had turned to a steady rain, creating rivulets on my umbrella and dampening my skirts. My eye was drawn across the river once again to the grey walls of Millbank Prison. I felt a heavy sadness in my stomach, which was followed by a snap of impatience at my feeling so sorry for myself.

How could I possibly work with James once he was married to Charlotte? I couldn't bear the thought of it.

Travelling to Colombia had been a fanciful idea of mine, though it would have been almost impossible for me to fund it. But what about America? There was a good chance I could earn a living there.

I continued on my way and soon reached The Crown Tavern, where Benjamin Taylor's inquest had been held. From there I turned away from the river and walked back toward Lambeth police station. I had seen no sign of Catherine, but I wasn't surprised. So far she had managed to evade and outwit everybody.

Back at the busy police station I found James speaking to the sergeant in the parade room.

"Penny!" He greeted me with a smile, but his eyes lingered on mine as if he had noticed the sadness lurking there.

"No news of Catherine yet?" I asked.

"No, unfortunately not. As you can see we have everyone searching, but I don't know how long we can sustain this for. This isn't the only case the south London police divisions have to deal with, and she isn't making it easy for us to find her, is she?"

"No, she isn't. I have just taken a little wander myself, for all the good it's done. Wherever she is, I don't think it can be around here."

"And we have many more sightings than we can realistically follow up on. All I can think of now is enticing her to come to us."

"How would you do that?"

"By setting up a trap of some sort."

"A cage, perhaps?"

We both laughed.

"I think there must be someone else she's planning to poison next," I added.

"There could well be, couldn't there? We haven't discovered any more husbands, though. She appears to have stopped at four."

"What is happening with Molly Coutts?"

"Ah yes, I have news on her. Your theory was correct, Penny. Catherine had paid her to go on the run."

"She spoke at last?"

"At her mother's insistence. She marched Molly down to Bermondsey police station yesterday evening and made her give a full statement to the police. She said she didn't want her daughter caught up in any more of this unpleasant business, and the statement was given on the understanding that the police would not press charges against her daughter."

"Catherine used her as a decoy, didn't she?"

"Exactly."

"She'll be rather upset that Molly has told the police the truth."

"Yes, there is a risk to the girl's safety now. We have a constable keeping an eye on her while she stays at her mother's home."

"That's how you can lure Catherine in!" I exclaimed. "We can print Molly's confession in the *Morning Express* and then Catherine will be angered that someone is talking about her, just as she was irked when I printed Benjamin's interview. She'll try to get to Molly because she won't want the girl revealing all her plans. But we must be careful that Catherine doesn't harm her in any way."

"We will. We'll have to plan it extremely carefully. Sergeant Richards has her written confession at Bermondsey. If you could write a summary of it and have it published tomorrow that will hopefully encourage Catherine to come after Molly."

"But you will look after Molly, won't you?"

"Absolutely. We can have officers in plain clothes close by at all times. We'll need to ask Molly to go somewhere her drink could be tampered with. A public house would make sense. That's how Catherine found Benjamin Taylor, isn't it?"

I watched James' face brighten as he considered this plan.

"I'll discuss it now with Inspector Austen," he continued. "He'll need to set the plan in motion as I won't be on duty tomorrow..."

There was a pause.

"Because you'll be at your wedding," I said.

"Yes." He held my gaze. "I'm sorry—"

"Don't." I turned away so that he couldn't see my face.

"Inspector Blakely, may I have a word please?" asked one of the sergeants.

I couldn't bring myself to look at James, but I felt his eyes on me as I turned and left the parade room. By the time I reached the street my vision was blurred with tears.

I composed myself during the short horse tram journey up to Borough. From there I walked to the police station on Bermondsey Street.

Every few moments a rush of tears threatened to disrupt my composure, but I swallowed them back and marched on.

I couldn't think about James any more. I had to put him out of my mind. The relationship we had enjoyed for the past year could no longer exist.

I pictured James' face at some point in the future when he was told that I was working as a news reporter in America. I imagined him stopping for a moment and pausing to think about the huge mistake he had made.

He would recall all the times I had told him to call off his wedding and would finally realise that I had been right.

But by then it would be too late.

I gulped back more tears as I marched up the steps outside Bermondsey police station.

CHAPTER 50

"Penelope!" said my sister Eliza as her maid showed me into her drawing room that evening. "How are you? You don't need to tell me why you're here."

"How do you know why I'm here?"

"Because it's Inspector Blakely's wedding tomorrow and you need a shoulder to cry on."

"I've done all the crying I intend to do."

"Oh dear. Really? For a moment I was hopeful that he had seen sense and called it off."

"He would never call it off. After all, it might harm his father's health, and his brother has travelled all the way from Scotland."

"Hopeless excuses."

"He doesn't care enough for me," I said, sitting on the settee. "If he really cared for me he would have put a stop to it by now. But he hasn't, and that tells us all we need to know. So I haven't come here to cry and feel sorry for myself, Ellie. I have already progressed beyond that stage."

Eliza gave me a sceptical look. "Really?"

"Yes, really. I came here for a different reason entirely. We need to talk about money."

"Oh dear. I haven't any to spare if that's what you were hoping."

"No, I'm not asking you for any. However, I recall that Mother and Father might have put something in trust for us."

"But that will only be released after they have died, Penelope."

"That's rather complicated for us, given that we don't know whether Father has died or not."

"Hopefully we shall find out soon. Anyway, Mother is still very much alive."

"What's the use in us waiting until after they're dead? That could be a long time yet, and what happens if we're never able to prove whether Father is dead or not?"

"I hope Francis will find that out. And even if he can't manage it, I suppose a period of time will have passed that would mean he couldn't possibly be alive any longer."

"That could be another twenty years! It's no use at all. Oh, but this talk of Francis reminds me that a letter arrived from him yesterday." I pulled it out of my carpet bag and handed it to her.

"Why are you so interested in the money, Penelope?"

"I don't need much; about twenty pounds. Perhaps thirty to be safe."

"Whatever for?"

"A steamship ticket to Philadelphia."

"*What?*" Eliza's mouth hung open. "You're going to *America?*"

"I may as well go somewhere. There's nothing left for me here. I had thought about following Francis to Colombia but it would cost too much, and I don't know whether I would be able to earn any money there. In America I could work as a news reporter. I hear there are a number of women reporters there, and just think of all the stories there must be in those great cities. Picture me working in New York! Can you imagine it, Ellie? In fact, I should be quite happy with Philadelphia to begin with. I could sail from Liverpool next Wednesday, and a travel agent told me I can buy a ticket for just seven pounds. It's the fastest route to the West."

"West? Since when did you ever want to go west?"

"Since it dawned on me that I cannot remain in the same city as Mr and Mrs James Blakely."

"But you needn't see them."

"But I will, Ellie, I know that I will. I'll come across James time and time again during the course of my work, and it will be awful. Then there's bound to be a time when I see him with Charlotte, and I cannot bear the thought of it. I feel sick just thinking about it; it turns my stomach. It's going to do that every single day after tomorrow. At least there will be plenty of other things to think about on the other side of the Atlantic. There will be so many new things to see and do. I won't have time to think about James or anyone else for that matter."

"Not even your sister?"

"Of course I'd think about you, Ellie. And the children. I might also think about Mother now and again."

"You can't leave Mother."

"She won't mind. I don't think she has ever really understood me, anyway."

"Oh, Penelope, how callous! I agree that she doesn't always understand you, but she loves you."

I felt a lump in my throat. "Well, she could come and visit me."

"She doesn't even like getting the train to London. There's no chance of her taking a boat across the Atlantic."

A thought leapt into my mind. "Why don't you come with me, Ellie? Then you'd be rid of that silly George. The children would love it! It's a big, exciting country, filled with opportunity."

"George and I have begun to see eye-to-eye a little more recently."

"Oh dear, I was hoping you would divorce him."

"I would only ever do so as a last resort, Penelope. What's got into you? You're excitable and flighty, and I'm worried that you're about to do something foolish."

"I'm not about to do anything foolish. I simply want to make the most of my life. I met a man and fell in love with him, and then he married someone else. I want a fresh start somewhere new, then maybe I shall meet someone who returns my love."

"Isn't that the same reason Francis gave for travelling to Colombia?"

"Yes, it is, now you come to mention it. I think I understand a little more of how he was feeling now. And once he's finished in Colombia he could come and find me in America! It's so much nearer than Britain. He could find a boat which sails up the coast from South America to North America. Perhaps I could find some affection in my heart for him the second time around."

"I'm going to call for the maid and have her fetch some laudanum. I've never heard you spout so much nonsense, Penny, and I fear for your state of mind."

She pulled the bell on the wall.

"Ellie, this is my moment of enlightenment! I've placed my hopes in futile things for too long. I admit that I feel a little light in the head, but it's only because I can see now what must be done. The rest of my life is waiting for me and I need to seize control of it! I'm already thirty-five years old. This may be the last chance I have to drastically change."

"I don't want you to drastically change, Penelope. I love you just the way you are." My sister's lower lip trembled.

"Thank you, Ellie." I got up from my seat and went over to embrace her in her easy chair. "We've had our differences over the years, but you're a good sister and I should very much like you to come to America with me."

"You need some money first, Penelope. I suggest you take the train to Derbyshire tomorrow and speak to Mother about the trust."

"That's likely to be the hardest part of all," I said, releasing myself from my sister's embrace. "But it must be done."

"Fetch the laudanum please, May," said my sister when the maid walked into the room.

She nodded and went off again.

"Now sit down, Penelope, and take some deep breaths," said Eliza. "You need to prepare yourself for your visit to Mother tomorrow."

CHAPTER 51

I stepped out of Eliza's home early the following morning with a thick head, wishing I hadn't agreed to take the laudanum. At the time it had helped my mood, but now my mind felt slow and foggy.

It was a cool morning and the sky was blue and cloudless. The day of James' wedding had dawned.

I travelled home on the underground railway, trying to push all thoughts of the wedding out of my mind. I needed to concentrate on my plan. I realised I wasn't even thinking about the Bermondsey poisoner case any more. I had written a summary of Molly Coutts' confession and handed it to Mr Sherman. I had done what I had said I would do, and now I would leave it up to Inspector Austen and his men to see it through. I hoped to be able to write about Catherine's arrest early the following week.

"I'm visiting my mother in Derbyshire," I said to Mrs Garnett once I had packed a few things into my travel bag and put on my light travelling coat. "I shall return on the train tomorrow evening."

"This is a sudden decision," she commented. "Is everything all right?"

"Yes, everything is fine. Thank you, Mrs Garnett."

I looked at her dark, enquiring face and felt a lump in my throat. *How could I bring myself to tell her that I was moving to America?* Although Mrs Garnett had irritating habits, I had rented a room from her for so long that she felt like a member of my family.

Without thinking, I stepped forward and gave her a quick embrace. Her entire body stiffened.

"What was that for?" she asked once I had stepped back again.

"Thank you for being such a good landlady," I said.

"Are you sure you're all right, Miss Green? I think you must be coming down with something. If you are, you're certainly not fit for a journey to Derbyshire. How far away is it? Five hundred miles?"

I laughed. "No, Mother lives about a hundred and fifty miles from here. The train journey to Derby takes just over three hours."

"Is that all? You should visit her more often in that case."

"Yes, I should," I replied curtly, feeling a pang of guilt. "Well, I must go and catch my train. See you tomorrow, Mrs Garnett."

I travelled on the underground railway to St Pancras station. When I purchased my ticket I was informed that I had just missed the ten o'clock train, and that I would have to wait for the next one at midday. I tucked the ticket into the pocket of my coat and made my way over to the refreshment room. It was hot inside, and noisy with voices and the clanking of crockery. Condensation ran down the windows and I decided that I couldn't bear to spend two hours in there.

I caught a glimpse of the Euston Road through the windows, and just beyond it lay Bloomsbury. The British Museum was only a twenty-minute walk away. I decided to walk there instead of sitting restlessly in the overheated refreshment room.

It was just after ten o'clock. *Was James already married?* I wondered. I hadn't asked him what time his wedding would take place, preferring not to know.

I made my way to Russell Square and thought about the walks Francis and I had taken here. Birds were singing in the trees and late summer flowers were in bloom. I took a diagonal path across the centre of the square and soon reached the British Museum.

I paused at the bottom of the steps and looked up at the enormous classical edifice. This was a place I visited most days, and I had grown so accustomed to it that I hadn't stopped to look at it in a long while. The triangular pediment resting on the columns was decorated with statues showing the evolution of man from a primitive being to one enlightened by the arts, mathematics and science. Beyond this great portico lay the reading room, which had become a second home to me over the years.

I walked up a few steps and paused again. A young couple pushed a perambulator past me and a scruffy pigeon waddled along a step. This was the spot where I had first met James the previous October.

Almost a year had passed since our first meeting.

I smiled as I remembered how he had nervously approached me, bowler hat in hand. I had been a different person back then; one who had been preoccupied only with herself and her work. I'd had no idea back then how much that meeting with James would change my life.

I took a breath, closed my eyes and turned away from the portico so that I was facing the bottom of the steps. A fanciful notion gripped me that if I slowly opened my eyes I would see James there waiting for me, just as he had been eleven months earlier.

The sun felt warm on my face and I breathed in, calming myself with a rare sense of hope. I slowly opened my eyes, praying that I would see him there. As my eyelids fluttered open I felt a sinking sense of disappointment when I saw that the space in front of me was empty.

I felt alone and completely foolish. *James was in Croydon marrying his sweetheart. How could I ever have imagined that he would come here?*

I wiped away a tear which had rolled down my cheek, and with my teeth tightly clenched I made my way down the steps again. I had about an hour before I needed to return to the train station.

I followed the route James and I had taken the afternoon we had met and made my way to the Museum Tavern at the corner on the other side of the road.

I was about to push against the doors and step inside, just as we had done that afternoon. But then I paused.

There were too many fond memories associated with the place. I couldn't bring myself to set foot in there and see it in the context of the new world that now existed for me; a world in which James was married.

I took a step back and walked on past the Museum Tavern in the direction of Covent Garden, feeling unsure where to go next.

A sudden hand on my arm made me cry out. I had experienced unpleasant encounters on the street before.

I grabbed my bag and leapt away, spinning around swiftly to see who my assailant was.

The man was smartly dressed but looked slightly dishevelled, with a loosened cravat and tousled hair.

"Penny?"

"James?"

Was it really him?

"What...?" my question tailed off before I could complete it.

"I saw you walking past the window!" He sounded breathless.

"But what about your wedding?"

"Forget about the wedding." He gave a relieved grin. "There *is* no wedding."

"And Charlotte?"

He stepped forward, held me by the shoulders and pressed his lips against mine.

CHAPTER 52

Some people gasped and others stared, surprised at our public show of affection.

"I do apologise," mumbled James. "That was completely inappropriate. Oh dear, now I've brought shame upon us both."

"There *is* no wedding?" I asked.

"I cancelled it."

He grinned, and I felt a smile spread across as my face as I looked at him in his wedding suit. A crumpled white flower was pinned to the lapel of his jacket.

"Oh James, I never thought you would... I can't quite believe it! What about your father?" I asked. "And your brother who travelled from Scotland?"

James gave a laugh. "They'll forgive me, I suppose. Eventually."

"And Charlotte?"

"Oh, she won't."

"Did you speak to her?"

"Oh yes, I had to speak to her. I was awake all night, and then I caught the first train down to Croydon this morning."

"You didn't sleep at all?"

"No. Sleep doesn't come easily when you're wondering if you're about to make the biggest mistake of your life. I made my way to St John's Church, convincing myself that it was my duty to go through with it. But on my way there I had the most awful sensation of impending doom, and I realised that I wasn't supposed to feel like that just before my wedding. I finally saw sense and stopped myself just in time. I went over to the Jenkins' home and broke the news."

"And what did they say?"

"Not a great deal. Charlotte hit me, then her father threw me out of the house."

"She *hit* you?"

"Yes, on the jaw just here." He rubbed it with his hand. "It's beginning to ache a little now."

"That's awful!"

"I deserved it, Penny."

"No one deserves to be struck!"

"She was extremely upset, and I can understand that. Anyway, I don't wish to dwell on it too much. Let's go inside." He gestured toward the door of the Museum Tavern.

I walked with James up to the pub, feeling as though I were walking on air. *Was this really happening?*

He paused outside the swing doors.

"You don't remember your recent words to me, do you?"

"Which ones?"

"In the Tower Subway. You told me you would be drowning your sorrows at the Museum Tavern today."

"Oh yes, so I did!" I felt a smile break out across my face. "You remembered!"

"Better than you, it seems. Come inside. We have company though, I'm afraid. Florence Burrell is here and she has been sharing some interesting theories on where Catherine might be hiding."

"Oh dear. Really? Poor you!" I said. "You never get a break from work, do you?"

"You'll be interested to hear this too, Penny. Come on."

We stepped inside the pub. The air was filled with tobacco smoke and I smiled at the familiarity of the place. *I was here with James once again. This was a moment I had waited a long time for; a moment I had thought would never happen again.*

James led me over to our usual table toward the back of the pub, and seated there was poor scar-faced Florence Burrell wearing a dark shawl and her usual thick-lensed spectacles. I considered her presence an inconvenience at a time like this, whether she had information about Catherine Curran's possible whereabouts or not.

"Would you like an East India sherry, Penny?" asked James.

"Yes please."

I greeted Florence and sat down at the table.

"It's a surprise to find you here, Miss Burrell," I said. "Is this the first time you have visited this public house?"

"No, I've been here before. Not for a few years, though. I used to like visiting the museum over the road. I went there with Tom once. I came in here today and saw the inspector, and he didn't look quite right."

"Today is his wedding day," I said.

"He didn't mention that!" she laughed. "Getting married at a church close by, is he?"

"No," I replied as James returned and handed me my glass of sherry.

Florence's eyebrows knotted together in puzzlement as he sat down at the table.

"You didn't tell me you were getting married, Inspector Blakely," she said.

"I'm not," he said curtly.

Florence gave a laugh. "I'm so confused!" she said, her eyes resting on his tankard of porter.

"I think we all are," I replied, watching her face intently and noticing how her dark eyes followed James' tankard as he lifted it to take a sip. Something about her expression caused a cold, gripping sensation to rise in my chest.

"Don't!" I yelled at James. I leaned forward and grasped hold of the tankard before he was able to drink from it.

CHAPTER 53

A look of alarm flashed across Florence's face. Then she leapt up from the table and ran out of the pub.

"What is it?" said James. "Where's she gone?"

We need to catch her!" I cried out.

We both followed in her footsteps, pushing past the other drinkers in the bar and falling through the doors onto Museum Street.

"There!" said James, pointing at a figure running down the street and swiftly turning left.

We followed Florence onto Little Russell Street only to see her dashing into a churchyard on the right.

"St George's," puffed James as we chased after her. I held onto my hat as we ran past the grand stone church and found ourselves on Bloomsbury Way.

"Over there!" I cried. She had already made it across the road and was running toward another side street.

As James and I swiftly followed we were berated by a cabman for frightening his horse.

The street opened out into the busy thoroughfare of High

Holborn. People thronged the pavements and the road was busy.

"Where's she gone now?" said James as we looked left and right, hoping to catch a glance of Florence's retreating form.

My heart thudded in my chest as I looked up and down the street.

"I can't see her!" I cried.

"We'd better not have lost her!" exclaimed James. "Let's cross the road."

We dashed between horses and carriage wheels. Once we reached the south side of the road my eye was drawn to a narrow passageway.

"I bet she's gone down there," I said.

"But what if she hasn't?"

"She'll be looking for places to hide. She won't want to stay on a busy street where her actions might attract the attention of a police constable."

James sighed. "We may as well take a look. I think we've lost her, though."

He took my hand and we ran down the passageway, which opened into a courtyard bordered by workshops and stables.

"It's a dead end," said James. "If she's here she won't be able to get out again. You search over there and I'll search this side."

We separated, and I peered over some discarded barrels and an old cart before reaching a tumbledown workshop with a grimy-faced man inside.

"Have you seen a woman hiding here?" I asked him.

He grunted in reply.

"She's wearing a dark shawl and a dark dress," I said, "and she has spectacles and dark hair. We think she ran down here just now."

The man gave another grunt and began hammering at a lump of stone.

"Thank you for your help!" I said with a sarcastic smile.

At that moment a movement caught my eye and Florence Burrell shot out from behind the workshop and made a run for the passageway as if her life depended on it.

I turned and gave chase, but James had already spotted her. He dashed across the courtyard and apprehended her just before she could reach the entrance. He launched himself at her and grabbed both arms.

"Let me go!" she screamed as she wriggled to get free.

I ran to catch up with them.

The grimy man from the workshop stepped out to see what was going on.

"Police!" James called out to him. "I'm making an arrest!"

"Get off me!" screeched Florence.

"Tell us why you were running away," said James.

"I don't have to tell you anything," she sneered.

"Did you put something in my drink?"

"No! Now let go of me."

"Cooperate with me please, Miss Burrell, or I shall be forced to arrest you."

"I will!" She squirmed. "Just let go!"

"If you attempt to run away again I will arrest you. Have I made myself clear?"

"Yes."

The scar on her face looked slightly different now. I couldn't work out why, but something about it didn't seem quite right. James slowly let go of her arms.

"Can you please explain why you were running away from us, Miss Burrell?" said James. "One moment you were about to tell me more about Catherine and the next you were gone."

"It's because she put something in your drink," I said. "Poison, probably. Is that what you did to Benjamin Taylor too?"

James was also looking at Florence's scar as if he had noticed something strange about it.

"What are you talking about?" she snarled at me. "I only met him once!"

In a swift move, James reached his hand up to Florence's face and rubbed at the scar.

"Get off!" She recoiled angrily, but when she looked at us again there was a red smear where James had touched her cheek.

"It's not real!" I exclaimed. "Why are you trying to disguise yourself, Florence?"

It felt as though her dark eyes might bore right through me. Then she pulled off her spectacles and rubbed at the false scar with her sleeve. Most of the red dye came off, but the skin remained oddly puckered.

"Funny 'ow easy it is to fool people with a bit o' glue and some beetroot juice." She gave a laugh and her voice suddenly sounded deeper, with no trace of a West Country burr at all. "The glue's ruined me face fer good, but it's served me well for long enough."

"Catherine Curran," I said. Her headscarf had slipped from her head in the struggle and I could see now that her hair had been artificially coloured dark brown.

"Me real name's Jane," she retorted. "And as I've done away with all me 'usbands I use the name Vincent now. Jane Vincent."

James grasped her arm again. "Miss Vincent, consider yourself in police custody for the murder of four men."

"Save it, Inspector," she spat. "You don't wanna be wastin' your time with me down the station. You were supposed to be getting married today, weren't you?" She gave me a knowing glance. "It's good you decided against it. I did it four times. Never 'ad a happy marriage."

"We're a five-minute walk from the police station on Bow

Street," said James. "If you could take Miss Vincent's other arm, Penny, we can walk her down there."

"No chance of it!" shouted Jane.

She bent her head down and sank her teeth into James' hand. He cried out and tried to keep hold of her, but his grip had loosened enough for her to get away.

We ran after her along the passageway back to High Holborn, and I felt sure we would be close enough to grab her as soon as she stopped beside the busy road.

Only she didn't stop. She kept on running and flung herself in front of a moving carriage.

"Jane!" I screamed as the horse managed to skip over her. I didn't have time to cover my eyes before the wheels of the carriage rolled across her as if she were a bundle of rags.

CHAPTER 54

J ames dashed over to where Jane lay in the road. The four-wheeled brougham stopped and the driver jumped down.

"I didn't see 'er!" he cried out, clearly distressed.

"She jumped in front of you. There was nothing you could have done," said James.

A group of people had gathered around, but I remained on the pavement, not wishing to get any closer. I could feel myself shaking. A well-dressed lady in a large red hat stepped out of the brougham and began to cry. I walked over to comfort her.

"She did it on purpose," I said. "There was nothing any of us could have done. It's probably best if you get back inside the carriage for now."

The lady did as I suggested.

James walked over to me, shaking his head sadly. "She probably died instantly," he said. "Someone has found a doctor, but there's nothing he can do."

I watched the group of people crowding around Jane's

body, then removed my spectacles so that the tragic scene wasn't so clear.

"I wish it hadn't ended this way," I said. "Perhaps we were wrong to chase her."

"There was no need for her to lose her life," said James sadly. "But we did what we had to do. We couldn't have allowed a serial murderer to escape justice."

"She almost poisoned you!" I said.

"It seems she did. What made you suspicious of her?"

I shivered. "I don't know, really. There was just something about her expression I didn't like. And the way she watched you as you picked up your drink. There was an odd smile on her face... I didn't like it at all."

"It's just as well you turned up when you did!" said James. "I hadn't expected to see her at the Museum Tavern this morning. She must have been following me."

"Just as you thought someone was."

"Yes, but I thought it was all in my imagination! Are you all right, Penny? You're shivering."

James removed his jacket and wrapped it around my shoulders.

"I've said it already, but I can't believe you cancelled your wedding," I said. "Is it really true that your engagement to Charlotte is over?"

"Of course it is!"

"I keep thinking you're somehow going to become engaged to her again."

James gave a snort of amusement. "I sincerely hope not."

A police constable arrived on the scene.

"What a strange day," I said, watching the sombre group in front of us.

"It is indeed," replied James. "More than enough has happened for one day, and it's not even noon yet."

"Oh, that reminds me," I put my hand inside my pocket

and pulled out the second-class ticket. "I have a train to catch."

"Where are you going?" His brow furrowed.

"Derby," I replied, "to see my mother. But don't worry, I think I'm going to give it a miss. Besides, my travel bag is still inside the Museum Tavern."

"Inspector Blakely?"

We turned to see the constable approaching us.

He cleared his throat before continuing. "I'm sorry for the interruption, sir, but do you have any idea what happened here?"

"I do, yes," replied James. "Would you like me to explain it all to you at Bow Street station?"

"If you wouldn't mind, sir."

⚬⚬⚬

"That's not your usual attire is it, Blakely?" asked Chief Inspector Fenton, surveying James' smart suit.

"No, I was supposed to be attending a wedding."

"And work interrupted you?"

"Something like that."

"Oh dear. Let's hope the bride and groom aren't too upset that you missed their big day!"

James smiled and said nothing more as we followed Inspector Fenton into the mess room at Bow Street police station. Sergeant Richards had joined us from Bermondsey, as had Inspector Austen from Lambeth. The mess room had a billiard table at the centre and a cloud of tobacco smoke hung in the air. It wasn't the sort of room many women saw the inside of, but James seemed keen to keep me with him.

We sat down at a table. Inspector Fenton had narrow eyes and dark, mutton-chop whiskers tinged with grey. I had come across him before when reporting on the murders down in St Giles.

"So the woman who now lies in the Macklin Street mortuary is the Bermondsey poisoner?" he asked.

"Yes, we are fairly sure it's her," said James.

"Did she confess before she died?"

"She said that she had *done away* with all her husbands," replied James. "That's as much of a confession as we could get from her."

"It sounds damning enough," replied Inspector Fenton. "What did her real name turn out to be?"

"Jane Vincent," said James. "She became Jane Taylor after she was married to Benjamin Taylor."

"Jane Taylor was the name she told Molly Coutts to use when she went 'on the run' to Kent," I added. "She told Molly to pretend to be her and to stay at a succession of inns and lodging houses in order to keep the police occupied. She had threatened to tell Molly's mother about an affair Molly was having with a married blacksmith, but her mother found out about it anyway! She needn't have gone to all that trouble for Catherine, I mean Jane."

"Jane gave Molly a fair amount of money, too," added James.

"When Benjamin Taylor told Jane to leave six years ago after she had failed to murder him, she changed her name to Catherine Vincent and simply married again," I said. "She was Catherine Vincent, then Catherine Peel, then Catherine Burrell and finally Catherine Curran."

"She managed to confuse just about everybody," said James. "And I'm still marvelling at what can be achieved with a little glue and beetroot juice."

"To the detriment of her skin, we might add," I said.

"She didn't care, though, did she?" said James. "In fact, I'm not sure Jane Vincent cared about anything much at all."

"Apart from money," I said. "How many life insurance policies did she take out in the end?"

"We found about ten in total," said James, "but there may have been many more."

"To think that she accumulated all that cash and then threw herself under the wheels of a carriage," I said.

"I don't suppose she ever thought she would be caught," replied James.

"We're satisfied that she is the woman who was seen with Benjamin Taylor at the Royal Vauxhall Tavern," said Inspector Austen. "But what about Inspector Martin's death?"

"I think I know the answer to that, sir," Sergeant Richards piped up. "The day Inspector Martin interviewed Sally Chadwick he asked me to make him some tea. I put the kettle on the stove in the constables' office, and a short while later Florence Burrell arrived. We had been expecting her as she'd sent a telegram to say she would be visiting. I explained to her that Inspector Martin was otherwise engaged, but that I'd let him know she had arrived when I took in his tea. I pointed in the direction of the waiting room and asked her to take a seat there."

"So she was unaccompanied for a while?" asked James.

"Yes, just for a short while," replied the sergeant. "I returned to the constables' office to fill the teapot with hot water, then left again to have a quick word with the desk sergeant about the paperwork relating to Sally Chadwick's confession. I went back to the constables' office to fetch the tea and found Miss Burrell walking along the corridor toward me looking rather lost and confused. I realise now that she must have been inside the constables' office."

"Then Florence Burrell was, in fact, Jane Vincent, the Bermondsey poisoner?" asked Inspector Fenton.

"Yes, sir. I assumed she was tired and had lost her way.

That's what she told me had happened, and I foolishly believed her."

"But in actual fact she had just tipped a large amount of arsenic into the teapot," said James.

"Yes. I didn't even think that she might have been in the constables' office," said Sergeant Richards. "She was walking away from it, so I assumed she was walking back from the other end of the corridor. I thought she had maybe walked down there, realised it was a dead end and then made her way back again. I should have realised sooner what had happened, but we were all so convinced that Sally Chadwick was responsible I didn't question it. I made a terrible mistake."

"We all did," said James.

"She did well to locate the teapot in the constables' office so swiftly," I said.

"She may have visited the police station before," said James. "In fact, she may have done so in another disguise to specifically plan the poisoning. Having got away with two murders, can you imagine how alarmed she must have felt when it was discovered that John Curran had been poisoned? What better way to disrupt the investigation than to target the investigating police officers?"

"And it did disrupt the investigation," I said with a sigh.

"That explains why we never found any evidence that Sally Chadwick had poisoned Inspector Martin," said James.

"And what of Sally now?" I asked.

"There's only one person who can really help her," said James, "and that's herself. Until now she has refused to implicate Jane Vincent – or Catherine Curran as she knew her – in any of this. Perhaps when she learns the woman is dead she will finally be at liberty to tell the truth."

CHAPTER 55

O nce James had assisted Inspector Fenton and his men with their paperwork, we walked back to the Museum Tavern to fetch my travel bag.

A bell close by chimed five o'clock.

"Well, I really have missed my train," I said. "I shall have to visit my mother another weekend."

"I don't recall you mentioning that you were going to see her," said James.

"It was a last-minute decision. I didn't particularly wish to remain in London."

"Why not?"

"Because I couldn't bear to stick around on your wedding day!"

"Oh yes, of course. I apologise, Penny. I can only imagine how it would have felt if the tables were turned. I have to say that it must have been... awful."

"I had planned to leave London," I said.

"For good?"

"Yes. I was going to see my mother about borrowing some money to buy a ticket to America."

"*America?*" James stopped and stared at me. "You were intending to leave the country?"

"You were about to get married!"

He sighed. "Yes, I suppose I was. Thank goodness I didn't go through with it. I would never have coped with you going to America. Never." Then he frowned. "You're not still planning to go, are you?"

"Of course not! If you're not still planning to marry Charlotte Jenkins I won't be going anywhere."

"Good." He grinned. "Then we have a deal."

There was a warmth in my chest which I only usually felt after a glass of sherry. I realised as we walked that I couldn't stop smiling.

I could still scarcely believe that the wedding had been called off. I hoped I would never have to see Charlotte again.

We retrieved my travel bag from the Museum Tavern, which had thankfully been handed to the bar tender for safe-keeping. An old man was dozing at the table we had been seated at.

"My beer has been cleared away," said James. "I suppose it was a few hours ago now. Goodness, I hope no one else drank it."

I looked nervously at the dozing man, concerned that he might have drunk the poisoned beer while James went to confirm with the bar tender that the drink had been tipped away.

"Thank goodness for that," he said when he returned. "No one else drank it. Though if it had been kept we could have had it tested for arsenic."

"I think enough arsenic testing has been done for the time being," I said. "Anyway, she cannot poison anyone else now."

"Let's go and have dinner," said James. "I'm not supposed to be on duty, but I told Sergeant Richards we'd be at the

Whitmore Restaurant in case anything important comes up. Hopefully it won't."

The Whitmore was a cosy little restaurant with red wallpaper and a low-slung, beamed ceiling. The candle on our table gave James' face a warm glow, and although he looked tired I could see a sparkle of happiness in his eyes.

"We must prepare ourselves for a few days of unpleasantness," he said. "My former fiancée won't have taken kindly to being abandoned at the altar."

"She didn't get quite that far, did she?" I said. "At least you managed to speak to her at home and saved her the indignity of turning up at the church in front of all your guests."

James laughed. "Oh dear. It's terrible, it really is." He rested his head in his hands. "Dreadful, really. I didn't think I was capable of doing something like that. I must be the most unpopular man in Croydon at this moment."

He placed his hands back on the table and I rested my hand on his, feeling my fingers tingle as I did so. Although this physical contact wasn't entirely appropriate, I felt happy that it no longer felt forbidden.

"It's probably best if you stay away from Croydon for a while," I said.

"Oh, I intend to. And I shouldn't think it would be terribly safe for me to return home either. Mr Jenkins is no doubt hammering angrily at my door as we speak."

We both laughed, then he fixed me with his earnest gaze.

"I made the right decision, Penny, I know that. I'm sorry I kept you waiting for so long."

"I'd hazard a bet that you are worth the wait, James."

We managed to dine for an hour or so before the inevitable interruption came.

"Oh no," groaned James as the lanky form of Sergeant Richards stepped into the restaurant.

He approached us, visibly breathless.

"I'm very sorry to interrupt, sir, but you did say—"

"Yes, I did," said James impatiently. "What's happened?"

"We're needed in Bermondsey. We've just received a telegram down at Bow Street. News of Sally Chadwick, apparently."

❧

"This is Maggie," I said to James as we sat in the spartan interview room at Bermondsey police station. "I've just realised I don't know your full name, Maggie," I added.

"It's Mrs Maggie Westcott." She looked smaller and older than I recalled her being.

"Nice to meet you, Mrs Westcott," said James. "I've seen you around, and at the magistrate's court with Miss Chadwick."

"Yer did," she nodded. "I 'eard the news about Mrs Curran."

"News travels quickly around here," said James.

"Mr Clark the verger 'appened to see Sergeant Richards runnin' outta this 'ere station and into a carriage early this afternoon," replied Maggie.

"He did indeed," replied the sergeant. "It was shortly after I received your telegram from Bow Street, sir. Mr Clark asked me what the emergency was, and I told him that Catherine Curran had died after being hit by a carriage on High Holborn."

"As soon as I 'eard it from Mr Clark I got meself over to Clerkenwell to see Sally," said Maggie. "I told 'er what 'ad 'appened, and I'm sad to say she cried about it. I dunno why really, considerin' what she told me after."

"Which was what?" asked James.

"That Catherine told 'er she 'ad ter say as she'd murdered all them 'usbands! She 'ad 'er terrible frightened. All them poisons in Sally's 'ouse was Catherine's; that was where she made 'em all up. She done it for years. Told Sally she could 'ave some o' the money, but I dunno as Sally ever saw any of it. She pretended to be 'er friend but she weren't, and she made Sally take the blame 'cause Sally's got a child's mind. She don't know no different, and she ain't got no ma or pa. And ter fink she's in that 'orrible prison! You need ter get 'er outta there."

I felt great relief on hearing confirmation that Sally was no murderess.

"We do indeed need to get her out of there," said James. "Sally has made a false confession, but we need to hear the truth from her now. Presumably Catherine Curran's death will have prompted her to talk."

"She can't be scared of 'er no more," Maggie agreed.

"I'll go and see her now," said James, getting up from his seat. "And I'll telegram the doctor, Dr Sherman. The hour is already rather late, but hopefully he'll be able to meet me there and assess her condition. I feel I could have done a little more for Miss Chadwick. I was so convinced that she had murdered a colleague of mine my sympathy for her had diminished. I'll attempt to rectify that by doing what I can for her now, and I shall ask Dr Sherman for some advice on how we can best look after her."

"She can go back 'ome," said Maggie. "She's capable enough o' livin' back there. I'll keep an eye on 'er. I ain't gonna be around forever 'cause I'm old, but me daughter'll do the same. We'll look after 'er, Inspector."

"Thank you, Mrs Westcott."

CHAPTER 56

"Well, Penelope, I don't really know what to say. I can't say that I approve. I think it dreadfully unfair of a groom to abandon his bride on her wedding day."

I had met my sister on Parliament Hill, where a brisk wind tugged at our skirts and hats. Copper-coloured leaves scurried across the grass.

"It's quite thoughtless, in fact," continued Eliza. "Are you sure you can love a man who is as thoughtless as that?"

"He's not thoughtless, Ellie. He was just worried about upsetting his fiancée. And his father, and his brother who had travelled—"

"All the way from Scotland. Yes, I remember you telling me. He's upset them all now anyway, so he should have just done it sooner. He would have caused slightly less upset had he done so."

"I'm not going to disagree with you, Ellie, but it is a lot easier, with hindsight, to reflect on a better way of doing things."

"Oh, isn't it just? None of us is perfect, I suppose."

"Far from it." I surveyed the view. "I love looking at London from here."

Shafts of sunlight caught the dome of St Paul's Cathedral, which nestled among the many church spires and chimneys across the London skyline.

"I prefer Hyde Park to Hampstead Heath," said Eliza. "It's rather rustic up here, isn't it? It reminds me of that book... Oh, what's it called again? That's it, *Wuthering Heights*."

I laughed. "A hill in London is quite different from the Yorkshire moors!"

"I consider it strikingly similar as we watch your very own Heathcliff approach."

James walked toward us, holding his bowler hat on his head to stop the wind whisking it away.

"Oh, he's nothing like Heathcliff, Ellie. Don't be so silly." I felt a flip of happiness in my chest.

"Good afternoon," said James with a grin. "Windy, isn't it?"

"It is indeed. How did the meeting go?" I asked.

"Rather dreadfully. I tried my best to explain matters to the Jenkins family, but... Well there is no nice way of explaining it, is there? Mr Jenkins' face grew so red and angry at one point that I became concerned he might explode. I don't think I shall bother visiting them again. What's done is done."

"It certainly is," said Eliza. "It's quite an unconventional thing to do, you know. In fact, I don't think I've ever known anyone to walk out on their wedding before. I'm beginning to wish I had done it myself!"

"Come on, Ellie," I said, taking her arm. "Let's go and find some shelter out of the wind. Thank you for being our chaperone today."

Eliza laughed. "I don't know why I'm bothering. You've

spent much of the past year together unchaperoned. It's quite scandalous! I'm quite sure Mother wouldn't approve. And as for Father..."

"Hopefully we'll find out what he thinks some day soon," I said.

EPILOGUE

FOUR WEEKS LATER

Heavy rain began to fall on the two men on horseback as they followed the winding river south west from Bogotá.

One of the men pulled up his collar and tucked his head down into his jacket. "I suppose you must be used to all this rain in England," he commented.

"In some ways," replied the other man. "Although it's still very warm today, isn't it? It's not usually warm when it rains back home."

"It never rains in Spain," said the first man with a grin. "The sun always shines there!"

"Of course it rains in Spain. All those delightful oranges you grow there must get their water from somewhere."

"Yes, perhaps you are right, Francis. But it certainly doesn't rain in the way that it does in England. And not as much as here, either. I didn't know we would arrive here just as the rains came!"

"The rains will pass soon enough, Anselmo."

The river to their right began to descend into a deep valley. To their left the land rose steeply, rich with lush vegetation.

"We must watch out for landslides," said Francis, surveying the slopes. "The risk is considerable when there has been a lot of rain."

He noticed a dilapidated hut high up on the hillside which looked as though it were gradually slumping toward the road.

"Oh! I hear it!" said Anselmo excitedly.

Francis listened and, sure enough he could hear the distant rumble of falling water.

The track bent sharply to the right.

"I think we're negotiating our way around the hillside now," said Francis. "I hope the road remains stable."

He glanced nervously over the drop to his right, hoping his horse wouldn't suddenly become startled by something and canter off the road as it had done the previous day.

"I hear it! I hear it!" sang Anselmo.

Another bend in the road brought them to the edge of a large basin lined with rock and scrub. Mist rolled above the steep, forested hills on the far side.

The hiss of an enormous waterfall filled their ears as white water cascaded down the rock face into the unseen river below.

"Salto Del Tequendama!" Anselmo called out, giving a loud whistle.

Francis felt as though his breath had briefly been extinguished within him.

Frederick Brinsley Green had likely watched the falls from this very same spot!

It was a beautiful, breathtaking place; so much more than he had expected when he'd first researched the Tequendama Falls for Penny. He had discovered many new worlds within the books he had immersed himself in, but nothing could compare to seeing these places with his own eyes.

They watched the waterfall for a while and Francis wondered what Penny was doing at that moment.

How would she fare now that Inspector Blakely was married?

He decided to write to her as soon as they reached El Charqito.

"Come on, Anselmo!" he called to his friend. "We're almost at the place where Mr Green was last seen. The real work is about to begin!"

THE END

HISTORICAL NOTE

Female poisoners seem to have been more prevalent in Victorian times than any other time, and I'm not sure whether this is a fact or just my perception! While writing this book I read about an interesting case which became known as the Black Widows of Liverpool. In 1884 two Irish sisters, Catherine Flannagan and Margaret Higgins, were hanged for four murders.

Margaret's husband of 10 months, Thomas, died in October 1883 after an illness of about three weeks. During that time he had been 'nursed' by both sisters. His brother, Patrick, had suspicions about his death and alerted a doctor who in turn informed the coroner. At the coroner's request an autopsy was carried out on Thomas Higgins and Catherine Flannagan immediately fled.

When the autopsy revealed that Thomas was poisoned by arsenic, Margaret Higgins was arrested. Catherine Flannagan, meanwhile, managed to evade the police for eleven days, stopping at various friends' houses and lodging houses in Liverpool. By the time she was finally arrested it was found that five life insurance policies had been taken out on Thomas Higgins' life – only one of them with his permission.

Growing suspicion led police to exhume and examine the body of 18 year old Margaret Jennings who had lodged with Catherine Flannagan. They also exhumed the bodies of John Flannagan – Catherine's 22 year old son, and Mary Higgins – Margaret Higgins' 10 year old stepdaughter.

Analysis of the victims showed that, tragically, all had died from arsenic poisoning. Life insurance policies had also been effected on their lives.

Arsenic was not an easy poison to come by in the late 19th century as it had been a controlled poison for many years by then. Flannagan and Higgins had obtained the arsenic by soaking fly papers in water (fly papers are sticky strips of paper treated with poison to catch and kill flies indoors). The arsenic laced water had then been stored in bottles and administered to their victims, arsenic was found in bottles, bowls and on spoons which the two women had used.

Reporting on the execution of the two women in March 1884, the *Liverpool Mercury* reported that they'd been "aided by a loose system of insurance which calls for immediate remedial legislation". It was also reported that the judge in the case, Mr Aspinall stated, "how many people might there be at that moment lying in the burial ground who, if their lives had never been insured, might be living at that moment?" Source: *Liverpool Mercury*, 4th March 1884.

There are rumours that the Black Widows of Liverpool were part of a wider poisoning network and that many deaths may have been undetected. And there's no denying that a life insurance payout is still a motive for murder these days, often carried out by people who think they'll escape suspicion.

Industry which was deemed too noisy or smelly to be carried out in the City of London was banished south of the river to

Bermondsey many centuries ago. The area's riverside location also led to the development of wharves and warehousing to serve the port of London. This industrial past meant that Bermondsey was a hive of manufacturing by the late 19th century. Leather, beer, gin, vinegar, biscuits, preserves, hats, glue, gunpowder and rubber were just some of the products processed in Bermondsey's factories and their chimneys constantly pumped smoke and malodorous smells into the south London air. Bermondsey was also home to some notorious slums which received a mention in Charles Dickens' Oliver Twist. My interest in the area grew when I discovered that several generations of my family worked as coopers in Bermondsey - so far I've managed to trace them there back to the early 17th century.

Nowadays much of the industry has left Bermondsey and redevelopment in the area has seen some streets become very expensive, desirable places to live. Poorer parts also remain and this mix continues the tradition of Bermondsey's diverse and interesting appeal.

The ancient church of St Mary Magdalen in Bermondsey has a striking appearance, both inside and out. A church has been on this site since the 13th century and the current building dates from the 1600s. The churchyard was closed for burials in 1854 which was the case with many central London churches because they had run out of space.

In the second half of the 19th century, people were usually buried in the large, newly built cemeteries in London's suburbs. It's therefore impossible that Catherine Curran's husbands would have been buried at St Mary Magdalen, however I engineered it that way to keep the location of the story within Bermondsey.

With the emergence of photography in the second half of the 19th century, post-mortem photographs became quite common. Few people had many photographs taken of them during their lifetime, and the purpose of a post-mortem photograph was to provide the family with a lasting memento of their loved one.

The deceased would usually be dressed in their best clothes and photographed with their family at the photographer's studio or in their home. They would often be posed as if sleeping and this was very common with post-mortem photographs of babies and children. Sometimes they would be posed as if they were awake and the photographer would add touches to the photograph to make their eyes and face seem more lifelike. Often a post-mortem photograph was the only photograph taken of someone, particularly if they had died at a young age. For this reason the photographs were very much treasured by families.

A visit to the baths was not only a popular pastime for Victorians but a necessity at a time when only the extremely wealthy had plumbing in their homes. Turkish baths were inspired by those found in Turkey, Greece and Spain and the London versions boasted magnificent themed interiors.

The Hammam Turkish Baths in Jermyn Street opened in 1862 and were said, for a time, to be the finest in Europe. The popularity of these facilities declined in the twentieth century as bathrooms were installed in homes and the Hammam was completely destroyed by a bomb landing on Jermyn Street during the Second World War.

I can't find any record that the Hammam Turkish baths were visited by the gay community, but the Savoy Baths in the same street had a long association with the community and were visited by many famous men including the composer Benjamin Britten, the writer WH Auden, the actor Rock Hudson and the young politician Harold Macmillan before he became Prime Minister.

The police raid on the Hammam Turkish baths is fictional, but inspired by a real-life event in 1880 in Manchester. On 25th September police raided a private party at the Temperance Hall in Hulme where 47 men were guests: around half of them wore women's clothing. All the men were arrested and charged with 'soliciting and inciting each other to commit an unnameable offence'. In court they were fined on the surety of 'good behaviour' for the following twelve months, if they defaulted then the punishment was imprisonment for three months. The incident was widely reported in the press with The Illustrated Police News headline being: 'Disgraceful Proceedings in Manchester - Men dressed as Women.'

The most extreme punishment in 1884 for homosexuality was imprisonment from ten years to life. In 1885 the Criminal Law Amendment Act recriminalized male homosexuality, one of the most famous cases tried under this act was the trial of playwright Oscar Wilde in 1895 for 'gross indecency'. He was sentenced to two years' hard labour which led to poor health and undoubtedly his premature death at the age of 46.

The once magnificent Euston railway station opened in 1837. It was notable for its beautiful, classically styled Great Hall in which a statue of George Stephenson - who the Victorians called 'Father of Railways' – once stood. At the entrance to the station stood Euston Arch which was a large, impressive structure built of sandstone.

The station was demolished and redeveloped in the 1960s to the upset of many. The statue of George Stephenson and the gates from Euston Arch are on display at the National Railway Museum in York in the north of England.

Tower Subway was the main route for crossing the Thames by the Tower of London before Tower Bridge opened in 1894.

The subway is a narrow iron tube which opened in 1870 and originally had a small rail carriage for people to travel on.

This early subway train failed to make money so the tunnel became a foot tunnel and was apparently a damp, echoey claustrophobic walk with a halfpenny toll.

It was used little once Tower Bridge opened and it closed in 1898 - but it's still there! It's now used for water mains.

The Royal Doulton Pottery was established on London's south bank in the early nineteenth century and became a major employer in the area. Some of the buildings, including the showroom, had a beautiful, ornamental style designed to reflect the products the factory made.

The factory was targeted by bombs in the Second World War and was demolished in the 1950s. A small part of the pottery complex still stands, including Southbank House - its exterior gives you an idea of how beautiful some of these buildings were.

Chislehurst Caves are actually mines which were first excavated in the 13th century to mine chalk and flint. Mining finally ended in the 1830s and left a network of tunnels beneath suburban south-east London covering 22 miles. The caves were used to store ammunition during the First World War and became an underground city during the Second World War when thousands of families slept there to escape the bombs. During this time the caves accommodated 15,000 people and had a cinema, three canteens, a barber, a hospital and a chapel.

Other unlikely uses over the years included mushroom cultivation in the 1930s and an underground music venue in the 1960s hosting bands such as The Rolling Stones, Jimi Hendrix, David Bowie and Pink Floyd. The caves are now open as a tourist attraction.

If *The Bermondsey Poisoner* is the first Penny Green book you've read, then you may find the following historical background interesting. It's compiled from the historical notes published in the previous books in the series:

Women journalists in the nineteenth century were not as scarce as people may think. In fact they were numerous enough by 1898 for Arnold Bennett to write *Journalism for Women: A Practical Guide* in which he was keen to raise the standard of women's journalism:-

"The women-journalists as a body have faults... They seem to me to be traceable either to an imperfect development of the sense of order, or to a certain lack of self-control."

Eliza Linton became the first salaried female journalist in Britain when she began writing for *the Morning Chronicle* in 1851. She was a prolific writer and contributor to periodicals for many years including Charles Dickens' magazine *Household Words*. George Eliot – her real name was Mary Anne Evans - is most famous for novels such as *Middlemarch*, however she also became assistant editor of *The Westminster Review* in 1852.

In the United States Margaret Fuller became the *New York Tribune*'s first female editor in 1846. Intrepid journalist Nellie Bly worked in Mexico as a foreign correspondent for the *Pittsburgh Despatch* in the 1880s before writing for *New York World* and feigning insanity to go undercover and investigate reports of brutality at a New York asylum. Later, in 1889-90, she became a household name by setting a world record for travelling around the globe in seventy two days.

The iconic circular Reading Room at the British Museum was

in use from 1857 until 1997. During that time it was also used a filming location and has been referenced in many works of fiction. The Reading Room has been closed since 2014 but it's recently been announced that it will reopen and display some of the museum's permanent collections. It could be a while yet until we're able to step inside it but I'm looking forward to it!

The Museum Tavern, where Penny and James enjoy a drink, is a well-preserved Victorian pub opposite the British Museum. Although a pub was first built here in the eighteenth century much of the current pub (including its name) dates back to 1855. Celebrity drinkers here are said to have included Arthur Conan Doyle and Karl Marx.

Publishing began in Fleet Street in the 1500s and by the twentieth century the street was the hub of the British press. However newspapers began moving away in the 1980s to bigger premises. Nowadays just a few publishers remain in Fleet Street but the many pubs and bars once frequented by journalists – including the pub Ye Olde Cheshire Cheese - are still popular with city workers.

Penny Green lives in Milton Street in Cripplegate which was one of the areas worst hit by bombing during the Blitz in the Second World War and few original streets remain. Milton Street was known as Grub Street in the eighteenth century and was famous as a home to impoverished writers at the time. The street had a long association with writers and was home to Anthony Trollope among many others. A small stretch of Milton Street remains but the 1960s Barbican development has been built over the bombed remains.

Plant hunting became an increasingly commercial enterprise

as the nineteenth century progressed. Victorians were fascinated by exotic plants and, if they were wealthy enough, they had their own glasshouses built to show them off. Plant hunters were employed by Kew Gardens, companies such as Veitch Nurseries or wealthy individuals to seek out exotic specimens in places such as South America and the Himalayas. These plant hunters took great personal risks to collect their plants and some perished on their travels. The *Travels and Adventures of an Orchid Hunter* by Albert Millican is worth a read. Written in 1891 it documents his journeys in Colombia and demonstrates how plant hunting became little short of pillaging. Some areas he travelled to had already lost their orchids to plant hunters and Millican himself spent several months felling 4,000 trees to collect 10,000 plants. Even after all this plundering many of the orchids didn't survive the trip across the Atlantic to Britain. Plant hunters were not always welcome: Millican had arrows fired at him as he navigated rivers, had his camp attacked one night and was eventually killed during a fight in a Colombian tavern.

My research for The Penny Green series has come from sources too numerous to list in detail, but the following books have been very useful: *A Brief History of Life in Victorian Britain* by Michael Patterson, *London in the Nineteenth Century* by Jerry White, *London in 1880* by Herbert Fry, *London a Travel Guide through Time* by Dr Matthew Green, *Women of the Press in Nineteenth-Century Britain* by Barbara Onslow, *A Very British Murder* by Lucy Worsley, *The Suspicions of Mr Whicher* by Kate Summerscale, *Journalism for Women: A Practical Guide* by Arnold Bennett and *Seventy Years a Showman* by Lord George Sanger, *Dottings of a Dosser* by Howard Goldsmid, *Travels and Adventures of an Orchid Hunter* by Albert Millican, *The Bitter Cry of Outcast London* by Andrew Mearns, *The Complete History of Jack the Ripper* by Philip Sugden, *The Necropolis Railway* by

Andrew Martin, *The Diaries of Hannah Cullwick, Victorian Maidservant* edited by Liz Stanley, *Mrs Woolf & the Servants* by Alison Light, *Revelations of a Lady Detective* by William Stephens Hayward, *A is for Arsenic* by Kathryn Harkup, *In an Opium Factory* by Rudyard Kipling, *Drugging a Nation: The Story of China and the Opium Curse* by Samuel Merwin and *Confessions of an Opium Eater* by Thomas de Quincy. The *British Newspaper Archive* is also an invaluable resource.

THANK YOU

Thank you for reading *The Bermondsey Poisoner*, I really hope you enjoyed it!

Would you like to know when I release new books? Here are some ways to stay updated:

- Join my mailing list and receive a free short mystery: *Westminster Bridge* emilyorgan.co.uk/short-mystery
- Like my Facebook page: facebook.com/emilyorganwriter
- View my other books here: emilyorgan.co.uk/books

And if you have a moment, I would be very grateful if you would leave a quick review of *The Bermondsey Poisoner* online. Honest reviews of my books help other readers discover them too!

GET A FREE SHORT MYSTERY

Want more of Penny Green? Get a copy of my free short mystery *Westminster Bridge* and sit down to enjoy a thirty minute read.

News reporter Penny Green is committed to her job. But should she impose on a grieving widow?

The brutal murder of a doctor has shocked 1880s London and Fleet Street is clamouring for news. Penny has orders from her editor to get the story all the papers want.

She must decide what comes first. Compassion or duty?

The murder case is not as simple as it seems. And whichever decision Penny makes, it's unlikely to be the right one.

Visit my website to claim your FREE copy:
emilyorgan.co.uk/short-mystery

THE RUNAWAY GIRL SERIES

৩৯৩

Also by Emily Organ. A series of three historical thrillers set in Medieval London.

Book 1: Runaway Girl

A missing girl. The treacherous streets of Medieval London. Only one woman is brave enough to try and bring her home.

Book 2: Forgotten Child

Her husband took a fatal secret to the grave. Two friends are murdered. She has only one chance to stop the killing.

Book 3: Sins of the Father

An enemy returns. And this time he has her fooled. If he gets his own way then a little girl will never be seen again.

Available as separate books or a three book box set. Find out more at emilyorgan.co.uk/books

67790603R00202

Made in the USA
Columbia, SC
31 July 2019